A HARD HEAD MAKES A SOFT ASS

The First Law of Nature - part II

PaPa Sak

A HARD HEAD MAKES A SOFT ASS

TABLE OF CONTENTS

Introduction

Is it really necessary to write a part two to 'The First Law of Nature'? The character study of Pooh the infamous hustler out of San Bernardino was a look into the life a relatively good guy that at times does villainous things. In the first book I explored the trials of a man that refuses to work a 9 to 5 but determined to have what he wants. By achieving what he wants he takes to the road of crime and drug selling. Many will determine him a bad guy once he made the decision to become a drug dealer; but I disagree. The rap artist DMX once said in his lyrics something that I thought was very profound. 'There is a difference in doing wrong and being wrong'. I'm not saying that it should be justified but it is definitely understood. In my stories I want to display Black people at their best and at their worse and still show the beauty we possess. We thrive in some of the most inhumane conditions. This says a lot about our power and our regal status in the universal order of things.

Though Pooh is a criminal he is willing to overcome every obstacle to survive. In the process he never compromises his principles. How many of us can truly say that? I gave you a brief background check into his mother and what led to the direction he chose. Some pressures are put on a person and they fall into them without blinking. Pooh's dilemma was that he was actually good at hustling so everyone expected him to do just that. Through his trials he realized he had the ability to be a boss in crime. He accepted his role and proved he had the will to survive and conquer. Once we come into this revelation, something inside of us still likes Pooh as a person. He becomes an ally and you actually want him to win. Maybe he is meant to win and maybe he is not but regardless you want him to win. Reason is, as his story is being told you see the humanity in this character. Based upon his circumstances you understand why decisions are made. You may not always agree with his decision but reading his story gives you an opportunity to walk in his shoes. That was the goal of the

3

first book. I wanted you to not only sympathize but also empathize with this character.

In part two, I follow the same themes. I still want him to be a likable criminal that has to sometimes make hard and ruthless decisions. Now that he is in a position to be boss we see how he handles power. You also get to see how limited his power is. In the bible, it points out in Ecclesiastes chapter three that there is a time or a season for everything. I believe that in the life of every man that chooses to be a criminal he has a period of grace before he has to change. In my experiences in the street lifestyle I remember vividly the many times that I was warned it was time for me to slow down. Eventually I took heed to these warnings and now I'm able to tell these stories. In the book 'Blue Rage, Black Redemption' by Stanley 'Tookie' Williams he points out how many times he was warned of impending danger if he didn't change his ways. But since he was so addicted to the lifestyle and the power he never followed an exit strategy. In this book you experience the signs and the trials that lets Pooh know that he needs to get out the game. The question is if he heeds these signs. Those that don't listen learn the hard way that 'A Hard Head Makes A Soft Ass!'

First and Foremost I would like to thank God if you call him Jehovah, Allah, Yahweh, Christ, The Supreme Being or simply The Most High. I hope those that support my writing enjoy this story. This book is dedicated to everyone that bought the first one and supports my literature. I am once again thankful to Latosha Hoffman and Herschel Finger for posing for this book cover and 'The First Law of Nature'. I want to thank everyone working at Etched N Stone Books & Entertainment. Particularly I want to thank my brother Brian Duckett for their efforts to make this publishing company a success. I also want to thank D. Gibbs for her insight about the great city of San Bernardino. I want to also thank the greatest graphic artist in the world Rafael Rodriguez.

Sincerely
PaPa Sak
The Kingpin of the Inkpen!!!

Weary

The weakened heart and the weary soul
Locked horns with the beast and endured the cold
His eyes lost innocence vividly depicting hell
His eyes swell his tears fell, hidden in despair
Under his hard stare
Thorns picking at his flesh he's grown accustomed to the pain
Numbing his senses while death pinches and pinches
Knocking at his brow
Tangled in jungle debris praying for God to set him free
Weary withered heals for his journey is long
Though his will is strong he can't go on
His time is up and something is calling him home
Thorns piercing his skin, scarring his flesh
The fire coming from the asphalt brings him closer to death
Only children and fools because proper warning is given
A hustler gets a certain time before he's punished for how he's
living
A fatal addiction that can plague the brain
Drive you insane with more side effects than cocaine
And it wears on his body heavy is the woe
Corrupted by his friend and sharpened by his foe
Asking for deliverance but not in so many words
Tired of the life that's picking at his nerves
Shaping his demeanor growing livid at a whim
Will he recognize when the game is becoming weary of him?

There is a time for everything!

1
KING OF THE VALLEY

Damn it feels good to see people up on it!
Biz Markie

The party was something else at my new house. I had a house warming party at my new spot in Redlands, California. Redlands is one of the surrounding cities of San Bernardino in the Inland Empire. My family came out and a few of my homies in my clique. I invited my big cousin Big Mel and his fiancée Maria. They had two babies together and he still hadn't set the wedding date. He was really playing the family role though. My mother Shirley also came out with her new boyfriend William Stover. He was a retired sergeant in the Army and a divorcee. All his children were grown and he was making a living with a plumbing business. He met my mother when she hired his company to do work on her house. Five years ago I wondered if my mother would have even given him the time of day. Now that she was getting older her requirements had scaled down some. But for the most part, I thought William was a pretty cool person. My sister Sharon and her husband Marcus also came out to my party.

I invited my homeboy Nelly and his girl April; he was running the Dorjil Apartments for me. He started calling shots on the dope spot after my homeboy Fab-Five got arrested for a murder charge. He was still in the County fighting his case after two years. We had good lawyers but we couldn't get the judge to change his mind. He had agreed with the District Attorney that Fab-Five be held without bail for fear of scaring potential witnesses. His government name was Fabian Gilmore and he was muscle for me while I was in war a couple of years back. I had major love for the nigga but it was nothing I could do but put money on his books while he sat up in the County. I also took care of his girl Shanell and his daughter Déjà. I invited Shanell out to the party because she was using the same babysitter that my girl Janice was using. She and Janice were friends from Beauty College; though they would have their disagreements from time to time and wouldn't speak to each other for the most part they were friends.

I considered inviting out my right hand man Lonnie but I knew he would have brought along his cousin Chris. I was beginning to wonder about Chris. Something inside of me was telling me not to trust him so I listened to my instincts. I couldn't prove anything but I had a feeling he was into some underhanded shit. I still had Chris running my dope spot off Mt. Vernon Blvd down the street and around the corner from Valley College in San Bernardino. But his cousin Lonnie was a buffer between the two of us. I think he has always held a grudge with me ever since his road dog Chucky got killed a few years back at a dope spot they were hustling at for me. Chris had gotten shot as well but he had survived. He was doing a pretty good job far as I could tell with the spot but I was still leery. So I opted not to tell Lonnie or Chris about the new house.

My new house was in my girl Janice's name because she was my legitimate girl. She kept all the paperwork clean and everything up to par. We had a four bedroom house with two bathrooms. Both the front yard and back yard was large with well groomed landscaping. We had a jungle gym in the backyard for my daughter Shanee. She would play with Déjà or my son Joshua from my baby mama Vanessa, when he would come by to visit. Janice would give me hell about my relationship with Vanessa but I would always check her quick when she involved my son. He was now almost eight years old and he could fully comprehend arguments.

The party had started around seven in the evening. The house was stocked with a full bar, brand new furniture and new carpet. It was actually a fix-up house for a really good deal. I had the surround sound in the house and we played plenty of oldies to cater to my mother's taste. She wasn't too fond of Hip Hop so we played Marvin Gaye, The O'Jays, Barry White and a bunch of old school R & B artist. We also had a bunch of Neo Soul music from Jill Scott, Erica Badu, Maxwell and R. Kelly. The vibe was real good because everyone was drinking and dancing on the floor. I could tell instantly that my mother had too much to drink. She always slurred her words and talked loud when she was drunk.

"Oooh William you play your cards right, you might get you some tonight." She announced while grooving to Love Train from the O'Jays.

"Is that so?" William replied.

"You damn right" She staggered into Marcus and Sharon dancing right next to her.

"That is too much information Mama." Sharon protested.

"Mind ya business and stay out of grown folks business, ya hear? I have to admit Marcus, yo black ass end up being a real good man to my daughter. I wouldn't have thought that shit for a million years." She announced.

I calmly walked over to my mother and tapped her on the shoulder. It took her some time to turn around.

"Go ahead and take a seat Mama, you done had too much to drink." I calmly replied.

"Boy if you don't go somewhere. No better yet come dance with yo Mama. William baby, excuse me for a minute while I cut the rug with my only son." She smiled.

William eased away from her as I took her hand so I could take lead. I glanced at Sharon and she shook her head. Marcus just chuckled to himself. They say the truth comes out of a person when they are drunk; whoever came up with that statement knew that it applied to my mother. We danced through several songs until she couldn't stand any longer. Then I helped her stagger to the love seat. She glanced around the room to recognize the spread that was laid out.

10

"This is a pretty nice layout Winnie." My mother commented.

My nickname in the family is Winnie, my nickname on the streets is Pooh and my government name is Sherwin Jerome Daniels. I glanced up to admire my own house. The theme colors were burgundy and gold. Our living room had burgundy carpet with a couch and love seat that was burgundy and gold. We had an oak burgundy dining room table and a bar off in the corner that was also burgundy and gold. My girl Janice had candles that matched the décor. She had a painting that accentuated the home from the great Black painter 'WAK'. The frames blended in perfectly with the color scheme. She had a gold coat rack at the door and the walls were a lighter gold more similar to tan. At the bar, she had finger sandwiches, chips and dip, dishes of lasagna and of course liquor. When I glanced at my bar I noticed a tall bottle of Jack Daniels and I thought about my uncle Ace. He was my deceased father's youngest brother. In fact he was the only living uncle I had on my father's side. He was my confidant and advisor. He was supposed to come tonight but was battling cancer in the hospital. It seemed to me that the chemotherapy was making it worse than better. I planned to go see him again on Sunday.

"What are you thinking about Winnie?" Janice asked out the blue.

"I was thinking about my Uncle Ace, that's all." I replied.

"Aw, that's right; he couldn't be here because he is in the hospital. Don't worry; you were planning to see him on Sunday anyway. He would want you to have a good time tonight though." She replied.

"Yeah, my nigga it's Friday night and we just got paid for real." Nelly sung along to the Johnny Kemp song.

I chuckled as he glided across the floor with April in his arms. They were a handsome couple to me. He threw up I.E. which stood for the Inland Empire and kept it pushing. Janice grabbed me by the arm and escorted me to the kitchen while everyone else was grooving. Once we were inside the kitchen we

11

began kissing and touching. I knew what was going to take place after everyone went home. She put me on punishment several times because of my relationship with Vanessa. I didn't really care because there was always opportunity to mess with new females. It was still good to know that my 'in house pussy' was acting right though. After several episodes of intimacy we finally stepped away from each other patiently waiting for everyone to leave.

The party didn't clear out until around midnight. Last ones to leave was Nelly and his girl April. Everyone else left shortly after my mother and William left around eleven. I sat on the porch and chopped it up with Nelly for about twenty minutes before he left.

"So the Dorjil's is moving real good nowadays huh?" I asked.

"Man, we making so much money that I'm thinking about asking Lonnie to drop off more at a time." Nelly smiled.

"Is he making the drops on time and making sure ya'll taken care of?" I asked while sipping on a beer.

"Yeah, he's doing everything on point."

"You know not to mention this party to any one right?"

"Yeah you were telling me. I ain't speaking up on that shit to anyone. I got Jake running the shop right now and I just told him I was going to a party. That nigga got hustle in him to run a shop by himself soon. That's if anything opens up." Nelly glanced at me.

"We'll see, but I've been hearing that he's got some grind to him. I already got love for the little nigga. I'm giving all ya'll a bonus real soon so don't worry." I replied.

"You talk to Fab-Five? He called my mom's spot a few days ago but I keep missing his calls." Nelly commented.

"It's been a minute, but if I got to holler at him about something I tell his girl Shanell. I feel bad for the nigga because he's been in the County for two years fighting this case. County jail time is hard time. Whatever happened to the right to a speedy trial?"

12

"Yeah but his name precedes him; and you best believe them white folks at the court gon' play that all the way out." Nelly replied.

I shook my head in disgust knowing he was telling the truth. The cold air had picked up a breeze but all the alcohol I was drinking must have kept me warm. I didn't notice the breeze until Nelly's last comment. I stood up on the porch trying to warm up slightly.

"I know. We gon' hold him down until he's able to beat this case. It seems that something else is behind all these postponements and arraignment changes. The D.A. said he has grounds to believe that Fabian is a threat to society while on trial. Whatever the fuck that means?"

"You think someone is snitching?" Nelly stood up frowning.

"Could be! Murder cases never go away and the lawyers aren't able to get shit to sway in favor of Fab-Five. We just gon' have to wait it out."

A moment after I made that statement April and Janice stepped on the porch. It appeared they were talking about the house designs but I was half paying attention. Nelly and I embraced seeing that was the cue for him to leave. Janice and April talked about exchanging numbers and going shopping then they left. Once they drove off Janice wrapped her arms around me.

"I actually like that girl April, she's so sweet. I'm glad you invited them. Where are Lonnie and Renee?" Janice playfully asked.

"Lonnie couldn't make it. I think Renee is pregnant anyway so it wouldn't be good for her to be out like this." I replied.

"Oh, Okay. You ready to go inside now Winnie?" She asked.

"Yeah let's call it a night."

****

The breeze of the fall caused people to shiver in the California Gardens. Markell and his comrade Casey were leaving the California Gardens and walking through Rio Vista Park. They were wearing black sweat shirts trying to keep warm.

"So we gon' rob these niggas over here in the Dorjil's and make their spot hot in the process. We might come up on a nice package and some money." Markell explained.

"I know we've been planning to do this shit for weeks but you sure you want to hit one of Pooh's spots?" Casey asked.

"Yeah fuck that nigga Pooh. He's got paper but he ain't sharing it with us niggas in the Gardens. Besides, that snitch nigga Noony said that they muscle is locked up fighting a murder charge. He was the nigga holding it down in the Dorjil's. We creep up on these niggas real slow and we gon' strike gold. Trust me on this shit, and that nigga Pooh won't know who hit him."

"Well nigga you know I'm down for whatever, I just think we can rob easier niggas that's all." Casey replied.

"This is gon' be easy. We do enough of these licks we can have enough to cop a whole kilo. And why not get the nigga that got most of the shit?" Markell stated.

"Because he is one most likely to want to hunt the niggas down that stole his shit. I got yo back no matter what, but if we trying to jack to come up then we can get some niggas that ain't a part of that nigga Pooh's shit." Casey explained.

"Trust me this is the better way." Markell insisted.

They made it across Rio Vista Park quickly because they were engulfed in their conversation. Once they were at the edge of the Dorjil Apartments they slid on the masks.

"We ain't worn these masks since we smoked that nigga when we were with Boom-Boom at that hotel in downtown, remember that?" Casey whispered.

"I know. I wasn't even legal yet. Okay, now you go to the other side and we gon' catch these niggas from both sides once we

14

spot where they keep their stash. When I start dumping you follow from the other side." Markell explained in a low voice.

They slowly crept into the Dorjil apartments coming from both sides of the apartments. They waited patiently just as Markell had suggested. After a few deals it became obvious to them both where the stash was hidden. Markell had been creeping over in the Dorjil's for weeks trying to find the hustlers from over there. He noticed that there was one particular change. The main nigga that is always running the spot wasn't present. Markell considered he might be in the cut somewhere hiding out. But the more he observed the more he could tell that someone else was running the spot. He thought about canceling the entire move then reconsidered.

"Fuck it, we already over here now. We might as well go through with it." He pondered.

They still had the advantage in the element of surprise. His eyes narrowed as he signaled for Casey to meet him in the front. Casey caught the signal then quickly moved to the designated spot they had previously agreed to meet.

"I told you these niggas are prime for us to rob. They living off of Pooh's name so they think no one gon' get to them. You see how easy it was to find that stash?" Markell grinned.

"Yeah, they served a few smokers and I knew exactly where that muthafucka was. I'm ready my nigga. Let's move on these niggas then bounce back to the Gardens." Casey nodded.

They quickly crept back into position and slowly came in on both sides near the stash. Markell noticed that one of the young ones referred to as Jake was putting a fresh amount of dope in the same stash. He was a short stocky man with a light brown complexion. He wore a black wave cap and a black and red sweat suit. Markell imagined him to be about 5'6 to 5'7 in height with a goatee that hadn't fully connected yet. He had to be about seventeen or eighteen Markell considered. The other two curb servers had to be still in high school, maybe freshmen or sophomores. He realized after observing their youth that this was

15

the right time to strike. Without a second thought they crept up on all three of the curb servers with their pistols drawn.

"Come up out yo shit nigga." Markell demanded.

The one named Jake glanced up to see a nine-millimeter pointed at his head. He and the two others slowly raised their hands in the air. Casey ran up to the stash and pulled out a fresh bag of dope. Casey checked the bag then nodded his head and smiled.

"Now put yo hands on top of yo head like the police tell you to do." Markell demanded.

They did as they were told as Markell did a search on each one. He found a Kimber Covert Automatic in Jake's waist under his belt. He quickly relieved him of his weapon and studied the gun. He knew the gun was worth about fifteen hundred in the store. He checked the pockets to find that they all had several hundred dollars but not enough money to account for what they sold today.

"I'm asking you this only once. Where are you keeping the money?" Markell viciously asked.

Jake glanced at the bushes and Casey followed his direction and found a Staters Brother's plastic grocery bag. Inside the bag was at least twenty to thirty grand.

"Now get on your knees." Markell demanded.

Markell waited for them to comply. Then he leaned in on Jake just close enough for only he could hear.

"Does your strap have any murders on it?"

"Nah!" Jake nervously replied.

"I was asking because I need a new gun and mines got a murder on it." Markell whispered.

He slightly backed away then put the pistol to Jake's head and fired one shot into the back of his skull. His body instantly dropped to the ground like a bag of potatoes. Both of his homeboys jumped nervously as Markell and Casey ran off into the night. They stood frozen wondering if Markell and Casey would turn around to finish them off.

Markell and Casey were long gone running through Rio Vista Park without breaking stride. They were smiling at one another even though they still had their masks on. Neither one of them stopped until they reached the edge of the California Gardens. Once they stopped they gave each other time to catch their breath before anyone spoke. The cold air in the Valley revealed every time they breathed out with a cloud of smoke coming from their mouths.

"We got them niggas dog. And I know that stash plus the money is gon' put us on fa'sho." Markell gloated.

"Yeah, that was a nice lick my nigga. But let's call it a night and count this money inside your grandmother's house." Casey suggested.

"Yeah I'm with that. That nigga Pooh supposed to be the King of the Valley but he ain't even schooling his people right. That shit shouldn't have been that easy. You know what I'm saying?" Markell chuckled.

"That was proof right there that any nigga can get got." Casey replied.

2
STRESS MANAGEMENT

Where the number one cause of death is money!
Rakim

My cell phone began vibrating around three in the morning. I kept it on silence so it shook violently on the dresser next to my bed. It shook me out of a deep sleep. Janice and I had wild sex that night right after the party so I was damn near in a coma. When I glanced at my phone the number didn't look familiar. That was a good thing, because I didn't want any of my people hitting me from their cell phone. Reluctantly I picked up phone to see who was calling this late.

"Yeah?"

"This L, get at me 911"

After Lonnie hung up the phone I laid my head back on the pillow. My paranoia quickly got the best of me so I hopped out of the bed and threw on some sweats. I slipped on the top part to the sweat suit then grabbed my keys, some loose change and my wallet. Janice must have heard the noise of the loose change because she awoke from her sleep.

"Where are you going?"

"I got to step out for a minute. Go back to sleep and I'll talk to you in a little bit." I calmly replied.

She frowned but managed to do as she was told. I figured she wasn't in the mood to fight. I walked out of the bedroom door closing it behind me. Then I peeked into my daughter's room to give her a goodbye kiss. When I got inside the room I realized she was at the babysitter's house. I slowly crept out the house and only locked the bottom lock. Hopefully I would be right back. I found a phone booth at a local gas station and hit Lonnie back at the number he had called.

"What's crackin'?" I asked.

"I'm calling you from a phone booth homie."

"I'm doing the same. It's good to talk." I replied.

"Some niggas ran up in the Dorjil Apartments and robbed the stash. They took the dope and the money then smoked Lil Jake." His voice trembled.

"Aw nah! That little nigga wasn't any older than sixteen or seventeen. We need to talk in person; where are you?"

"I'm at the liquor store on Baseline. You know the one not too far from the Dorjil's." Lonnie replied.

"If you cool, I can be over there in about twenty minutes."

"I'm cool." He sighed.

I jumped on the freeway as quickly as possible to head over to the West Side. When I arrived Lonnie was in his black Dodge Charger. I pulled up in my Range Rover from the opposite side so that my driver's side could be next to his driver's side.

"Let's get out and talk my nigga." I said.

We walked a little ways from the cars so it would be easy to talk. I was more hurt than I was paranoid but I always tried to stay sharp. We walked on the rough gravel ground that surrounded the area. I could tell that he had just thrown on something as well. He also had on a sweat suit and a wave cap. His goatee had fully grown in good contrasting with his light brown complexion. He was only about an inch shorter than me. He put his head down and shook it before he spoke.

"Man the little young niggas Cory and Rasheed said two niggas came in on both sides with pistols drawn and caught all three of them slipping. Cory was telling me that they knew where the stash was and demanded that they give up the money. Once they got everything they thought that was it; but one of the niggas put a bullet right in the back of Lil Jake's head like it wasn't shit." Lonnie's voice trembled.

19

"They must have been scoping those niggas for a while. Who in the fuck would do that shit knowing that is one of our spots." I thought out loud.

"This shit is just like when Chucky got smoked. It was the same way even. The niggas that killed Chucky plugged him right in the head while he was on his knees." Lonnie reminisced about a comrade that got killed that was best friends with his cousin Chris.

"Yeah, 'Noodle Knockers' is what the young niggas from out in L.A. is calling them. Making sure they dead by putting one in the head. This is a fucked up thing because now we got to find these niggas and serve they ass. And all that does is bring more police. And if we don't serve them our people will look at us crazy and these crazy niggas whoever they might be will think they can keep doing the shit. What did Nelly say about that shit?" I replied.

"That nigga wasn't there. I asked him why in the fuck he wasn't there and he told me he went to some party or something that he told you about. Did that nigga tell you about a party?" Lonnie asked suspiciously.

"Yeah he told me. I can vouch for the nigga." I replied.

Lonnie took it as that and didn't say another word. I could tell he had some questions in his head from his facial expression. Lonnie was a buffer between me and the other niggas on the street so I didn't usually deal with them, he did.

"I was over here hollering at Tracy and he came up to talk to me in passing. That was when he mentioned the party. I knew about the party for weeks. He probably didn't think to mention it to you because he knew he had got at me." I lied.

He nodded his head appearing to accept my explanation. There was a brief moment of silence because we were both in thought.

"I think if the stick up niggas were scoping the spot out for a while they noticed Nelly wasn't there and decided it would be a good time to move on the spot. This is what I want you to do." I paused so we could make eye contact.

"Put money on the street about anyone all of a sudden moving weight. Get information but don't put a price on anyone's head just yet. Whoever did this shit is either real low key and under the radar or they were trying to bring some shit out for a war." I explained.

"Yeah I was wondering about that too. Why didn't they kill everybody then there wouldn't be any witnesses. They wanted to smoke one nigga then let the other two explain how it happened. Somebody is trying to get our attention. It would have been easier to kill everybody." Lonnie pondered.

"I know. Somebody is trying to test my name. They are trying to see what I'm willing to do for my people. When we catch up with these niggas I want them to be right in our hands. I don't want it to be a hunt down thing. Only place I'm worried about is the California Gardens. We don't have anybody from out of that hood to give us info." I considered.

The wind was starting to affect us but our mind was on the task at hand. It was three in the morning and we both were cold and drowsy. But our feelings were irrelevant considering we had a major problem brewing. We had walked a little distance from the cars so I casually turned around to start heading back to the vehicles.

"More than likely it might be some niggas from out of there. They the only niggas we not serving on the West Side." Lonnie pointed out.

"Yeah, but it could be some niggas that want us to think it was somebody out the California Gardens." I replied.

My mind was going in a thousand directions. The cold was beginning to take a toll on me and I actually began to shiver. What bothered me the most was that I didn't have a clue to who it could be. The last time I had beef with a nigga was when I was beefing with this nigga named King James. He grew up on the West Side but went to schools outside the city. He was dead now and most of his people had been wiped out. His main muscle was this nigga named Barry that everyone called Boom-Boom. He was doing time though for trying to smoke me at a shopping center. Word was out that I toppled King James so somebody was trying to make a statement. Maybe it was some nigga getting out of jail that was once down with King James.

"Find out if any niggas with a reputation just got out of the pen. You know what; get at Gregg's sister Monica too. Fat Gregg, the murder that they trying to pin on Fab-Five, you remember him right?" I asked.

"Yeah, I know his fat ass sister Monica. What about her? Ain't she sour at you because she knows you and Fabian are cool?" Lonnie asked.

"Nah, her and my sister talk all the time. She doesn't know what to believe. I told Sharon to slide some money her family's way when they were struggling. All she knows is Fab-Five was accused of the shit but she got doubts because they haven't proved shit. They don't have any witnesses just a gun. But she knows we took care of her family for sure. Get one of the little hood rats to get at Monica because she's got family in the California Gardens. That's how Gregg was able to sell dope over there. Don't do the shit directly but get a female to do it then let her speak up on some shit moving over in the Gardens." I explained.

"Alright that's cool, and then we can go from there."

By that time Lonnie and I was back near the cars. We quickly embraced then hopped in our rides. I had to rub my eyes before I started up the Range Rover. I yawned twice before I even pulled off. He honked his horn twice letting me know he was taking off and I did the same in response. I let the engine sit for a minute before pulling off.

There was a lot to think about driving on the freeway back to Redlands. I liked the new house and it was decorated beautifully but I needed to be near some of the spots I was serving. I was going to sleep in until about one or two then stay a few nights with Vanessa. She still had her apartment near Cal State San Bernardino. She was a simple girl that would prefer stacking her money than trying to upgrade every year. I knew she was sitting on a nice chunk of change by now. She still was even driving the Mercedes I bought her a few years back. She didn't even try to get an upgrade when I knew she could afford to. I was going to spend time with her at least until Monday. Janice worked on the weekend at this shop she owned with my sister called 'The Pleasure Palace.' I wanted to be close to the action just in case I found myself in a war.

When I got inside the house I tried to be as quiet as possible. Janice was definitely going to be up around nine this morning which was only a little over five hours away. When I opened the bedroom door I noticed her turn towards the clock that read 3:48. Then she turned in the opposite direction which was with her back towards me. I got undressed and climbed in bed wondering if she was going to stress me out about this shit.

Around nine in the morning I heard noise coming from out the bathroom and inside the bedroom. Janice was stomping through the house causing as much disturbance she possibly could. I was naturally irritated but tried to ignore it.

"Winnie wake up, you seen my hair care kit?" She growled.

"Why would I know where is your hair care kit. I'm trying to get some sleep Janice." I complained.

"You probably wouldn't be so sleepy if yo ass wouldn't have come home at 3:48 in the morning." She snapped.

"It was business Janice, so leave me the fuck alone." I fired back.

"You sure you wasn't making a late night creep to visit that bitch Vanessa?" She replied.

"I ain't got time to be doing all that fucking when I just got through fucking you all last night. Would you leave me alone, I told you it was business." I sneered.

There was a moment of silence as I wrapped myself in the bed covers. Then I heard her walk out of the bedroom. She must have thought about what I said. Besides, I knew that she didn't want to take it further because I had flared up with her. I rarely got upset with her because I knew no matter what; I was going to do what I wanted to do.

I awoke around one in the afternoon and stumbled around the house. I warmed up some breakfast that Janice had left on the stove. My mind was still too hazy to really make a move towards leaving. Plus I had the thoughts of what happened last night. I wanted to get all the niggas that was running corners for me together so that we could have a sit-down. I had four spots that I was serving dope to but three of them I trusted. There was Travon who I was serving up in the Delmont Heights. He had been working out for some time now. He was a short and stocky cat with a dark complexion. He was one of the shot callers over there and we went to Cajon High School together. Fab-Five had hooked up that connect before he was locked up on the murder charge. Then there was Nelly who I'd just seen the night before at my house warming party. He was named after the rapper Nelly but he resembled Juelz Santana, the rapper out of Harlem, New York. My homeboy Nelly was a little taller though and had me by an inch. He was a soldier through and through because he came up under Fab-Five. He didn't have a problem protecting what was his. Then there was Kramer who was a shot caller from out of the projects. He was once talented in football so everyone always called him by his last name. He was a year or two under Fab-Five and also had gone to Cajon High School. Kramer was a stocky cat about the same height as me at around 5'10. He could have gone all the way to the pros if his grades would have been better. I didn't have a problem meeting up with everybody except for that nigga Chris who was running my spot off of Mt. Vernon. He wasn't good at hiding his underlying animosity he had for me and he made me feel uncomfortable.

I had to arrange a meeting without him being there. I had to have Lonnie represent him without it being a problem. First thing I had to do was help arrange and pay for the funeral of Lil Jake. Then once I was out and finished with that, I could link up with Vanessa and carry out my plans. That made me jump up from the couch after making that resolve. I wanted to get in the streets by two-thirty.

I drove over by Cal State San Bernardino and called Vanessa from a nearby phone booth.

"Hello."

"What's going on beautiful?"

"You call me from a different number everyday Winnie." Vanessa purred through the phone.

"I always got to be sharp. I'm glad to know you are at the house. I'm right up the street." I replied.

"Why didn't you just stop by and just use your key?"

"I felt like somebody was following me after leaving the new spot out in Redlands. I think I lost them though but I wanted to make sure." I replied.

"Are you sure you wasn't just being paranoid?" She chided.

"Maybe so but something looked strange and I just wanted to make sure I wasn't giving up the spot of my baby." I playfully flirted.

"Well what's up; are you coming through or what?"

"I'll be there in five minutes."

I opened the door to Vanessa's apartment and she was in the kitchen. I heard her fumbling around in one of the drawers."

"You want something to eat?" She asked as I walked up to the kitchen doorway.

"Nah, I'm good. But I do want you to go somewhere with me."

She didn't say anything as we stood there in uncomfortable silence. Then she looked up at me as if to ask where we were going.

"I want you to roll with me to arrange this funeral. Lil Jake from over in the Dorjil's got smoked last night. You feel like going?"

25

"Damn Winnie, why you always have to call me when you have to bury one of your friends. Do I look like the Black Widow or something?" She teased.

"Nah, you're just my rock. I need to be with someone that I know is down with me when I got to take care of the ugly part of this here game."

"Okay, but is this cool what I got on?"

"You can work anything you wear." I replied.

She had on a loose fitted tan dress that still accentuated her curves. The color of the dress also complimented her complexion. She had a light colored tint that blended in with her pretty skin. She was slamming. I smiled as she walked past me to grab her purse from out the bedroom.

This time I told her to drive in her Mercedes because I was paranoid that someone followed me from my house. I thought I saw a couple of white guys tailing me from off the 215 Freeway. I looked around hoping that I could find a phone booth. That way I could hit Lonnie right after we went by the funeral home.

When we walked into Simpson Mortuary it brought memories when I lost my best friend Antoine. He had been killed in this game because deep down I knew he wasn't built for it. I paused at the door when I seen the same woman that took care of all the arrangements for his funeral. She smiled but I can tell that she vaguely remembered me. I wanted to ask her how many black bodies come through this funeral prematurely every year. But my second thought was that it was a futile question because she probably had lost count.

"Are you okay Winnie?" Vanessa asked while wrapping her arms around me.

"Yeah beautiful, I'm fine. I just thought about Antoine for a brief moment."

"Yeah I think about him from time to time also. But it is what it is." She shook her head.

We walked up to the counter and the young lady continued to smile. She always was a pretty woman, a light caramel

26

complexion. It appeared as though she always wore her hair in a bun. She had several small moles bunched up on her cheek. It was obvious that she was the religious type. Besides us having to deal with the deceased I could tell we were worlds apart.

"Can I help you?" She pleasantly asked.

"Yeah, I came to check on the body of a deceased by the name of Jacob Chandler."

"Oh yes, his family was in here earlier to view the body. We are having problems with the funeral arrangements because there is not enough money for a proper burial." She replied.

"Yes, well I'm here to make sure all the arrangements are made. Here is five thousand dollars and I will make the final payment a couple of days before the funeral."

"Should I put the name of the person paying for the burial?" She asked.

"No, just say that it was an anonymous donor."

It took her about fifteen minutes to arrange everything then she wrote me out a receipt. Vanessa wanted to stop and get something to eat so I told her to stop at a nearby restaurant where I could use the phone. I made sure I ordered my food then I hit Lonnie on his cell phone. He called me about ten minutes later from a phone booth.

"What's crackin'?"

"Tell everybody I want to meet up with them tomorrow at the Riverside Galleria. Tell Chris that during that time he can be talking with Oscar and make sure the Mexican homies is straight. You can speak for him at the meeting and give him one for them to take."

"What about that paper?"

"Tell Chris to get that from them and they will be expecting it." I replied.

"What are you talking about?"

That was Lonnie's way of asking me what time did I want us to meet up at the Riverside Galleria.

"When it's open, around seven." I replied.

27

That was my way of telling him that I was expecting them to be there at eleven in the morning. We had a code based upon how it was in shooting craps. Every number had a running mate. In dice, a seven had a running mate of eleven. Ten had the running mate of four; nine had the running mate of five; eight had a running mate of six; and twelve had a running mate of two or three. If we were to meet at three I would tell him high twelve and he would know. Only way that changed was if I was meeting with him right away. Then he would know to post up somewhere because it was an emergency meeting.

"Cool!" He replied.

Once we hung up I went back into the restaurant with Vanessa and our food was already there. It hadn't been there that long so it was still hot and steaming off the plate. My order was an enchilada platter that looked and smelled good. Vanessa ordered some sort of Spanish burrito dish that came with beans and rice on the side. She smiled when I sat down across from her.

"You are just in time."

"Yeah, I had to handle some business real fast. Now how is our son doing?"

"You will see him later on right?"

"Yeah but I just wanted you to tell me anything new since I've seen him on Monday." I replied while putting food in my mouth.

"Well, he is doing good except he got a D on his science project. He was complaining that he didn't like the class and the teacher was boring. So I plan on going down there on Monday. But he can't play his X-box 360 the entire weekend. I put it up in my room until I talk to his teacher and see what's going on." Vanessa explained.

"I'll go with you."

"Is Janice still picking arguments with you in front of Joshua? I'm trying to figure out why he is so distracted."

"I checked her on that real quick and haven't had a problem since. She still complains about shit but she knows not to do it around Joshua." I replied.

"Well that's good. I plan on figuring out what might be throwing him off because I don't want a trend. I know you got a daughter now but he's all I got."

"I know Vanessa, but I'm in your corner more than you believe. You got me too." I sincerely stated.

"I know there is love there Winnie but now you got your life with Janice. Ya'll just bought a house out in Redlands and it's just a different type of thing. I'm not complaining because I know we hold a place in each other's heart. But the game is going to eventually give you an end result. It always does baby." Vanessa compassionately explained.

"I'm getting tired myself. I know that the game got too many potholes for a nigga to last forever in this shit. I'm trying to get out of being locked in but it ain't easy. But trust and believe I got my mind on ways to get out. As far as that house that Janice and I got, I don't have a problem walking away from that house in a heartbeat. That was something Janice wanted real bad."

"Yeah but you have something invested together. That makes people stick it out even when it's not good. We have love Winnie; we have Joshua but what is it that makes you want to make it work with me? You understand what I'm saying?"

"I told you that you were my rock. Just wait it out a little longer Vanessa and everything is going to fall into place. In this game stress is another thing added to the long list of ways to die. You help me manage my stress. That is more valuable than a house, money or a piece of ass. As far as my daughter is concerned, I'll always take care of her as long as I have the means to do so. But as far as Janice goes, my heart is with you." I assured her.

She smiled as we discussed other things in our life.

29

3
LOYALTY

These devils find a way to get at you!
Lil Kim

It was a chilly morning in Riverside when I arrived at the Galleria mall. I showed up about an hour earlier so that I could clear my mind and contemplate how to get at these niggas. You always got to be a few steps ahead so that the game doesn't swallow you. As I roamed around the mall I reminisced about the last day I talked to my homeboy Antoine. He was walking through this mall when I had hit him up. Then later that night a punk bitch named Karen had him set up. It felt like his ghost was protecting me as I watched the shops setting up for the day. The peaceful morning was appreciated. Vanessa had cooked me a really good breakfast so it was good that I was walking it off. We were supposed to meet outside in the parking lot near Macy's. But I made sure to park on the other side of the mall just in case someone was watching me.

By the time I made it to the other side of the mall near Macy's it was thirty-five minutes after ten. I walked through Macy's breezing through things until I reached the parking lot. The strong wind hit me right when I opened the door. Lonnie was leaning on his Dodge Charger and what appeared to be him counting money. He looked up at me when I was within a few yards from him.

"What's Crackin' Pooh? Inland Empire until I die?" He jovially greeted.

"Always! Is Chris taking care of that move with Oscar and them?" I asked.

"Yeah but he was a little sour about not being able to come to the meet. He said he had some issues he had to discuss."

"Did he relay that shit to you?"

"A little bit but it wasn't anything that I couldn't handle. He wants some more muscle over there off of Mt. Vernon. He says the Mexicans ain't tripping but after hearing what happened with Lil Jake he wants to make sure nobody is tripping." He replied.

"That makes sense. I'll see what's up on some homies from out of the Delmont Heights. I got a few homies that can hold it down over there if I put some paper in their pocket. I'll send them at you tomorrow."

"Fa'sho!"

At that moment Kramer from the projects came walking up to us. That nigga walked like a linebacker or some shit like that. He was always talking about knocking someone out. We would go to a club and if a nigga rubbed him the wrong way the first thing came out his mouth.

"I'll knock that muthafucka out!"

He walked up and embraced Lonnie then he embraced me. It was ten-fifty by then because I glanced at my watch right after we embraced. Kramer always had a facial expression as though he was about to smile. Even when he was talking about knocking someone out. It wasn't an actual smile but it was more like he wanted to but never got around to doing it. But for the most part he was looking good and as far as I could tell he was feeling good.

"How are you doing my nigga?" I asked.

"Shit I've been doing real good. We got the projects popping right about now. Niggas is making some real money and feeling good about it. But I almost had to knock this nigga out the other day." Kramer replied.

Both Lonnie and I started laughing. We knew that was coming up in the conversation at some point.

"What's so funny?" Kramer looked confused.

31

"You nigga. You are always talking about knocking some nigga out. Yo ass should have been a boxer instead of a hustler." I replied.

Lonnie and I were still laughing when Nelly walked up. You could tell he was still sleepy.

"What's cracking Big Nelly?" Lonnie said enthusiastically.

"Nothing really, just sleepy than a muthafucka. We didn't close shop until four this morning." He mumbled.

"It was still buzzing over there even after what happened to Lil Jake?" Lonnie asked.

"It was like it didn't skip a beat. But his mom is real fucked up about that. Good looking on that funeral money Pooh. You are a real nigga through and through."

I nodded my head and shrugged my shoulders. That was something I thought I was supposed to do. He embraced Kramer last after embracing Lonnie and me.

"I was sorry to hear about your young comrade getting got like that." Kramer said.

Nelly nodded his head then let it drop as he briefly lamented. Travon came walking up last about a few minutes after eleven.

"You late, my nigga." Lonnie stated.

"My bad, I damn near overslept. A nigga like me don't be waking up until noon. I didn't get to brush my teeth or shit." Travon replied.

"Don't be bringing that bad breath over this way my nigga." Nelly teased.

"Aw nigga, I keep a pack of gum in the Cadillac. Aye but I am sorry to hear about Lil Jake. They were dirty ass niggas, whoever done that shit." Travon snarled.

"Everybody lift their shirts up." I said.

I was lifting my shirt up with everyone else. It was my way of letting them know that everybody has to be checked every now and then. This was to make sure no one was wearing a wire. After everyone complied then I continued.

32

"Lonnie and I talked about how whoever these niggas are that did this to Jake was trying to make a statement. If not they would have killed Cory and Rasheed right along with Jake. If they bold enough to kill one of our people then let two others live then we might have somebody that wants to give us problems. It was like they were waiting for a response, you feel me?"

"So what; we gon' go to war with these niggas?" Kramer asked.

"First we got to find out who the fuck they are. Chris pointed out to me that it was probably the same niggas that shot him and killed Chucky on Mt. Vernon. It was done the same way. They walked in on both sides then put in work." Lonnie interjected.

"Do we know who those niggas were that killed Chucky?" Travon cut in.

"We know who sent them but we never found out who pulled the trigger. If it was from that nigga Boom-Boom's people then they were probably out the California Gardens." I replied.

"Then let's go to war on them niggas from California Gardens and squash this shit once and for all." Kramer passionately replied.

"But we not a hundred." Lonnie pointed out.

He was basically saying that we weren't a hundred percent sure. I didn't speak for a moment because I was lost in my thoughts. We didn't even have any names and Kramer was ready to war. It would be good to be more tactful than that.

"We can't just sit on this shit because everybody gon' get to asking questions. Niggas gon' get to thinking we can't protect what's ours if we don't make some kind of statement. But I can't just ride on a whole neighborhood based on who I think did it. We got to be for sure then we go after the niggas responsible." I replied.

"Yeah, blasting on a neighborhood for the hell of it is on some gangbanging type shit." Lonnie added.

"Well bitches are already running their mouth up in the Dorjil's. You know Sissy that stays up in there? She got the younger sister named Felicia with the banging ass body. Sissy was saying that it was for sure some niggas from the Gardens because she was over there the other day to braid her home girl's hair and some young niggas was shot calling the next day. She said it took her two days to braid her friend's hair and one day it was nothing then the next day it was crackin'." Nelly explained.

"Did she say who the young niggas were?" I asked.

"Nah, but she said she might be able to find out."

"Did you get at Monica yet?" I asked Lonnie.

"Nah, I heard she was out of town." Lonnie replied.

"Yeah she's been gone for at least a week." Nelly added.

"Well I gathered you niggas together to let ya'll know that we lost one of our own, which ya'll already knew. But if we in this together then we in this all the way together; you feel me? So gather yo straps and let's see how these niggas hold up once we find out for sure who the fuck they are. But start getting ya people protected where if these niggas try to do that shit again, they gon' catch a surprise." I explained.

Everyone nodded in agreement after I finished. We all embraced before we went our separate ways. We needed a face to face because we hadn't done it in awhile. We had been good for two years without any problems. Every now and then someone would have an issue where they would want to directly talk to me. I always gave them an audience unless it was Chris. I avoided that nigga like the plague. But I hadn't gathered all of us together in about two years. It was also a meeting where I wanted to read them. I wanted to see if I had to worry about any one of them. This nigga Big Black, who I bought my dope from always, told me to watch the niggas around me from time to time. This was a meeting that was long overdue. Lonnie stayed a little bit after everyone left.

"What happened to Big Mel? Why wasn't he here for the meeting?" Lonnie asked out the blue.

"That nigga getting old so I told him he didn't have to come. Just like your cousin didn't come neither did mine." I replied.

"Well we gon' need to hook up some time tomorrow so I can make the drop offs. The first of the month is Tuesday." Lonnie reminded me.

I wasn't worried because I had enough dope to supply everybody I just hated having to rent a room with a kitchenette so that I could cook the shit. Back in the day I had this stripper broad get an apartment in her name so that I could cook the shit up at her house. But one day out of the blue she boned out with all my dope. I haven't seen the scandalous bitch since. All that shit came to mind when Lonnie reminded me I had to get that dope to him the next day.

"I'll have it for you tomorrow, my nigga." I sighed.

"Cool. What are you about to get into?"

"I'm going to holla at my uncle. I need to see how he's doing then after that I'll probably go chill with Janice's nagging ass." I replied.

We embraced one last time then I drove off. I was heading straight for the hospital to visit my Uncle Ace. I didn't like the way he was looking as of lately. He was suffering from cancer and the chemotherapy had him looking bad. My eyes watered just thinking about it. When I arrived in the hospital parking lot I took a little time to get out the car. I straightened up a few things in my car then reluctantly got out.

Once inside the hospital I hopped into the elevator with a few things on my mind. I pondered on Ace and how he was feeling but I also worried about my new enemies. Or should I say the enemies I didn't know about. It would be amazing to find out that Boom-Boom had that much influence even while in jail. My thoughts had me away from the present and suddenly the door was opening to the floor. I walked down the hallway and once I made it to Ace's door I stood in the doorway. I solemnly sighed anticipating seeing my uncle in this condition.

35

"Damn nigga I ain't dead yet." Ace said while coughing.

I strolled up to his bed without looking at him directly. He appeared half asleep but I knew he was still sharp as a tack.

"Well I seen you haven't loss your sense of humor. How are they treating you up here?"

"You got to keep a sense of humor up in this place. Hospitals are places of death and it always seems like everybody is waiting to die." Ace commented.

"You appear to be a little livelier than before. Are they changing something around here?"

"I had two Jell-O puddings today. Maybe the sugar has gotten me hyper or something. Shirley came up here Friday, the day you had your housewarming party. What do you think of her new boyfriend William?" Ace replied.

"Yeah she told me. I don't know what to think of the nigga. He ain't my pops but I don't have a problem with him." I sighed.

"That nigga seems too rigid to me. It's like he's got a broomstick up his ass. Twenty something years ago Shirley wouldn't have given that nigga the time of day. He's too fucking square for her. Yo pops had her in love with his ass."

"Yeah but you know how that goes Ace. A lot of niggas in the game don't live too long. The women that date them end up dating a square nigga when they get into them forties and fifties." I admitted.

"Yeah I know. Rest his soul but my brother was a hard headed nigga. He didn't know when to quit. He thought the game would carry him into old age. You know it's about that time you start thinking about another way of life. Niggas like Big Black are like one in a million. I remember how my brother, yo pops, would always talk about loyalty. 'If you loyal to the streets then they will be loyal to you'. My big brother was a soldier but he never knew when to quit." Ace reflected.

"Yeah time is probably running out for me too. But I got a few tricks up my sleeve before I bounce. You know the same

36

night I had the housewarming party some niggas came and robbed one of the spots. Check this shit out, they killed one of my little homies but left the other two alive to tell how it happened."

"Yeah that's some niggas trying to get at you. They want to see what you are willing to do for your people. If they that bold, that means they are ready for any kind of war you might want to bring on them. More than likely it's some niggas that know you took down James. Shit, they might be some of his people that resurfaced. You think you can make it through another war?" Ace glanced up at me.

"I don't know. I really ain't in the mood for this kind of shit. It seems like some never ending shit. I got in this game to live well and to survive but there is always a muthafucka out there trying to test you." I glanced down at him.

He had lost a lot of weight and appeared to be frail. All of his hair was gone and had fallen out during the chemo. This was the weakest I had ever seen Ace. But his council was invaluable.

"First thing you do is check on the people around you. See what the fuck is going on with them. Loyalty is a fragile thing in this world we live in Sherwin. Muthafuckas will think about their self before they think of anybody else. Then once you get a good read on the people around you then you start paying for information. Make people become loyal to their pockets and they'll lead you in the right direction." Ace explained with fervor.

"I checked on my people yesterday. They all seemed on the up and up. Except for this one cat named Chris but I didn't invite him to the meet." I replied.

"What's up with him? If he's a problem then he needs to be in a body bag. What do you think he's up to?"

"I just got a gut feeling about him that started back when that young cat Chucky got smoked a few years back."

"You've been feeling this way for a few years and this nigga is still in your circle? What the fuck is wrong with you?" Ace asked incredulously.

37

He coughed momentarily from getting more excited than he should. I looked at him and waited for him to calm.

"He's related to my main man Lonnie. Lonnie loves that nigga to death. If I get rid of that nigga it can't even appear as though it came from me. I don't think he had anything to do with this robbery though. I just wondered if he's talking to the police. In my homeboy Fabian's court papers the District Attorney is stating that it is a confidential informant. He's my number one suspect because I sensed animosity from him. For reasons I won't say but if he knew something for real I would have been implicated. So what I do for now is let Lonnie be a buffer between me and the nigga until I can come up with a way of finding out what's really up with him." I explained.

"Damn I wouldn't want to be in your shoes." Ace pondered.

"Yeah, but if I got to fall, I'd rather fall as a man than go against what I stand for. The game is fucked up nowadays because too many niggas compromise who they are. A bunch of bitch niggas." I sneered.

"Why don't you just walk away from this shit right now? I know you got enough money saved up to just relocate somewhere and start new."

"But I got too many people that depend on me. If I bounce now, there will be a bunch of people left out in the cold. I got to find a way to help my people so that I can ease up out this shit." I sighed.

"Heavy is the head that wears the crown. It's a fucked up situation because you got to be loyal to people that might feel they don't have to be loyal to you." Ace considered.

"I don't even want to talk about this shit anymore. How is the chemotherapy working? Are they considering a time and date when you might can go home?"

He climbed out the bed without replying. I helped him even though he appeared capable enough. He walked over to the restroom and closed the door. That gave me time to look around

38

the hospital room. He had a room all to himself. I noticed that he didn't have the television on despite him being in bed all day. Ace never was a big watcher of television. Only show I recall him watching faithfully was 'Sanford and Son'. My pops, Ace and their other brothers were all big Redd Foxx fans. That made me think about the old albums from Redd Foxx I used to sneak and listen to when I was little. Ace came out the restroom as I was chuckling to myself. He glared up at me.

"What's so funny?"

"I was just thinking about those old Redd Foxx albums ya'll used to have." I replied.

"Yeah, that's the funniest man in history. Before Richard Pryor, Eddie Murphy and Chris Rock it was Redd Foxx." He smiled while climbing into the bed.

It was good to see him in a good mood. We talked for about an hour and a half before I left. He told me before I left that he was hoping to see Big Black one day soon. I let him know that I was going to holla at him in about a week and I would let him know.

As I drove down the 10 Freeway I thought about everything Ace told me and wondered how things would play out. Knowing that I had to rent a room with a kitchenette I thought about not even going to Janice's house. Instead I made a detour and drove through the West Side of San Bernardino just to scope the scenery. It hadn't gotten dark yet by the time I rolled by the Dorjil Apartments.

I didn't want Nelly or any of the young homies to see me around there because then I would have to talk and hang out for awhile. It was buzzing but not that much since it was still daylight. I rolled up and parked across the street at the apartments known as Little Zion and sat inside my car. About twenty minutes into me sitting outside, Sissy came outside to walk to the store. I rolled down my passenger window.

"Ay Sissy, come holla at ya boy for a minute." I somewhat yelled.

39

She was skeptical at first but walked closer to the ride. I smiled to set her at ease a little. She smiled back when she realized it was me.

"Damn Pooh, I didn't know who the hell you were?" She sighed with a slight chuckle.

"Yeah, I hadn't seen you in a minute so I decided to say what's up."

Sissy was one of those real pretty girls that had a couple of babies but lost her shape. She was still voluptuous but she let her body go in a few places. She was still pretty as hell and she always wanted to throw me play. At the time I was with Vanessa and everybody knew it. She ended up messing around with this L7 (square) nigga I never really knew about. I was locked up a little after that. When I got out of jail she was married with two kids by the nigga. They must have broken up because she was back at her mother's house with her two kids.

"So what have you been up to Pooh? I heard through the grapevine that you were a shot caller now." She made light conversation.

"I'm just trying to survive that's really about it. People put too much on shit that's all. You trip off that young nigga Jake getting smoked like that?"

"Yeah that shit bothered me too. That little nigga had a crush on me when we were little. He was only like a year or two younger than Felicia." She referred to her younger sister.

"Who do you think would pull some crazy shit like that? I heard they didn't kill anyone but him." I subtly pried.

"I don't know who pulled the trigger but you best believe it was some niggas up in the California Gardens. I've been doing my homegirl Mercedes hair for years and it wasn't buzzing over there until Lil Jake got smoked." She continued.

"Who's the niggas calling shots over there?"

"Shit I don't know them niggas like that but I bet you Mercedes knows whose calling shots. Her brother Marquise is out in the streets with all those niggas." She replied.

"So how have you been doing? How is life treating you nowadays? I heard you were married and everything." I deliberately changed the subject.

"Yeah but I don't even want to talk about that trifling ass nigga. He's trying to get joint custody of my two daughters because I'm living with my mom again. But shit I'm alive." She shrugged.

"Yeah I got two kids now also. I got a boy from Vanessa and a girl from this other chick you don't know." I commented.

"You were with Vanessa for a long time. I didn't think ya'll would ever break up. You've always been a loyal nigga. Because back when I had my shape I sure was trying to fuck with you but you stayed on Vanessa." She replied.

"Yeah we decided to go our ways for awhile but you never know what might happen in the future."

"You look like you are doing well; this Range Rover is the business." She grinned.

"I'm alright. A few good things here and there but nothing that can't be gone in a day or two."

"Well I sure would like to have a few good things here and there. Times are hard right now, if you know what I mean." She admitted.

I dug in my pocket and pulled out five crisp one hundred dollar bills. I reached out and handed it to her while she was leaning in the passenger window.

"What are you giving me that for?" She looked surprised.

"So you can get you a few little things for yourself."

"What is it you want me to do for this Pooh?" She said suspiciously.

"Nothing really. Just stay cool with a nigga and keep a good conversation with a nigga that's all." I replied.

"That's it. Shit I can do that with you all day. Tell me something I can do for you; for real." She openly flirted.

I chuckled just a little bit trying not to insult her. I didn't have any interest in doing anything with her but I baited her good.

41

"I'll tell you what. If you find out anything about the niggas running shit over in the California Gardens then I'll make sure you keep money in your pocket. You feel me?"

"You ain't said shit but a word. In a few days I'll be able to let you know who all those niggas are." She promised.

"Alright then that's a deal."

Shortly after she walked away I drove to the hotel room with the kitchenette so that I could cook that raw to give to Lonnie.

4
SIXTEEN-FIVE

Fuck with my La Familia I will kill ya!
The Game

My cousin Big Mel came to hang out with me at the Ontario Mills mall. Ontario is another city in the Inland Empire area. We had been consistent with hanging out at least once or twice a week. When I stopped by to pick up his money for a couple of kilos he was buying we decided to hang out as well. I was going to see Big Black in a couple of days and Lonnie had already picked up the money from everyone else. For the most part Big Mel was laying low but I knew he was willing to smoke somebody if I asked him to. He had bought him a house in Fontana, another neighboring city. He started a plumbing business from a trade he learned in the pen. My brother in law Marcus showed him how to do all that shit and make it all legal. The crazy thing was that he was actually doing plumbing jobs but serving dope on the low. He was much different than he was about thirteen to fourteen years ago. I would tease him about his old age and he would just laugh.

"You know Maria's family is Catholic and they keep stressing me about us getting married." He commented out of nowhere.

"Why don't you go ahead and do that shit then?" I shrugged, not understanding the logic.

"It's still other bitches I want to fuck. I lost ten years in the pen. It's much more pussy out there besides Maria. Once I say I do, I'm going to feel like a hypocrite if I fuck other broads." Big Mel replied.

I knew he had gotten older because I would have never heard that from him back in the day. I tried to choose my words carefully.

"Do you want to be with Maria?"

"Yeah, but never fuck another broad is a hell of a commitment." He sighed.

All I could do was laugh. That was a decision he would have to make on his own.

"Look man, I think we need to ride on those California Garden niggas for what they did to Lil Jake. We gon' roll through there tomorrow night and light up any hustlers that we see. I've been having someone give me an update on them niggas around the clock. We gon' bring out the heavy shit too. You know the Mack 10s, M11 and this shit I got a hold of called TP-9. We gon' give those niggas the blues since it's buzzing over there." I explained.

"You know all you gon' do is make it hot on the West Side? You sure you don't want to catch them slipping first?"

"I just want to make a statement first. Then we gon' see how they deal with it. Once they see the firepower we're working with they might reconsider who their fucking with." I replied.

"Or they might be ready to retaliate." He considered.

"I think it's some young niggas that was once down with Boom-Boom. He's still locked up but he's probably still able to call shots from lock down." I explained.

"Even if he is calling shots ain't that many niggas gon' do murder unless they got it in them. I could see Boom-Boom...why are we calling that nigga that? I know him as Barry. He ain't never Boom-Boomed me. Anyway, the way you told me the story it's in your face that they don't have a problem killing a nigga. These ain't niggas that did a lick then accidentally smoked Lil Jake. That shit was calculated. They wanted you to know how it was done so that you would know that they don't have a problem with killing to get what they want."

He had a real good point. I still had to respond to these niggas in a good or bad way. We had sat down in the food court by this time. We were both quiet as we observed the mall patrons. Big Mel was giving me time to process what he was saying.

"I still got to serve them niggas because if I don't they gon' try to pull some shit again." I said.

"I didn't say you shouldn't serve those niggas. I'm just saying that don't expect for it to be kick back after that. They knew who they were stealing from and they knew whose people they were killing. You gotta blast back but brace yourself for the worse is all I'm saying." Big Mel explained.

I had already pondered on that. I was going to see Big Black right after we served those niggas then we would see what they came with. Its some parts of the game you hate having to deal with. The money is good but the world is tainted. When you make a decision you have to consider the effects for years to come. Sometimes you are forced into a decision and you can lose everything. My world was a place where bad decisions could get you in the morgue or stuck in the penitentiary for the rest of your life. But I've always been the type of nigga that would rather be judged by twelve then carried by six. Those California Garden niggas had to feel the pain before it was all said and done.

It was late when we drove through the California Gardens. It had to be around eleven at night and we can tell that it was still buzzing. Somebody had dope up in the Gardens and it was just like someone told me. I had Lonnie parked down the street from the spot with Travon. We had Kramer driving in with PoMo who was from the projects under him; and Main Man who worked under Chris at the Mt. Vernon spot. The plan was for them to roll up and start blasting on the dope spot from one side forcing the ones that didn't get hit to run in the direction of Travon and Lonnie. We thought about having a third shooter but we didn't want to chance any cross fire. If my homeboy Fabian was out he would walk right in the Gardens and start dumping.

As expected when Kramer pulled up he had his lights on so it appeared as though another car was just rolling through. Their security in the California Gardens wasn't that tight because my people were able to roll by. Then they suddenly popped out the window at the opportune time and started blasting in a crowd with heavy artillery. The bullets were tearing holes in the walls of a vacant house they were serving at. Two were already down by the time a few niggas ran in the direction of Travon and Lonnie. Lonnie didn't even cut on the engine to the car. He and Travon got out the car and started emptying loads at niggas running their way. At least three niggas was hit that ran in their direction. They mowed them down with precision then hopped into the bucket and sped off.

I was around the corner in hiding waiting to hear the results from Lonnie. Lonnie dumped the car in an empty lot then he and Travon drove off in two separate cars. Kramer used an old school Monte Carlo that he was fixing up. He put one of those dealership slides in the license plate so they couldn't remember the car. He had plans of getting the car painted the day after we put in work. I thought it was a little risky but I wasn't there to put in the work. When Lonnie pulled up I heard the sirens from the police and ambulance. He seemed as calm as day when he hopped out his car. We quickly embraced.

"Man we put in work tonight. Those niggas got at least four or five niggas dead behind what we did tonight. Now we can wait and see what they about to do next. If we're lucky we've got the niggas that smoked Lil Jake. If not we at least sent a message that we were ready for war. That new gun you gave me was the shit. That's some Green Beret type shit right there." He said enthusiastically.

"How did PoMo and Main Man do? Did they show and prove tonight or was it you and Travon doing all the work?" I seriously asked.

"Nah, they laid some niggas down tonight. I think they at least got two while me and Travon might have gotten three. They did their share if you know what I mean my nigga." He replied.

"Okay, then we gon' lay low for a while and see what happens. Make sure we got security on all four spots so tight that if a nigga steps at us wrong in the least bit we gon' light his ass up. We hurt them niggas a lot worse than they hurt us."

"Yeah they're hurting right now."

We smiled for a split second then embraced and we both drove off in our separate cars. I headed back to the house in Redlands because I wanted to lay low for a while. Only thing I always wondered about was if someone was following me from that house. If someone was scoping the Redlands house they wouldn't find anything. That was my good home where everything was legitimate. What scared me though was if they knew about where Vanessa lived. I had planned on going to see Big Black the next day and I couldn't lead them to him. I thought about not even going home to Janice but I knew eventually I had to. Twice I felt like I was being followed so I did some driving maneuvers so that if I was being followed it would have been obvious. But I knew I couldn't keep doing that. Besides, if the DEA was watching that house they would bump me up if they had something big. I didn't want to give them anything big. I figured I would go ahead and go home since I hadn't shown my face at the house and my daughter would probably be calling for her daddy.

When I walked in the door all the lights were out. I slowly crept into the master bedroom and began taking off my clothes. When I sat on the bed to take off my shoes the light suddenly came on. It startled me for a moment because I thought it was law enforcement. I grabbed my chest breathing out a sigh of relief when I realized it was Janice.

"Damn Sherwin, you have a tendency not to show up home nowadays. Are you over that bitch Vanessa's house when you're not at home with me?" She growled.

47

"I'm taking care of business when I'm not with you. Come on Janice I've had a rough night and the last thing I need is for…"

"You think I give a damn about you having a rough night? Every night you don't come home to see your daughter is a rough night for me. I'm not even getting into how you are with me. You haven't been much of a boyfriend and we got this house together. What kind of nigga are you…?"

"Would you shut the fuck up? My little homeboy Jake got smoked the other night. He's DEAD, and you talking about coming home at night. I don't need this shit right now Janice. I'm there for my daughter but I'll walk away from this house like it ain't shit. You best believe that." I snapped.

Janice very rarely had seen me lose my temper. When I did then she knew that I wasn't in the mood to argue. She slowly cut off the light and laid her head back on the pillow. I put my face in my hands as I sat on the edge of the bed. My sentiment was that I didn't need this shit. I was trying to be a father for my daughter Shanee but Janice was becoming another problem. And who in the fuck wants another problem? I slowly undressed and lied down in the bed. Later on that night she came and cuddled under me as I tried to rest my mind. I wish I didn't have to deal with her like that. But it is what it is.

The following day I went into the kitchen and found that Janice had fixed a hardy breakfast. I was ready to throw down when I seen all that food. She must have felt bad about bringing out the worse in me. I sat down and took my time to slowly eat up my food. I wasn't planning on meeting Big Black until around eight that night. So I basically had a whole day ahead of me until that time. He was irritated by tardiness. But since I had a feeling that I would be followed from the house I decided to give myself a two hour head start.

I sat around the house until about four in the afternoon watching television. I went to pick up Shanee from daycare at four-thirty. One of the babysitters at her daycare had a thing for me but I wouldn't take the bait. She was a pretty girl with a

48

caramel complexion and a nice petite frame. She always would smile from ear to ear when I arrived. She had freckles on her face and wore a shoulder length bob hairstyle. There was days that she would even walk me out to discuss 'how smart my daughter Shanee was'. I knew she wouldn't speak to Janice about it if we did fool around. But I was careful not to shit where I eat. Besides, she didn't serve any purpose for me but sex. The safe thing to do was keep it platonic.

If I had something to do I would then take Shanee to my mother's house. Then Janice would pick her up from there or she would spend the night at her grandmother's house. When I arrived today my mother was already waiting at the door. I peaked in for a little while to see William on the sofa drinking a Heineken. I talked with both of them for a few moments then left. By that time it was close to five-thirty in the afternoon. I stopped at a phone booth and made a couple of calls. Then I drove to this underground parking structure and sat there for about twenty minutes.

Suddenly a blue Avalanche pulled up beside me in the parking lot. When I hopped out he was all smiles. My brother in law was on the straight and narrow his whole life but he was the coolest nigga I knew.

"What's up Marcus? How have you been lately?"

"What's going on my nigga?" We embraced.

"Nothing; but a few tails that's all. What I want you to do is drive the car to my moms' house and park it in her underground parking structure. Leave it in there and have Sharon pick you up from my moms' house. You don't even have to go inside if you don't want to. I'll take care of my business and give you the car tomorrow. Is that cool?" I explained.

"Yeah it's cool; I'll just take the Mercedes when I drop Sharon and Jr. off in the morning." He referred to Sharon's car.

"How is my nephew? Both Joshua and Shanee been asking to see him." I asked.

"He's getting big. I can't wait to put him in Pop Warner football. He might mess around and be a linebacker or some shit. But they all supposed to do something with Shirley this weekend. She told Sharon she wants all three of her grandbabies over her house. William and she got something special planned for them. I think they're taking them to Disneyland." Marcus replied.

"That's right; mama mentioned that to me before I left her house tonight. Well I'll holla at you later. I got some business to handle."

"Alright Sherwin stay up."

It felt funny him calling me Sherwin even though he did it all the time. I'm used to people either calling me Winnie or Pooh. I quickly exchanged keys with him and drove off in the Avalanche.

I always wore a sweat suit when I met with Big Black. I never knew when he was in the mood to have me do a strip search. It was random at times. He could go months without searching me then pop it up at a whim the very next time he sees me. He was still a cool muthafucka I just knew he took every precaution. He always gave me game about subtle things that I could pay attention to. I pulled up to the hotel he told me to meet up with him at about fifteen minutes before time. I made sure I got off a few exits ahead of my exit just in case I was being followed in the Avalanche. At times I thought that I was just being paranoid but after meeting with Big Black I knew I wasn't alone.

"This game is real nigga. The day you decide to ignore the signs is the day you are in the back of a squad car. A smart nigga don't want his name ringing out unless it has to. That reputation shit is a liability and that shot calling shit is a bull's eye for any Drug Enforcement Agent. Watch ya back always." He would say.

"But what can a nigga do when his name is ringing out already?" I would ask.

"Try to make people believe that it's just rumors and not true. Downplay that shit because it could come to bite you in the ass."

50

When I walked inside the room he was in a sour mood. I could tell the way he sighed when I walked in. I knew then that he was going to be cut and dry and strictly business. I might have to prove I'm not wearing a wire. But I was determined to have council with the nigga no matter what.

"You got that one ninety two?"

"Yeah, right here." I said as I sat the duffle bag on the bed.

"Am I gon' have to count this shit?"

"Not really but you gon' do what you want to." I shrugged my shoulders.

"I'm going up next time we meet. Each one is going for sixteen-five." He nonchalantly commented.

"What happened?" I asked out of surprise.

"You didn't hear about the law catching a shipment off the Long Beach port? It was a lot of fucking work. It had to be a good two hundred of them things. DEA agents were all over the place. It was all over the news. We're in a drought nigga." Big Black stated.

He said it so calm that you would have thought he was asking for a cup of coffee. I couldn't say anything for a few moments. I could afford the bump up in prices but I wasn't expecting it. I knew it wasn't coming out of my pocket. I would have to let my people know.

"I'll let my people know. I'm getting bad news after the next. You know one of my young workers got smoked over at one of my spots?" I commented.

"What for?"

"Some niggas ran in on the spot and smoked him but left two of my other workers alive." I explained.

"That's the same shit I was talking to you about having a name. When niggas know your name they do dumb shit like that. Now you got to put in work or your name is gon' look weak and every nigga gon' test you. I'd hate to be in your shoes." He shook his head.

"We handled those niggas the other night." I replied.

51

"You think you can handle another war? War brings police and all of a sudden niggas is doing things they ain't supposed to do. You might want to back up out this shit. A hard head makes a soft ass."

"We might not have to go to war. We might have finished those niggas off the other night." I optimistically suggested.

"Are you sure that you killed the niggas that did that shit to yo peoples?"

"I ain't for sure."

"Then you probably are going to war."

It was as simple as that for Big Black. He didn't have time to beat around the bush. One plus one equals two was his logic. If the shit didn't add up then he went straight for what did.

"Is it a way out this shit?"

"Yo name got you in too deep. You got niggas that answer to you. So that means they depending on you to come through for them to make their paper. If you don't hold up to that then they get to resenting you. You don't know what a nigga might do when he resents you." He explained.

"So if I just left tomorrow and niggas never heard from me, how would they get at me?"

"They will go after yo family. This game keeps going even if you on the gravy train or not. Money, Mackin' and Murder is the life we chose. The way to get out of this is pass the ball to someone you can trust that won't turn state's evidence on you."

My thoughts wandered when he dropped that on me. All the niggas that copped from me was down as far as I could see. Naturally Lonnie would be my first choice. But what was going on with his cousin Chris made me worry about him. Kramer wasn't a boss nigga when it came to running shit on a big scale because of his temperament. Nelly was a down little comrade but he was still young and his decisions were sometimes young. Now Travon was a solid nigga but he wasn't that ambitious. Then there was Chris, he just wasn't built for this game and I realized that after we lost Chucky. All of them had their good and bad qualities

52

but I would have to decide which one if I had any intentions on getting out the game alive and free.

"We're done here nigga. You know where you can get what's yours. Next time we will hit that spot over in Montclair. Be safe nigga." Big Black interrupted my thoughts.

I went back to my thoughts as he got up to leave. He grabbed the duffle bag of money since he did a quick once over in front of me. He walked towards the door and before he opened it he looked back at me.

"Sometimes I feel like I'm earning the sixteen-five by dropping shit on you that you should know from the gate. You one of the smartest young hustlers I've came across and Ace's blood runs through yo veins. But there comes a time when the game doesn't want you anymore. Yo time is up."

With that he walked out the door and closed it behind him. I sat at the edge of the queen sized bed stunned. I went inside the closet and found what I was looking for and rolled back to a storage bin I had in Vanessa's name that was open twenty four hours. I needed an apartment where I could store the shit and cook it up when I needed to. Because I didn't want Vanessa's name that close to the product. I had a female in mind but I just didn't know how to approach her about it. When the time is right I'll make it work.

5
UP AND COMING

Because the street is where my heart is at!
Eazy-E

Markell paced back and forth in the backyard of his grandmother's house. He was infuriated but he needed to think things through. The weaponry that was used against his homeboys was some shit that he had never seen before. The firepower killed three of his homies and damn near killed the fourth. What bothered him more was the fact that Pooh found out too fast for his taste. Casey sat on the back porch watching his road dog pace without saying a word. Markell knew that the streets were talking but not that fast, he thought.

"Somebody from over on this side is running off at the muthafuckin' mouth." Markell blurted out.

"Who?"

"I don't know just yet but I'm gon' find out real soon." He assured Casey.

Markell picked up the curl bar that was lying on the concrete. It had twenty five pounds of steel dead weight on both sides of the bar. He began curling the bar while Casey continued to dwell on his thoughts.

"How are you gon' find out? It ain't like a nigga gon' admit that he's been talking too much. Besides, all we know that nigga Pooh was just being random. He scoped us out for awhile like we scoped him then decided that we were the niggas to get." Casey said.

"He doesn't even take me as that kind of nigga to just blast on niggas on some random shit. Pooh ain't trying to get the police

54

hot on the West Side right now because he's making his paper. He knows that if it gets too hot its gon' fuck up business for him. He went after us because somebody told him we were buzzing over here." Markell explained after setting down the curl bar.

Casey went after him and got up to lift the weights. Markell sat down in one of the backyard chairs trying to think. Just as soon as he sat down he stood up waiting for Casey to finish his set.

"Let's bounce my nigga."

They went to the side of the house and walked out the gate. Casey followed closely behind as Markell picked up his pace. It was one of those unusually warm California days when you considered the season. Normally it would be cold outside but today the sun was out focused in the Valley area. That stern facial expression reflected Markell's internal turmoil. He walked down the street with the walk of a predator. His 5'11 muscular frame and dark brown complexion emanated power and respect. He wore his New York Yankees fitted Starter cap lowered over his forehead barely above his eyes with the brim pointing forward. He wore a blue hoodie with blue khakis and black Converse Chuck Taylor's. His road dog and best friend Casey was an inch taller and more of a dark sandpaper complexion. His tight eyes and dark weed lips fitted his rough exterior that was painted with different tattoos. He also wore a baseball cap but his was black with the initials SD on the front for San Diego. He had it turned backwards with Black khakis, a Black Pro Five T-Shirt and some all Black K-Swiss.

When they arrived at their destination one of their workers was standing outside the new spot. He was a youngster around sixteen or seventeen named Kevin. He waited for Markell to say something before he opened his mouth.

"How is the block buzzing?"

"It's moving even though we changed spots." Kevin replied.

55

"Any new customers or the same smokers that live around here?"

"It's been muthafuckas I mostly know or at least seen around the hood." Kevin shrugged.

"Where the fuck is Marquise? Ain't he supposed to be on the block with you right about now?" Markell sounded irritated.

"Yeah, but that nigga just ran to the house so that he could get his strap. I told him earlier that I had mine so he didn't bring his but I told that nigga he needs to keep a strap at all times now that the homies got smoked. I just sent him to go get his strap after it slowed down because it was buzzing a lot earlier." Kevin explained.

"Yeah we gon' make them niggas pay for that shit. Tim, Pokey and Shawn were some down ass niggas." Casey cut in.

"I went to go see Travis in the hospital and he will have to learn how to walk again. But that nigga was in some serious pain." Markell added.

Suddenly Marquise came walking up with his pistol tucked away under his belt. It was barely covered over his Black Pro Club T- shirt.

"What's up Markell my nigga?" He embraced Markell.

"Nothing. But I got to ask why a nigga got to tell you to get yo strap after you know what happened the other night?" Markell asked out of curiosity.

"My thirty-eight wouldn't make a difference against the shit they had anyway. But real talk my nigga I just forgot." He chuckled.

Markell smirked because he knew that was the reason anyhow. Marquise embraced Casey then they walked over in the cut against a brick wall by the new dope spot.

"Ya'll checking up on us or what?" Marquise asked.

"Nah not really. I just wanted to see how the new spot was buzzing after that shit that happened the other night. I think somebody is running off at the mouth. You know of somebody that might be talking about what's going on in the Gardens?" Markell asked.

"I haven't really seen anything that made me think somebody is talking. Only thing I was tripping off of was that fat bitch Sissy that braids my sister's hair. She's always asking questions. She gossips too fucking much for my taste." Marquise frowned.

"Sissy? I don't know any bitch around here named Sissy." Markell replied.

"She stays over in the Dorjil's. She's a square bitch that was married to some L7 nigga. She grew up over there but moved away when she got married. She and Mercedes went to High School together."

"Hold the fuck up. This bitch stays in the Dorjil's and she's running off at the mouth about what's going on over here?" Markell flared up.

"Nah, not like that, the bitch just asks too many questions for my taste. Mercedes says the bitch is looking for a man with paper because her nigga ain't fucking with her anymore." Marquise explained.

"What kind of shit she asking?" Casey cut in.

"Yeah, I'm wondering what she's asking too." Markell glanced back at his road dog.

"Just the other day she was asking whose the high rollers over here because she needs to hook up with one. I told the bitch I didn't know any high rollers around here. Then she asked Mercedes to hook her up with a shot caller but I knew none of my homeboys wanted to fuck that fat bitch." Marquise continued to explain.

"That's it? That's all the bitch asked." Markell asked.

Marquise tried to focus on anything else Sissy might of said. He rubbed his chin trying to remember anything else. It took him a few moments before he remembered.

"I remember one day they were in the kitchen and Sissy asked my sister if she could hook her up with some Ridah type niggas. I ignored it because I remember thinking that she doesn't even really like thug type niggas now all of a sudden she wants a Ridah."

"Oh I need to meet this broad. Tell her to come through for some reason or another so we can holla at her. Because that nigga Pooh, the one we think sent those niggas over here, might be having that bitch find out shit." Markell stated.

"How am I supposed to get her fat ass over here when she just put some braids in my sister's hair the other day?" Marquise asked.

"Tell the bitch you got the perfect dude for her that you want her to meet. Then we can question the broad." Markell replied.

"I just think she runs off at the mouth that's all. I don't think she had anything to do with what happened..."

"Let's just find out. You might be right but we need to know what she knows." Markell interrupted him.

A few nights later Sissy walked through Rio Vista Park wondering what guy Marquise wanted her to meet. According to Marquise he fit all the requirements to what she was looking for. She figured she would flirt with the nigga just long enough to find out his name and maybe where he lived. Then she could shoot the information right back at Pooh. Pooh was a cool ass nigga she thought. He was giving her nice amounts of cash just to tell him what was happening in the California Gardens. It wasn't really a big deal and God knows she sure could use the money. She had her hair in a bun and she took the time to put on a little make-up. She decided to wear a corset to accentuate her body. She had ass and titties but she also had a bunch of baby fat. Her ass had turned into cottage cheese but it still looked shapely in some jeans. She wore a peach colored blouse with small heel shoes that had peach color in the shoes.

"I look good. Whoever he is, he's at least gon' want to fuck. If he's cute enough we might just do that." She said to herself.

She made it across the grass near the California Gardens to be greeted by Marquise and another man. He was about six feet tall with a dark tan complexion. She instantly thought he was cute but was a little irritated by the severe weed lips. Even though he had on a thermal she could tell he had a bunch of tattoos. They were even on his neck. That really wasn't her type of nigga at all but she was going along with the ride.

"Ay Sissy, this is the nigga I was telling you about." Marquise greeted her.

"Nice to meet you, but I thought you said that Mercedes was supposed to come?" She asked while shaking the guy's hand.

"Nice to meet you too sweetheart." The guy replied.

"What is your name? Remember my name is Sissy not sweetheart." Sissy calmly scolded.

"My name is Casey. I was just trying to break the ice." Casey smiled.

"You can still break the ice but just call me Sissy. So are we going back to your house or what Marquise?" She showed little interest in Casey.

"What's up Sissy? You're not feeling me or what? I'm trying to get to know you and you talking about going back to Marquise's house." Casey said.

"Nah it's not like that. I think you're cute and everything, it's just that I don't know you so I would rather…"

A gunshot goes off and Sissy's body slumps to the ground. Looming over her body is Markell with a pistol in his hand still smoking from the gunshot. All three men glanced down at Sissy's body to see the bullet wound to the head had blood leaking into the grass. Markell was the first to step away then Casey and Marquise followed closely behind.

Chris glanced at his brand new burgundy Dodge Charger with pride as he sat down inside the Chinese Restaurant in Yorba Linda. Yorba Linda was a city in Riverside County about thirty-five to forty minutes away from San Bernardino. Chris had to take every precaution possible. Though he grew tired of having to meet with these people he sat in the restaurant nevertheless. A streak of fear ran through his body as he seen the familiar crew cut walk in the door followed by his partner. Their military disposition and no nonsense attitude didn't make things better. He tried to relax as they both sat across from him in the same booth.

"How is everything Chris? You've been a difficult man to catch up with. I hope everything is fine." Detective Yates said in a condescending tone.

"I'm fine how about you Detective Yates and Detective Hudson. I hope your new year has been pleasant." Chris replied being equally condescending.

"Let's get down to the point. What have you got on Mr. Daniels? We've been trying to get charges on him for some time now and nothing can hold." Detective Yates frowned.

"I told ya'll that I don't ever deal with him because he always has someone else that deals with me directly. He's been like that for the last few years." Chris replied.

"Well it's about time you stepped it up and found a way for us to get to him. Give us some information about some of his whereabouts and some people in his organization besides you. And who is the person that he has to deal with you?" Detective Yates continued.

"I'm not giving him up so don't even ask. As far as Pooh, I think I showed my card at my homeboy Chucky's funeral. Pooh is not a dumb muthafucka; he can read into shit that most niggas can't and that's why he is calling shots." Chris sighed.

"Well we know he has ties to several murders like that of James Stuart. He also has ties to a recent shooting that took place in the California Gardens leaving three dead and one wounded. It is a clear motive behind the shootings in the California Gardens. It was in retaliation for a young man in the Dorjil's by the name of Jacob Chandler." Detective Hudson explained.

"Shit, ya'll know more than me. I knew about a meeting but I was told to do something else. I heard that there is an up and

60

coming nigga out the California Gardens that put in work against Jake. He was the only one that got smoked that night so it was some kind of message being sent." Chris explained.

"So that probably explains the killing of Sissy Lattimore." Yates said to Hudson.

"Do you know the up and coming over in the California Gardens?" Hudson asked Chris.

"Nah, that's probably why three niggas got killed instead of one. If they knew who he was they would have went after him. But Sissy I remember her in the Dorjil's she had a sister named Felicia. When I would visit my cousin I remember they were cool. That's fucked up. You think she had some connection to Pooh?" Chris asked.

"You're supposed to be giving us information but it appears that we are the ones giving you all the information." Yates said sounding frustrated.

"I'm not even supposed to be dealing with ya'll. I only talked to Detective Barnes then he passed me off to ya'll. Matter of fact I don't think I even want to do this shit anymore. I was sour at Pooh but when I really think about it he didn't really wrong me." Chris firmly replied.

"Well that's tough fucking luck. You're already working for us and you will continue because we've been allowing your ass to sell drugs with immunity for years." Yates retorted.

"You don't have any drug charges on me. I'm not under your thumb because I'm working off a charge. I don't have to do anything with you from now on. Matter of fact, ya'll have a good day because I'm out." Chris stood up to leave.

"I don't think so Mr. Jackson. We can definitely let your partners know that you've been working for us for some time. I don't think your friend 'Pooh' or anyone else will look at you in a favorable light if they knew that." Yates replied.

Chris gave Yates a vicious look then as if defeated slowly slumped back into his chair. Chris really didn't have anything else to say so he stared at the ceiling.

"Look here Chris, we just want Mr. Daniels. Once we are able to get him then you can resume your life however you please." Hudson tried to soften the blow.

"Why do you want Pooh so bad? He's just like any other nigga trying to hustle for a living." Chris said.

"He's murdered people to be in the position he's in and we want to wipe that silly smirk off his face. We had gotten a lead on him years ago but we later found out it was a set up for a rival of his." Hudson replied.

"Yeah, but he's got a new rival and ya'll can tie two murders to him. Why not go after him?"

"We will, but it is one case at a time. We want the people that killed your friend Sissy but they are small time. Pooh is someone big that we could really tie to some things." Yates lustfully replied.

"So since Pooh is the bigger fish ya'll want to get him first? Well I don't know where he lives or anything." Chris sighed.

Yates and Hudson could tell that they were at a stalemate. There must be a way to penetrate his organization where they could tie him into something. If only Chris could get inside or be motivated to find something.

"So how did you feel about not being invited to the housewarming party in Redlands? Cornell Young was able to attend why weren't you invited." Hudson asked.

"Pooh got a house out in Redlands? I didn't know anything about that. I once heard he had an apartment in Colton but that's about it. Is everything in his name?" Chris asked more out of curiosity than anger.

"Nothing is in his name. It is in the name of his girl Janice Jenkins I believe." Yates replied.

Both detectives were tired of talking to Chris at this point. He hadn't served any real purpose but they knew they had a few tricks up their sleeve. They looked at each other without saying a word. They both stood up simultaneously while Detective Yates handed Chris another business card.

"What are you giving me this for? I already have your business card." Chris stressed.

"But I'm giving you another one with the date and time we are supposed to meet up again." Yates replied.

"This is some bullshit. You know and I know that you got more information than I do. I'm calling Detective Barnes about this shit." Chris threatened.

"I doubt if he takes your side." Hudson laughed.

"Ya'll need to fuck with the up and coming nigga and leave everything else alone. Pooh knows he's a target so he's not gon' dump on a nigga unless he has to. Ya'll going after the wrong dude. You go after that nigga in the California Gardens then everything else is gon' come full circle." Chris said out of frustration.

"That's the best thing you've said since we've been in here." Yates replied.

They walked out the door while Chris put his head down on the table. He didn't have a clue to how he was getting out of this.

6
HEAVY IS THE HEAD

I got a six sense, I stack dead people!
Young Jeezy

I can't believe this nigga. Now he's messed around and started shooting females in the head. It bothered me that he found out so fast that she was talking to me? I was sad when the word came down that Sissy had gotten smoked in Rio Vista Park. Whoever this nigga is; he's a different type of breed. In this game, sometimes you got to kill but then there are times you can avoid the drama and handle it a different way. He had to know that the police was going to get hot. That's the difference between a boss nigga and a common thug. A boss will consider the consequences if he got to peel somebody's cap. Crazy thing is Sissy wasn't giving me that much anyway. I figured it was niggas from the California Gardens that killed Jake because everybody else was eating off my plate. I thought about the projects but as long as Kramer was in that bitch I knew we were okay.

I just buried my little homie Jake so now I would have to attend another funeral for my homegirl Sissy. She was really a square female that shouldn't have even been in this mess. Only reason I decided to use her was because of what Nelly told me. I figured somebody might be playing both sides. It made me nervous because that kind of nigga is more dangerous than anyone. It didn't sit right with Lonnie that Nelly happened to go to a party the night Jake was killed. I considered what he said but I also knew that Nelly was at my housewarming party. But now this was something else that Nelly was involved in where someone ended up dead. Lonnie definitely would have that on his mind when we

64

met. I was driving on my way to meet up with him. But his judgment was clouded when it came to Chris so that had to be considered. All these thoughts were racing through my head as I drove to the Riverside Galleria Mall.

Now I was looking under my Range Rover every morning to see if there was a tracking device under it. I only felt that way when I was leaving the house where Janice and I lived. These young niggas from out the Gardens was making old feelings come back up. This was what I was feeling when I was dealing with the King James war. Maybe Big Black was right; my time is about up in this game. When I pulled in the parking lot at Macy's I seen Lonnie already outside leaning on the wall. He was in the cut but I recognized him right away. He nodded his head when he noticed the Range Rover.

I hopped out the car and when I reached him we embraced. No one said anything for a moment. We were both trying to pick the right words for the situation. Shit was getting real hectic and we were trying to tread lightly on everything.

"I've known Sissy all my life. I can't believe that someone would even do her like that. Now both her daughters got to grow up without a mother." Lonnie lamented.

"I know! I feel real fucked up about it because she was talking to me and those punk ass niggas probably found out and killed her to get to me."

"But who could have said anything about you talking to her. You think there's somebody whose playing both sides?" Lonnie asked.

"I was thinking the same shit." I shook my head.

I began rubbing my eyes as we both contemplated. Lonnie was a smart young comrade so I figured what was coming next.

"There are a lot of fingers pointing at your boy Nelly. I think he's a cool nigga and everything but too many things look suspect around him. I mean...he goes to a party the night his spot gets robbed. He's the one that mentions Sissy to you and she ends up dead...what the fuck?"

"Let's don't jump to conclusions about the nigga just yet. We got to look into what he's been doing and see how that shit plays out before we accuse him of shit."

He made some good points and what bothered me more was the fact that he knew about the spot where Janice and I live. Nelly only been over there once but every time I walk out the door I feel like I'm being followed. But Lonnie and I have known Nelly since we were all kids and I haven't ever seen him show love to niggas from out the California Gardens. But I had to admit he was our number one suspect.

"I thought about Kramer but that nigga too stupid to be playing both sides. Plus he didn't know that Nelly wasn't going to be there that day Jake was killed and he definitely didn't know if Sissy was spying for us." Lonnie continued.

"And Travon is a Delmont Heights soldier so I know he wouldn't play both sides. Yo Cousin Chris hates those niggas from back in the day. I'll tell you what; we gon' start watching that nigga from now on. If he does something that is suspect then we handle that shit from there." I replied.

"Okay, but who are we going to put on that shit? Who's going to have the time to watch this nigga's movements all the damn time?" Lonnie asked with a look saying he had no suggestions.

"What about Jermaine who we call 'Main Man' that works under Chris over there off of Mt. Vernon? You pull that nigga to the side and don't let anyone know what you are doing but him. If niggas get to suspecting Nelly off the bat they might do something stupid. Main Man done put in work with us and he knows how to keep his mouth shut." I explained.

"I didn't even think of him. Yeah I'll tell Chris that he's gon' run some errand for me and he won't trip if I take him off the corner."

I nodded as if I agreed but truthfully I didn't give a damn what he told Chris. As long as he knew not to tell Chris the truth I was cool. At this point I was ready to wrap it up with Lonnie and head back to San Bernardino to pick up my daughter.

"Oh yeah, some broad named Mercedes came up into the Dorjil's telling Cory that the California Garden niggas want to sit down with you." Lonnie said.

"They asked to speak to me by name?" I asked in surprise.

"Not yo government name but they knew you as Pooh."

"When did this shit happen?"

"Yesterday when I went to pick up the bread from the Dorjil's Cory was telling me."

"Ain't Mercedes the girl that Sissy knew up in the California Gardens?" I suddenly remembered.

"That's sounds about right. So what you want me to do?"

"Fuck them niggas. If they want to sit down with me they have to build they weight up first. I don't know them niggas like that anyway and what do they want from me?" I replied.

Lonnie nodded and slightly smiled. There was nothing left to say at this point so we embraced and went our separate ways. As I drove off I thought about the California Garden niggas wanting to meet. It wasn't cool that they knew my name but I didn't know their name. I swerved through traffic trying to pick my daughter up from school while this shit was on my mind.

The same routine was taking place about a week after I met up with Lonnie. I had the California Garden niggas on my mind right before picking up Shanee. I thought I might be acting arrogant by not meeting with them. But if they were suggesting a meeting then that meant that they looked at themselves as my equal. To me they were a bunch of punks that shoot women in the head. They were worried more about killing than they were about hustling. Plus I didn't know if they were working for the police or what. They couldn't be trusted. As I continued to sort out my problems I realized suddenly that I was pulling up in front of the school. It was just in time. Shanee was one of the first to walk out the door. She ran up to the car and opened the backdoor of the car with no problem. Then she waved goodbye to one of her friends

67

and climbed in the child seat. After strapping herself in she looked up at me.

"Hi daddy, are we going to Grandma Shirley's house?"

"What do you want to do?"

"I want to at least go by there daddy because Grandma Shirley and Mr. William are making banana pudding."

I chuckled to myself after she said that.

"What's so funny?"

"I love you."

"I love you too." She giggled.

She began showing me a drawing she did in school. I didn't have the heart to tell her that I had to drive. So I pulled over to look at her drawing and tell her how beautiful it was.

"Okay daddy, now that you seen it let's hurry up so we can get some pudding."

I quickly started up the Range Rover and sped off. I had to turn down the music as we drove so that she could tell me about her day. When we pulled up in my mother's parking structure I had an earful to tell me how smart my daughter really was. I knew that this game I was in had me risking my life and freedom but my hunger was even more motivated by my children. I definitely wanted her and Joshua to have a better life than me. Those thoughts made me consider my opponents who were trying to meet up with me. His hunger had him willing to do anything to get ahead. This made me consider meeting up with him if not just to see how he looked and feel is vibe. I could read niggas a lot of times when they couldn't read themselves. But my second thought was not to even give him the idea that we were equals. That nigga was trying to establish something with me as though he could really war with me. I didn't have time for that bullshit.

When I got inside my mother's house I noticed William sitting on the couch. He was in comfortable house clothes with a beer while watching the Lakers. Shanee came running inside the house to hug my mother. Shanee really loved her grandmother. But I noticed that she was much nicer to her and Joshua than she was to Sharon and me. I guess since she doesn't have to deal with them every day she can be nice every time she sees them.

"How are you doing Winnie baby? You gon' stay a little while and have some of this banana pudding William and I made?" Mama walked in the living room.

"Yeah, I want to see what Shanee is so excited about. How is everything with you?" I made conversation.

"I'm doing good baby. Yo sister came by and we talked for about an hour or so while William and Marcus talked on the balcony. That boy Marcus Jr. is going to be something else. The Lord has blessed me with three beautiful grandbabies." Mama replied while still hugging Shanee.

"Oooh is my cousin Marcus and my brother Joshua coming through grandma?" Shanee asked.

"You know she's the only one that can call me grandma and get away with it. I always tell Joshua and Marcus Jr. to call me Big Mama. But no matter what I can't get this little girl to do the same." Mama chuckled.

"That's Janice that calls you grandma in front of her. She wants Joshua and Marcus over here with her so she can get all the attention. Both of them are crazy about Shanee." I commented.

"I know my grandbaby spoiled but I love her to death anyway." They finally broke their embrace.

I walked over into the living room while Mama and Shanee went into the kitchen. I sat down to watch the game with William. Then I jumped up for a minute to grab a beer from out the refrigerator after he asked me if I wanted one. We talked about how the Lakers were going to make the playoffs and might do some things this year. For the most part I thought William was a cool laid back person. He blended in good with the environment of my mother's household. He hadn't moved in but I could tell he had spent the night a few times. It was somewhat bizarre because I hardly seen my mother with other men besides my father. I always would hear about them after she broke up with them. Then her and Paula her best friend would get in the living room and talk badly about men. William was probably the second guy I've met after my father was killed. I talked with him for about an hour then I left.

About thirty minutes after I left my mother's house Lonnie called me. I stopped to grab something to eat so that I could use the phone booth. My plan was to holler at Vanessa and Joshua for a little while but not spend the night. But there was no telling what Lonnie had on his mind. I called him at the phone booth right away.

"What's crackin' with you L?"

"You got a little time on yo hands? It's some shit that you might want to peep out." Lonnie replied.

"We can meet up on Baseline Boulevard at the shopping center. Is that cool with you?"

"Truthfully big homie, I was hoping to meet you near Colton over there near Valley College." He replied.

"Alright then I'm on my way."

That was when I knew the shit was serious. He never suggested to meet somewhere other than the spot I designated. I drove over to Valley College as quickly as possible. When I pulled up he once again was already outside the car. This time he had rented a Chevy Impala late model. I thought about asking him what was up with the rental but chose to listen first. Once I walked up to him we embraced.

"What's up Pooh? I need you to check something out for yourself. It should be getting dark real soon." Lonnie said.

"Where we headed?"

"To this spot over in Colton."

I walked over to the passenger side of the Impala and hopped in. We drove for a good half a mile before he pulled up near some apartments. The apartments were familiar but I couldn't put my mind on it instantly then it dawned on me.

"Why are we over here near Shanell's place?" I asked.

"I can show you better than I can tell you." He replied.

Now I was intrigued but I was still somewhat nervous. I was hoping that it was something that I wouldn't mind seeing. But in my heart of hearts I knew that it was something that might piss me off. Nevertheless I sat patiently waiting for whatever was going to happen. It took about twenty minutes before we saw some movement. It hadn't gotten all the way dark but it was on its way. I seen Shanell walk out the door and that didn't surprise me that much. Then I seen Nelly follow closely behind her and he had his arms wrapped around her waist. My mouth dropped. They were laughing about something then he turned her around to face him. They began kissing right on the porch of her apartment. I slowly shook my head and somberly sighed. This was really bad for business. He waited for her to walk down stairs with him then they kissed again. It was long passionate kisses that they both were into.

"Look at this shit." Lonnie mumbled.

It was best for me not to say shit at this point because I was pissed off. I was liable to jump out on both of them and start swinging. Nelly had always been a good dude. I couldn't understand for the life of me why he was doing this shit to Fab-Five. I couldn't even imagine what Fabian might do if he was to find out. This was some really messy shit.

"Drive the fuck off." I demanded.

Lonnie started up the engine and drove down the street. They were so preoccupied with each other they didn't notice the Impala rolling down the street right by them. I felt like exploding. Neither Lonnie nor I said a word on our way back to my car. We were lost in our thoughts. He pulled up right next to my car in the Valley College parking lot. He was about to speak but I indicated with my hand that we get out and walk. The wind was sharp and it had just gotten dark when we made it back. We were going to be cold for a little while.

"How did you find out about that shit?" I asked.

"I had Main Man on him since we met up last week. He told me the only thing he saw was that Nelly would sneak away from the dope spot and drive over this female's house in Colton. He just figured it was some broad he was fucking with. But when he said Colton it rang a bell in my head. I didn't think much of it but I wanted to see who he was seeing. When Main Man took me to the apartment complex I still was thinking it was some other broad but when he came out kissing on Shanell I must have wigged out." Lonnie passionately explained.

"Yeah that's some scandalous shit to be fucking yo boy's girl while he's locked up fighting a murder charge."

"We need to serve this nigga for that shit. I'm telling you Pooh this nigga is probably up to some other shit if he is willing to stoop that low to do in Fab-Five."

"That don't mean he's fucking with some California Garden niggas. We got to handle this shit but I can't just smoke the nigga behind this shit." I replied. My thoughts were racing.

"Fab-Five would smoke that nigga if he was out." Lonnie protested.

"Look here nigga, you might not like every decision I make but that don't mean that you know everything I'm dealing with. Calm the fuck down; I'm just as pissed off about this as you are but I can't just jump the gun. Let me think this through." I stated firmly.

Lonnie didn't respond. He sat back and thought about what I said and remained quiet until I indicated that we should walk back to the car. I wish I could have seen this shit on my own without Lonnie and Main Man. I could take my time with this information. Now everyone would want results. Besides that, contrary to popular belief men gossip just as much as women. If word got around to certain homies then something would have to be done. Just one wrong nigga could turn this shit into a disaster.

"Look here Lonnie, I know your loyalty to Fabian is strong and so is mine. But don't speak on this shit to no one."

Lonnie grudgingly nodded his head. He was a sincere nigga and I knew his loyalty was strong. I had to respect that but it wasn't the right time to move on something like this. If word was to get back to Travon from out of the Delmont Heights I knew it would be hell to pay. Travon loved Fabian like a brother. Nelly and Fab-Five were supposed to be like brothers. Fab-Five put him on and recommended to me that it was okay to let Nelly run the shop in the Dorjil's. This was the ultimate betrayal.

Lonnie and I hopped into our perspective vehicles and drove off. If Fab-Five knew about this he would kill Nelly slow. He might even kill Shanell behind this shit. Fab-Five was a cold ass killer. He believed in killing a nigga if he was a problem. I had to make decisions that were clear and precise.

When I pulled up in the driveway I noticed that Janice was still in the kitchen. Her pretty blue BMW sitting in the driveway next to my car with a light mist covering it made me think of Antoine. Those were some tough times and it seemed as though I was going through them all over again. As I walked into the front door I thought about this Fifty Cent lyric that said. 'Death got to be easy because life is hard' and I understood what he meant at that very moment. Once the door was closed behind me Janice greeted me at the door. She seemed like she was in a good mood. I decided to sit in the kitchen and talk to her since all we had been doing was passing each other. She hugged and kissed me on the cheek and everything.

"Shanee was telling me that you hung out a little while over Mama Shirley's house?" She started talking while fixing me a plate.

"Yeah, I decided to try some of that banana pudding Shanee was so excited about. Plus I would get a chance to watch the game."

"That's good you were spending quality time with yo family. I hope you and I can spend some quality time together soon." She playfully replied.

"That would be good. We should go to an amusement park or Universal City Walk." I smiled.

"That will be good. How about we go to the R. Kelly concert at the Orange Show later this month? All the girls in the shop are talking about going."

"I can't really do the Orange Show crowd because I know too many people."

"How about we go to Anaheim to go see him?" She quickly asked.

"That's cool. Let me know when and we will rent a room down there and have Sharon and Marcus watch Shanee."

She was on cloud nine after my response. I figured she knew that I wouldn't want to go to the Orange Show so she had the Anaheim show as a back-up plan. But I had some concerns of my own.

"How is everything at the shop?" I asked.

"Business is real good. We have a steady stream of customers and we keep attracting more customers."

"How is your girl doing? Uh-Uh what's her name? How is Fabian's girlfriend that works up there with you?"

"You are talking about Shanell? Yeah that bitch doesn't come in regular anymore. Her regular customers are looking for her long after their scheduled appointments and everything. We got into it again the other day because she had this girl waiting an hour after her scheduled time. I told her stupid ass that she's making the business look bad and she keeps talking shit. I don't know how she's paying her bills with all the shit she is buying."

"Is she still paying her booth rent?" I asked.

"She pays her booth rent every month and she is on time too. It's some girls that struggle to pay the booth rent but not Shanell. She's the one who told me about the R. Kelly concert in Anaheim."

"She's going to the concert?"

"That crazy bitch already got her tickets." Janice responded.

"She's not going the same night we are going is she?"

74

"I'll find out what day she's going so we can go on another day. She might peak her head in the shop on Friday or Saturday."

I gobbled down the food she had sat in front of me and decided to give Janice the high hard one. I figured that Nelly was tricking on Shanell. I paid her rent and gave her some extra cash to hold down Fabian's household while he was fighting his case. It definitely was not enough to be missing work and going on shopping sprees. Nelly was in too deep, he wasn't just hitting that ass he was also investing in her. I guess he believed Fab-Five wasn't getting out and neither did she. I put my plate in the dishwasher and went in the room to release some of my frustration. Janice had wanted it for some time but she called herself putting me on punishment again since the housewarming party. Now I was off punishment.

It was several days after finding out the bad news about Shanell and Nelly that I attended Sissy's funeral. It took a little longer because they had to raise money for the funeral. I would have paid for everything like I did with Jake. The only problem with that was I didn't want them to think I was guilty of something. So I gathered a few of the homies and we all donated to help with the funeral arrangements. Her ex-husband was in the front row at the church crying his heart out. Sissy's two daughters were there which I didn't agree with. That was their mother but they were too young to have that last impression of their moms. A few of the homies from out the Dorjil's came through. It was Lonnie, Chris, Nelly, Corey, Rasheed and I that showed up. Everyone went their separate ways after the church services but I followed the procession to the cemetery grounds. I stayed in the cut until her younger sister Felicia walked up to me.

"I'm glad you came Pooh." She attempted to smile.

"Yeah I had to come. Sissy was good peoples." I replied.

"She always thought you were cool ever since we were little. She used to say Pooh is so fine." She slyly grinned.

"How do you know she wanted you to tell me that?" I returned the smile.

"Shit she was right. We both felt that way. She probably would have told you one day if it wasn't for those punk ass California Garden niggas." She scowled.

The tears began to fall from her face again. It wasn't anything I could do at this point. I let her pour it all out.

"I know this won't make you feel better but it is a little something to help you out." I handed her a bag.

"What's this?" She opened the bag.

"It's about twenty-five hundred in one hundred dollar bills. Sissy was good people and she didn't deserve this."

"Thank you Pooh, give me your number so that I can keep in touch with you."

I slid her my number and then she logged her number in my phone. I embraced her one last time before I dipped out.

7
SAN BERNARDINO LIVING

What about you eating dinner in the devil's kitchen?
Big Boi from Outkast

"Ooh Pooh, I'm so glad that you called me. I've had a crush on you since I was a little girl. My sister Sissy 'Rest in Peace' had a crush on you too." Felicia enthusiastically explained.

"Is that so? Well you all grown up nowadays. Everything about you lets me know that you are a woman." I replied.

"You should let me show you how much of a woman I am."

"Maybe you can do that a little later. I was hoping we could get something to eat then maybe chill somewhere." I smiled.

"That's cool with me."

I took her out to a fancy restaurant so that I could wine and dine her. Felicia was pretty as hell and I remembered her as a little girl but now she was all woman. I knew eventually I would have to tap that ass. But I had other plans. First thing I wanted to do was get her addicted to the lifestyle I was introducing her to. Make her crave then hook her into me with fierce loyalty. Not the kind of loyalty a square broad would have for her man. I wanted her to be loyal to the nigga that gave her game. I also wanted her to be loyal to the nigga that gave her revenge.

"Are you enjoying your steak?" I asked while we sat in the restaurant.

"This is the best steak I've ever had in life. I ain't ever been in a place like this before. Thank you Pooh." She whispered.

"Don't even worry about this." I smiled.

After we left the restaurant I told her I would take her home if she liked. She adamantly refused and wanted to know what I was doing tonight. I already rented a hotel room that was four hundred dollars a night. It was a suite with all the amenities that one could ask for. I ordered it for two nights just in case something went a little longer than one night.

"So what were you planning to do later tonight Pooh?" She eagerly asked.

Her youth was beginning to show. It reminded me of a hustler I had to take down. He was a boss nigga named James that I had to go to war with back in the day. He was dead now but his words rang in my head. Young girls for babies and older women for relationships was what he would say. It made sense after spending a few hours with Felicia. She was good looking but she wasn't used to having things. So everything I did was like wow to her. Then her youth would show in the way she would react. I considered her youth when I took her out so I remained patient with her.

"I was going to wind it down and go back to my room. I'm staying in a room for right now. You want to come chill with me for the night?" I glanced at her.

"Hell yeah!"

I pulled into the hotel parking lot with valet parking. Everything I was doing was to hook her to the flash. I wanted her on my team and I wanted her to love what I had to offer. I knew the moment we left that I had her on the hook. The final touches would take place inside the hotel room. She wrapped her arm around mine as we went up to the top floor. As I slid in the card key she glanced one last time in the hallway then smiled when she saw the room. She looked inside the restroom to see the Jacuzzi bathtub and the other amenities that you wouldn't see in people's apartment.

"Man Pooh, you are really living it up. This is the kind of life I want to have one day." She said while taking off her shoes.

"You can have something like this real soon. We gon' see about you having a few things you might want and need, you feel me?" I asked.

"I was feeling you before the restaurant then even more after the restaurant. But now I'm feeling you even more now that we are up in this room." She smiled.

There was nothing left for me to say. I slid off my Nike Air Force Ones then slid off the top to my sweat suit and collapsed on the bed. She climbed on the bed right after me and began rubbing my chest. I just laid back as she slid her hands down my sweat pants. She eased her head down towards my pants then wrapped her mouth around my dick. She began licking slowly allowing her tongue to slide across the shaft. She worked her way down to my balls and continued to work her tongue. I loved every bit of it but I could tell she was trying to impress me. She kept glancing up at me to see my reaction to the oral pleasure she was providing. Sorry to disappoint you honey but I've had someone give me head before. I had to hold in my smirk as I thought about how seductive she was trying to act. No baby I'm seducing you but you don't even know it.

By now she had slid my pants down to my ankles with my help. I didn't tell her to stop but she took a small break to get totally nude. I glanced at her perky titties and small waist and my tongue got sticky. She climbed on the bed as her plump ass bounced as she came closer to me. I couldn't help but grab her ass while she began kissing on my neck and chest. She worked her way down to my stomach and back down to the main target. I moaned in satisfaction as she continued her phenomenal blow job. Then she worked her way back up to kissing on my neck and climbed on top of me. She guided my manhood inside of her and I plunged right in. As she rode me she let down her hair that was in a bun and held together by chopsticks. She moaned in satisfaction while rubbing on my chest. I had to admit that she was good at riding me. So young yet so gifted.

"Ooh Pooh that's it right there." She moaned.

79

I grabbed hold of those huge hips as she bounced up and down. Then I turned her over doggy style and put in work. She moaned and whined while I had her fat ass on the edge of the bed sticking up in the air. We continued our sex episode in several different positions until I realized she was satisfied. When I finally came, we both collapsed on the bed. We laid there momentarily while panting and trying to catch our breath.

"You good about everything you do? Why you ain't got a woman?" She asked.

"I have plenty of women. But you and your sister are special to me. So I just want to make sure you are alright." I replied.

"I can see how bitches are chasing after you. But you done already made me feel good in more ways than one."

"Well what about where you live? You still like living with your moms up in the Dorjil's?"

"Hell nah, especially after the girls are gone. My nieces went to live with their daddy now that Sissy is gone." She shook her head in disbelief.

"It's gon' be alright. I'll make sure some homeboys I know will find out who did that to yo sister. You want them locked up for life?" I asked.

"Fuck no, I want they muthafuckin' asses dead. A homicide detective came by my mama's house asking did Sissy have any enemies. My mama looked at him like he was crazy. Tears fell from my eyes because they probably won't ever find out who killed my sister." She began to sob.

"We'll find them I promise. What was the detective's name that came by to visit yo moms?" I consoled her.

"He was an old black dude named Barber or Barnes or some shit like that."

I didn't say anything after that. I thought about Detective Barnes snooping around the Dorjil's a few years back when my mother stayed over there. That was one muthafucka I was trying

80

to avoid. Felicia was in her own thoughts probably dwelling on the loss of her sister. I decided to lighten up the mood.

"What if I told you that you could get your own spot and move out of your mom's house?"

"Yeah right! How would I be able to do that?"

"I'll help you pay the rent and everything. I'll come through every now and then to take care of some business but it will be your spot." I replied.

"When are you talking about doing this?"

"In about a week or so the month will be up. We can find a place and set you up good with furniture and everything. I'll even get you a ride but you got to get a job to pay utilities and shit like that."

I really wanted her to get a job so that I could use that time to cook up the raw. I didn't want her around when I was cooking up all that cocaine into crack. Even though she probably knew what I did to make money it was wise not to have it in her face. This would be perfect if she was down. I wouldn't have to rent a hotel room with a kitchenette any more. This was cheaper in the long run. I was basically taking care of three households already so one more wasn't shit. Another good thing about Felicia was that I knew where her mother lived. I knew where her people were from. So I didn't have to worry about her taking off with my shit. Felicia didn't take me as that type anyway but it was still good to know I could locate her if she disappeared.

"Thank You Pooh." She reached over to hug and kiss me.

Now that I would be set up again I could concentrate on other things. I still had to serve those niggas in the California Gardens. Then I had to handle some shit in my own clique. This Nelly shit was the worse. If Fabian was to find out about this and knew that we knew about it he would be pissed off. He'd really be hurt if I didn't deal with the shit. Out of all the niggas she could fuck with she decided to mess with his homeboy. Shanell was a good looking broad. It was all kinds of niggas that she could holla at while Fab-Five was locked down. But you don't ever do a nigga like that. Especially a killer like Fab-Five. I dialed the numbers contemplating my next move.

"Hello?"

"What's up Gangster Nelly? This is Pooh."

"What's crackin' my nigga?"

"Why don't you let Cory and Rasheed handle the spot for a while? Then me and you can chop it up and get something to eat." I suggested.

"Where do you want me to meet you?"

"Meet me over there on Pepper Street in about ten minutes. Do you need more time?"

"Nah that's cool, I'll be over there in about ten minutes."

"Alright then!" I replied then hung up the phone.

I knew he was over Shanell's house that was why I only gave him ten minutes. That was my way of confirming if he was over there or not. When he pulled up in his Suburban Truck he looked serious. He took his time getting out the car as if he was preparing for something. I wondered if he thought I knew. I would have to play it by ear. When he got out the car he walked up to me smelling like that Michael Jordan cologne. We quickly embraced and walked into the fast food restaurant.

"Carl's Jr. got this bomb ass chicken sandwich that I want to get." I broke the ice.

"Yeah, that shit got a pepper in it. I'm about to order one too." He smiled.

We sat down across from each other inside of a booth. There were a couple of people waiting in line but the dining area was basically empty. We waited for our food to come before we really said anything.

"So what do you think about what those California Garden niggas did to Sissy?" I asked.

"Those niggas were foul for shooting a female in the head. It wasn't like she set somebody up or something. Sissy talked a lot but that wasn't worth her getting killed especially since she wasn't in the game. I felt real fucked up about her two daughters." Nelly explained.

"Yeah, but I heard they were with their daddy now."

"But still, they won't never get to see they mama again. I know she wasn't in our clique but I wouldn't mind serving those niggas for what they done." He commented.

"Yeah, I got shooters in the clique but I don't have any killers like Fab-Five. He would walk his crazy ass over there in a heartbeat and peel a nigga's cap." I said.

I glanced at him after that statement while taking a bite of my sandwich. I seen him glance around nervously and swallow his food hard. I didn't want to push the issue too much.

"So what's up with you Nelly; how has life been treating a young Baller like you?"

"Baller? I'm doing cool but I ain't a Baller like yo ass." He smiled.

"Yeah, but if you stack yo bread right you can be there. I might back up out this game real soon and decide to pass on my connect." I shrugged.

"Shit if you decide to get out the game I thought you might want to pass yo connect to Lonnie. I didn't think you would be thinking about me." He sincerely replied.

"Well you and Lonnie are the best at grinding for this money in the clique. It might be good if both of ya'll had the connect if you know what I mean."

"That would be straight." He nodded his head.

"But you know a boss nigga can't violate the code. He's got to live by the code or he ain't shit. You know what I'm saying? We chose this life so we ain't men when we ain't following what we chose to walk. Now if we walk away from the life that's different. But as far as I can tell you've been a stand up nigga. That's why I got major love for you." I explained.

"I got love for you too, my nigga." Nelly smiled.

I nodded as we finished our food. That was basically my way of reading him the riot act. He was on the up and up as far as

I can tell except for this Shanell situation. I knew I couldn't get at her because females can get emotional about shit. Next thing I knew she could be telling Fab-Five and Nelly that I tried to holla at her. She might even take it a step further and tell Janice some shit. I was hoping that his conscious would have him make the right decision.

We talked a little more then went our separate ways. I decided to pay Vanessa a visit when I left Carl's Jr. I rolled into her apartment complex and parked the Range Rover next to her Benz. When I walked upstairs she was in the bedroom talking to my son. I peaked in the bedroom then kissed her on the cheek. After joining in the conversation for a while I led Vanessa back into the living room and out into the balcony. She had grabbed me a beer before she came outside.

"What's on your mind, Winnie?"

"I wanted to ask your opinion about something. Tell me what you really think." I replied.

"Don't I always tell you what I really think?"

I nodded and leaned over the rail. I sipped on my beer before saying anything. She patiently waited for me to gather myself.

"What if you had two homeboys working under you and you found out somehow that one of your homeboys was fucking your other homeboy's woman behind his back?" I asked.

"Whoa, you came out the gate with some crazy shit. I wasn't expecting that. Let me think about that for a minute."

She let the thought run through her head for a moment. She leaned on the rail and looked out into the mountain scenery.

"You have a loyalty problem. If he's fucking his homeboy's woman than he must have some snake in him. That means he's capable of doing some other shit as well. You got to get rid of him." She replied.

"Just like that. I mean what if that is his only fault in this game? What if he's been on the up and up about everything else?" I asked.

84

"There is a thin line in the game and anything can push a nigga over the edge. Let's say that he gets caught up by the law. They pressure him to talk by threatening to expose his secret. Once there is an opening for weakness you always have to get rid of it or it becomes your weakness too." She calmly explained.

"Every man has a weakness. I should get rid of a man because I've found out one of his? It's seems a little hypocritical."

"Look Winnie, you asked my opinion so I gave it to you. You better believe that he's got something in him to go after another's man woman if that is his homeboy. Especially if they are in the game together. As fragile as loyalty can be in this shit you have to question other shit about him. But you gon' do what you want to do." She said with slight irritation.

"This game makes you lose who you are. Just to stay above water you got to be hard hearted at times. Sometimes I feel like my soul has been stolen from me." I complained.

"Yeah, but this is the life we chose. Many of us choose this life and don't want to take the good with the bad. The money and the nice things are what turns people to the game but once they fall on hard times they turn on the game." Vanessa replied.

"Yeah, if I got to die let me die standing and not on my knees. So what you know good?" I changed the subject.

"I am glad you came by. You didn't even compliment me on my hair. Do you like it?" Vanessa posed for me.

"It looks beautiful every time you get it done. I even like the burgundy highlights as well."

"Thank you. But I was hearing people in the beauty salon talking about some young niggas in the California Gardens moving weight. Some niggas named Markell and Casey. One of the little young bitches in there is fucking with Markell. Her name is Tanya but they call her Pebbles. She was bragging in the salon about how her man is running shit nowadays. She's dating Markell and her friend Bernice is dating some nigga named Marquise. That little young hoodrat couldn't keep her mouth shut. She is definitely a liability to her man."

"You never cease to amaze me. I've been trying to get the names of the niggas moving weight over there for some time. Then there you go with the name of three niggas over there. So Markell and Casey are the ones I need to be asking about?" I rhetorically asked in disbelief.

"Yeah, she was talking about how they are living it up San Bernardino style. She said that her man Markell is a shot calling nigga."

"What about Casey?"

"He's Markell's road dog. According to 'Ms. Pebbles' he's too grimy for one of her homegirls even though he's making money too. But it sounds like Casey is his number two."

"What about this nigga Marquise the one her homegirl is getting at?" I continued to probe.

"I don't know much about him because his girl didn't talk as much as Markell's girl. But he has to be one of the niggas that got some kind of rank because he was mentioned with the other two. If he was a curb serving nigga he wouldn't have…"

"Mama, can I fix me a peanut butter and jelly sandwich? I just finished my homework." Joshua asked out of nowhere.

"Go ahead baby; you startled me for a minute." Vanessa glanced back at our son.

I did the same and he smiled at both of us. It didn't look like he heard our conversation but you never know. He was getting older so he might catch on to things a little faster. Both Vanessa and I watched him walk into the kitchen before we continued.

"Like I was saying, he ain't just curb serving. He's probably right under them."

"How often do those young broads come into the shop?" I glanced back to see where my son was.

"I've seen them in there before. They usually come in on Saturdays and they have been coming in a lot since her man is a shot caller." Vanessa chuckled.

"Cool. Let me know if they are up in there the next time you go in and I will put some people on them."

"So what are you going to do about your homeboy fucking another one of your homeboys?"

I smiled without replying. She understood what I meant and we both left it at that. I stuck around for dinner and decided to spend the night. It was one of those moments where Vanessa and I connected that night. She and I made love until the early morning. Then we laughed and joked about different things. I had a house with Janice but Vanessa was my bottom bitch without a doubt. It was a night to remember.

The following morning I got up early and hit Lonnie on his cell phone from a phone booth. He hit me back in about ten minutes and we chopped it up.

"So is Main Man still sitting on what we seen the other night?" I asked.

"Yeah, and he says ain't shit changed. They still got this thing going on and it ain't about to stop." Lonnie insisted.

"Okay tell Main Man to back off of him and I'll handle the shit from here."

"Are you sure my nigga? I don't mean any disrespect but are you sure you want to do that?" Lonnie strongly asked.

"Don't worry about it. I got it under control."

He left it at that. We discussed another time we would meet up and then we got off the phone. I waited a few days before I even moved on anything. The difficulty was trying to figure out how things could happen. Those few days I took was good for me because that was the time I moved Felicia into her spot in Colton. She was loving the idea of having her own place. She had gotten herself a job and was on cloud nine. Then it dawned on me while I moved her few things in; how I would take care of my problem. All we had to do was move her clothes and a few more miscellaneous things. I spent the night with her on a blow up mattress so she wouldn't feel so alone in her empty apartment.

87

The very next day I went up to the phone booth and called up my homeboy Travon. He was one of my comrades that I could rely on. I told him that I would meet him at a particular time and that it was real important. He agreed to meet up at that time then I went from there. I figured we'd have a long talk over some food. Then we would walk outside to discuss business.

By the time I went home to Janice a few days had passed. I laid in my bed pondering on the things I had in place. My eyes stared at our bedroom ceiling like I was in a trance. Janice laid next to me tossing and turning and basically fuming. I had spent the night out a few more days than usual. She probably wanted to get it off her chest. I ignored her for as long as I could because I wasn't in the mood for an argument.

"Winnie we need to talk."

"About what?"

"About you spending the night out like you do. Do you have to be out and about like you do when you know we got a daughter at home?" She pleaded.

"I do baby. You just will have to understand that I'm always on the move. I sleep where I can and when I can. It's not that I don't want to come home I'm just living in these San Bernardino streets and I got to be one step ahead of everyone else." I replied.

"Well if this continues you will end up losing me and our daughter. Because I need something stable in my life and so does Shanee."

"This house is not stable enough for you?" I replied.

"Not if I don't have my man with me half the time. Who wants to come home to an empty house?" She snapped.

"This is the life we chose so I don't want to hear anything else about it." I replied calmly.

"This is the life *you* chose." She mumbled under her breath.

"What did you say?"

"Nothing, let's just go to sleep." She suggested.

I heard what she said but didn't push the issue any further. The bitch was getting on my nerves. I had all this shit to deal with and she wants to nag about me coming home. It could be a whole lot worse. I just rolled over and went to sleep. I'll deal with this later.

8
DEL MONT HEIGHTS MURDER

Misfortune is attached to the debris of total chaos!
PaPa Sak

Nelly felt good about making some of the rounds now. It let him know that Pooh was beginning to recognize his hard work. He climbed out of Shanell's bed regretting once again that he had slept with his homeboy's girl. Fabian would kill me if he knew what I was doing, he pondered. He wiped his eyes to clear the sleep crust that had formed. He sat on the edge of the bed thinking about his life. His thoughts raced as he drank some water sitting next to the bed.

"You want me to fix you something to eat before you leave?" Shanell asked while entering the room.

He told her to wake him up in a couple of hours because of a run he had to make. He nodded his head to confirm her suggestion. He wasn't much in the mood for talking. He thought Shanell was a cool ass female though. She had hooked her claws into him and he couldn't break loose. She had that pretty caramel complexion that blended in with her conservative hairstyle. The highlights in her hair blended in with her complexion perfectly. Her 5'2 frame was petite but impressive in all the right places. But she was much more conservative than her body suggested. She was one of those types of women that didn't like to show off her body though she couldn't help it. Nelly smiled at the thought of seeing her. He finally lifted himself from the bed so that he could walk into the restroom.

He thought about ending his affair with Shanell. After he had the talk with Pooh at Carl's Jr.; he considered not ever going to see her again. It would be best he thought. He had it in his mind that he would go right to her house and tell her it was over. Then he seen her and everything changed. It had him perplexed because his homeboy's baby mama was the perfect woman to him.

"What are you doing over here Cornell? I wasn't expecting you to come through until later on tonight. But it's good to see you baby, come on in." Shanell opened the door.

"What were you doing? I just came to talk to you about something." Nelly asked while walking inside.

"I just got off the phone with Janice. You know Sherwin is taking her through the ringer. He has all kinds of women he's chasing after and some nights he doesn't even come home to the new house they bought together. It's sad but between you and me, I think Janice is staying for the money and the status. She is always complaining about the things he does." She gossiped.

"Yeah but Pooh is a hood nigga she should know that he might act like that."

"You are a hood nigga and I'm always able to talk to you if I need to. If we didn't have this secret wouldn't you come home to me every night?" She asked.

Nelly painfully nodded his head. He was quickly developing a headache. He felt dizzy for a spell. Shanell had him open.

"What's wrong baby? You said you came over here to talk to me about something?" She walked over towards him.

"I sometimes wonder if Pooh knows that we are seeing each other. I just came from hanging with him and he was talking about how he needs to trust me because he might need me to take over one day." Nelly laid his head on her stomach and wrapped his arms around her.

She stood next to him while he sat in the chair holding her tightly. She felt the frustration and could sense the desperation. She kept her arms around his head and gently rubbed on his face.

"If Pooh does know then I might have fucked up real bad. He may have some loyalty to me but he also has loyalty to Fabian.

91

If he tells Fabian, then that nigga won't rest until I'm dead. I can kill but I ain't a killer; you know what I mean?" Nelly explained.

"Yeah but how do you know that he knows? He could just be promoting you without even suspecting anything. Besides, he would probably tell you or me that he knows what we are doing. And I haven't mentioned it to anyone even Janice." She sadly replied.

"Why would he tell me something that he feels I should know better? I have a loyalty to Fabian too, I don't know. If I was in his shoes I would want to get rid of a problem."

"I think you are just worried about nothing. He probably trusts what you are doing and wants to give you more responsibility. Stop worrying about it Cornell." She assured him.

Nelly stood in the mirror contemplating the events of that afternoon. He still wondered if he should have just ended it. But now he was being promoted to do drop offs like Lonnie. He would start off in the Delmont Heights delivering to Travon. He walked into the living room after washing his face and brushing his hair.

"You look so handsome right now." Shanell smiled.

"Come here."

He wrapped his arm around her waist and they passionately kissed. The aroma from the pasta dish is what stopped their passionate embrace. The hunger pangs in his stomach began to call out to him. She rubbed his bare chest then walked in the kitchen to fix his plate. He was ready to get out there and prove himself once again.

Marquise was rolling down the street in his new Impala with twenty inch rims. He was feeling good while playing that Rick Ross. He had to pick his girl Bernice up from the beauty salon. He planned on getting him some pussy before he hit the block. He smiled at the idea. Bernice was a chocolate bombshell with an athletic body. She kept her hair short to accentuate her beautiful face. Her homegirl Tanya was supposed to hook her up with Casey but she wasn't feeling him like that. Tanya a.k.a.

Pebbles was Markell's girl; who Marquise and everyone else called Killa Kell. He was moving the weight up in the California Gardens and Marquise was his number three. Markell, Casey and Marquise all grew up together but he wasn't as close as Markell and Casey. But there was love there just the same. He was feeling good about his position in the new organization. They had particularly grown close when they lost a few homeboys that was ambushed. Marquise never met the man but he hated the nigga they called Pooh. Everybody on the West Side knew that he was the one moving weight in most neighborhoods. Some people were saying he even had people hustling for him in the city of Rialto. But because of that ambush he lost his road dog Cornbread. He and Cornbread were close like Markell and Casey.

"I know that nigga ordered the shit that killed my peoples." Marquise said aloud.

He pulled up in front of the 'Beauty Divas' Hair Salon expecting Bernice to walk out any minute. Then out comes the chocolate bombshell he had seen before when he came to pick up Bernice. She was even prettier than Bernice and that wasn't an easy task. She kind of reminded him of that Miss America girl Kenya Moore. She was even built like her. He stared in amazement as the girl walked down the street. He looked through his rearview window as she crossed the street.

"The nigga that's fucking her probably got major paper. She's finer than frog hair." He shook his head in disbelief.

A moment later he heard a knock on his passenger side window. He glanced up to see Bernice staring at him through the window.

"You gon' let me in or keep staring at Vanessa?"

He pushed the automatic unlock on his door and she climbed inside. He grinned knowing he was caught staring at the attractive woman.

"Aw baby you tripping off of a nigga looking at a bitch?" Marquise chided.

"No not really, because that bitch is pretty than a muthafucka. I can't hate even if I wanted to." She replied.

"Her dude must got paper huh?" Marquise asked out of curiosity.

"I don't know who her man is. She's quiet all the time when she's in the salon but she's so nice. All she does is speak to people but Pebbles was running off at the mouth last weekend. I couldn't get the bitch to shut up." Bernice commented.

"What was she saying? Killa Kell is the last nigga she wants to be talking too much about."

"I know; that nigga's crazy. But she was talking about how her nigga is a boss and everything. She wasn't even calling them Killa Kell and Cay. She was calling them Markell and Casey. I was like damn why don't this bitch shut the fuck up?" Bernice laughed.

"Yeah I'm gon' have to talk to Killa Kell about that shit. She gon' need to know when to shut the fuck up." Marquise replied.

"I'm knowing. I know we some fly ass bitches and we shitting on these hoes but don't talk about it; be about it. You know what I'm saying?" Bernice replied.

Marquise didn't respond he just cruised down the street and lit up a blunt. The sweet aroma of Kush Chronic Marijuana floated throughout the car. He puffed on the blunt three or four times then passed it to Bernice. She puffed on it as they made their way to the hotel room. They were both in their thoughts passing the weed back and forth.

"I know we gon' get a room tonight but when are we getting our own place?" Bernice asked out of nowhere.

Here this bitch go again, Marquise thought. He didn't say anything as he drove into the hotel parking lot. He turned off the engine and just stared at her for a brief moment. She knew he wasn't in the mood when he gave her that look. She grabbed her overnight bag and didn't say anything else. He carried her bags inside then led her to the upstairs room he had already paid for.

94

In a black Camry with tinted windows and a dealer's license plate two men sat outside the very same hotel. Oblivious to Marquise these two men had followed him all the way from the beauty salon.

"Look here, you gon' light this nigga up then we gon' speed off." Lonnie said to Main Man.

"I got the nine-millimeter ready to go."

"Yeah, my nigga you gon' win some points with Pooh for taking care of this shit. You got a good look of the nigga when he got out the car. All you need to do is start dumping on that nigga when you see him coming down the stairs." Lonnie explained.

"What if he doesn't come back down here tonight? He might not come downstairs until the morning." Main Man replied.

"Well then we gon' have to wait until he comes out of that room in the morning."

"If he's with that female should I just blast her too?" Main Man inquired.

"Nah, we ain't into blasting on females like those niggas. We just gon' have to put this stocking over yo face if it's daylight. It's gon' be harder for her to point you out with a cap and a stocking. But don't smoke the broad." Lonnie explained.

"How you know Pooh don't want her dead also?" Main Man insisted.

"I just know." Lonnie grew impatient.

It didn't take long for Marquise to walk out of the hotel room. He opened the door and stood in the door. It appeared he was having a conversation with the woman he had upstairs. Lonnie touched Main Man on the shoulder to indicate it was time to move. Main Man quickly hopped out of the car. He was able to make it near the soda machine right under Marquise's room. After a few more words was exchanged with Bernice, Marquise came walking down the stairs. He walked down the stairs counting money without a worry in the world. He glanced up when he reached the bottom of the stairs to see Main Man fondling with the soda machine. He walked past him without giving it a second thought.

In a flash Main Man walked up behind him and plugged two bullets to the back of his head. Marquise's body fell to the ground and Main Man quickly walked off. He made sure not to run but walked extremely fast. Lonnie already had the door opened when he was ready to climb in. They then drove off without speeding away.

Bernice had the television up loud but she thought she heard gunshots. She decided to peak outside and when she did she noticed that Marquise's car was still in the parking lot. She opened the curtains all the way and thought she saw someone's leg. She threw on her jeans and one of his T-Shirts to inquire why he hadn't left yet. She also wanted to know if he heard the gunshots as well. When she went downstairs she could tell that he wasn't inside the car. As she drew closer she realized that Marquise was lying on the concrete next to the driver's side.

She suddenly screamed as loud as she could. Her body began to shake as she stared at his body in horror. Suddenly people came out of their rooms to see who was screaming. She continued to scream. She continued to shake uncontrollably as the very man she had just made love to laid dead next to his car. Someone eventually called the ambulance while other hotel patrons came to her aid.

Finally the police sectioned everything off with yellow tape. The marked police cars swarmed the area within minutes securing the perimeter. By that time Bernice was wrapped up in a blanket still noticeably shaken. An unmarked car pulled up and a Hispanic man in a suit and tie hopped out the car. He talked to one of the uniformed cops who pointed towards the body. Once he looked over the body he glanced up to see Bernice still standing nearby. He sighed then walked over to her calmly.

"I'm Homicide Detective Hector Levya of the San Bernardino Sheriff Department. Can I speak to you for a moment? Let's start off with your name."

"My name is Bernice Ambrose." She replied.

Nelly drove up in his suburban with all smiles. He noticed Travon standing outside the spot in the Delmont Heights waiting on him. He was standing next to someone he didn't know. It must have been one of his curb servers working under him. He pulled up right in front of him and climbed out the car.

"What's cracking Travon my nigga?" Nelly said enthusiastically.

"Just trying to get that paper. What's up with you?"

They shook hands but Travon held him out so they couldn't embrace. Nelly looked at him in a bizarre way then chose to ignore it. Travon could be a hard ass at times, he considered. He looked around and observed his surroundings; it was the Delmont Heights after all.

"Where the shit at?" Travon asked.

"In the back seat of the car. Look under the seat and you'll find a half for you." Nelly replied.

"Why you drive yo own shit up in here when you delivering a package. When Lonnie comes up in this bitch, he is always in a bucket or a rental. That way they can't seize yo shit." Travon explained.

"I don't plan on doing that shit all the time. But break me off that bread so that I can bounce up out of here." Nelly said.

"Alright follow me."

Travon led him down the street then took him to the back yard of a vacant house.

"So you've been fucking with any new bitches lately?" Travon asked out the blue.

"A few here and there. Nothing too much because I've been trying to make this money."

"Are you bullshitting me? As many women I've seen you pull back in the day you ain't fucking with any bad bitches?" Travon insisted.

"I said no nigga; now get me the bread so I can bounce." Nelly said sounding irritable.

"Damn nigga quit tripping. You sure you haven't been fucking with any new females? You ain't fucking with a female named Shanell?"

"Aw shit...you know about that? It ain't what you think my nigga..."

POW!!!

One bullet pierced a hole in the back of Nelly's head. His body dropped to the ground crushing some of the tall weeds in the backyard. A young shooter named Willie was looming over the body. He looked down at the corpse as if he was admiring his work.

"Look here nigga, get the keys to his car and dump that shit somewhere on the street. Dre you follow this nigga to wherever he decides to dump the car and ya'll get back here. We gon' close up shop tonight because the police is about get hot." Travon ordered.

They moved out without saying another word. About twenty minutes later the police arrived at the vacant house. They taped off the backyard with yellow tape until the homicide detective showed up. After about thirty minutes a brown Crown Victoria pulled up in front of the vacant house. A handsome middle aged Black man hopped out of his vehicle. He looked around at the crowd that had gathered around. He glanced at all the onlookers trying to do a brief scan of the crowd.

"More than likely our victim's killer is in this crowd." Detective Barnes said to himself.

He walked in the backyard and climbed over the tall weeds to reach the body. He looked at the body and noticed the bullet wound to the back of the head. He noticed the footprints left after the murder.

"There was one shooter but three people involved besides the victim. It appears that he was lured back here by someone. This is an obvious homicide. Close range to the back of the head.

98

The imprint of residue and powder indicates that it was close range." Detective Barnes said to another officer.

"Aye Barnes, since you are the primary on this murder here is his wallet." A uniformed cop said.

He handed Detective Barnes the wallet and he looked inside. He instantly recognized the picture on the identification. He frowned as he tried to place the name and face.

"Cornell Davenport!"

He rolled the body over trying to figure out where he knew the young man from. Then he thought about the Dorjil Apartment complex.

"You are outside of your neighborhood young man." Detective Barnes rhetorically spoke to the corpse.

"That's who you are! You are someone that works for Mr. Daniels. Mr. Sherwin Daniels. He lost another one of his people over in the Dorjil Apartments a little while back. I wonder if these murders are connected?"

By the time Detective Barnes walked outside the crowd had dispersed. He seen a few stragglers but they turned their head the moment he looked their way. He decided to call it a night and deal with his new revelation the next day. He also considered that he would have to pay Mr. Sherwin Daniels a.k.a. Pooh a visit real soon.

9
HOT

We watch for cops hopping out the back of vans!
Jay-Z

Once again after leaving the house Janice and I own, I felt the police were following me. Usually I'm able to switch cars or trip them up so they can lose my location. I brought my Range Rover to a mechanic to see if the police had put a Lojack on my car but they couldn't find anything. But this familiar brown Crown Victoria continued to follow me this day. It was an unmarked police car but I could tell that it was a cop car. Finally after allowing me to go several blocks he pulled me over.

When he got out the car it dawned on me that I knew the detective. He walked out with his hand on his pistol holster just in case something went down. He should have known better than that. Slowly Detective Barnes approached my car window.

"We need to talk." He stated firmly.

"What do we need to talk about?" I asked.

"We need to talk about these murders that have been taking place for the last few weeks. Knowing your position in this game, it is one of two things. Either you are a willing participant in these murders or you are an allowing participant in these murders." He replied.

"What if I don't know anything about these murders and it is just a bunch of niggas acting like damn fools?" I commented.

"Come on Mr. Daniels, you and I both know better than that."

I glanced into the sky when he said that. It was one of those gloomy days when it appeared as though it was about to rain.

It wasn't cold but it wasn't hot either. But that was only the weather because I was feeling the heat of the police. He allowed me to wander in my thoughts but he knew that I wasn't willing to talk.

"Mr. Daniels I know you are a strict believer in the code of the streets. But what's going on right about now is something that is going to bring law enforcement at your doorsteps. I had a woman that is the mother of two killed in the California Gardens. A few weeks ago a partner of mine caught a murder of a young man by the name of Jacob Chandler that I know worked for you. Then another one of my colleagues caught a murder from a young man named Marquise Caldwell. He was from out the California Gardens. Then last but definitely not least a few nights ago I ran across a guy that I know is one of your workers. His name is Cornell Davenport and he was found dead in the back yard of a vacant house."

I listened to him explain the details of these murders without responding. I glanced at him with a look as though I was asking him what he expected me to do.

"I'll tell you what Mr. Daniels; since you're such a smart ass. If these murders don't stop somehow you will find yourself the blame for them all. I remember that young man talking to you the day we arrested Fabian Gilmore. You kept it peaceful for years so you might want to keep it that way." He firmly stated.

"You are preaching to the choir. You think I want bodies so that I can get pulled over by you fine folks. Believe it or not Detective Barnes; I don't control everything that happens in the streets."

He backed away from the window in defeat. He lowered his head then shook it. I understood what he was trying to do. He just wanted the killings to stop and I actually felt for him. For the most part he was a good cop trying to do the right thing. But he and I belonged to two different governments as far as I was concerned. Truthfully I wanted the killings to stop as well but it wasn't entirely up to me.

101

"Look, I will see what I can do. But it's not up to me like you might think." I said.

"I'm starting to think that you are all the same; a bunch of criminals that kill one another and disgrace our people. Hard working Black people that abide by the law have to live with the stereotypes you guys reinforce." He sadly replied.

"So I'm supposed to live by the rules that govern yo life? I'm supposed to get exploited by giving someone forty hours or more a week so I can have bad credit. Then have to kiss the ass of someone less intelligent in order to get ahead. At least I'm not a hypocrite. I know the world I chose and the consequences that come with it. You don't understand my stress or my perspective yet you judge me. If that's all DETECTIVE BARNES then I would like to leave now."

He glanced at me and we made brief eye contact. Then he waved his hand indicating that I could leave. It had been a long time since I was able to vent my anger and frustration. It felt good to do so. But my second thought was that what I said might bite me in the ass one day. I had bigger problems than Detective Barnes pulling me over. I had to prepare for Nelly's funeral. I knew that Janice would want to go because she met him and everything. What bothered me was that she might have known that Nelly and Shanell were messing around. It wouldn't benefit her to tell me because she knew I wouldn't like it. All these things raced through my head on my way to Simpson Mortuary. The young woman at the front desk would probably start thinking something after seeing me in there twice in the last few weeks. I had a few errands to run before the day ended so I couldn't let it bother me.

After I prepared everything for Nelly's funeral I stopped by Felicia's house to cook up the dope. I knew she had to work today so I had several hours to do my thing. Lonnie would pick up the dope from me around three or four in the afternoon. I already changed cars and was rolling around in the Caprice when I went to Felicia's house. Lonnie and I decided that it would be best that we let Main Man take over the Dorjil's. We then could still move the weight and promote him in the process. I thought the young soldier was loyal and had earned his spot. I wasn't trying to step on Corey and Rasheed's toes so I suggested that we give them a bonus to pacify them. Lonnie was going to add more money to their cut that way everyone would be happy.

We also had to explain the Nelly murder. What I decided was that we told everyone in our crew that some California Garden niggas were responsible. I knew that Lonnie, Main Man and Travon knew better but that was because they knew about Nelly fucking with Shanell. Everyone else didn't need to know that we took care of one of our own for fucking up. I wasn't trying to send that kind of message. I had to also worry about the niggas from out the Gardens retaliating for us getting one of their people. We wanted to get the niggas Killa Kell and Casey but we could only get one of their peoples. This game kept tugging at my conscious even though a lot of it was necessary. I used to envy the position of a nigga I once took down. James was the top dog then but now I was living the stress he had endured. I worked to get to the top spot and with a little luck and a few smart moves I made it. But now police came to me to solve the problems of the San Bernardino streets. It bothered me even more while I cooked up the raw cocaine into crack. I was getting a contact from all that dope and I guess it made me more sensitive. It made me worry more than usual.

Even after I cooked up everything I still wondered how I would be able to touch Killa Kell and Casey. If I got rid of them then I won't have to worry about the violence as much. They were some hungry upstarts that were unpredictable. From what I was hearing we had gotten their number three. But whenever you fucking with some people in the game its best to get number one or number two. Number two is usually the buffer between the number one and everyone else. If you know the game of chess, it is the queen that can move all around while the king just relaxes. But you have to trap the king in order to win the game.

103

Going after the number one is very difficult because more than likely there is a reason he is number one. You can't just have a connection to get dope and become a boss. You have to be able to make niggas want to follow you. You can do it either through fear, confidence or respect. The nigga that came before me had earned people's confidence as someone that took care of business. He didn't have to instill fear because he had people around that did that for him. Those that were feared had enough confidence in him that he would take care of them. James did exactly that until I took him down. The way I was respected as a boss was through respect. People seen me start from the rock bottom and work my way up to the top spot. I gave young hustlers hope that it could be done. I also showed them that I was the type that can do it. By living by that ethic and never violating the code of the streets I gained the respect of the people that worked for me.

But it was easy to tell that Markell was the type of cat that wanted to be a boss based upon fear. He wanted people that served under him or served under someone else to fear him. Niggas like Markell were too willing to kill to get that result. Murders always brought about police so the rule is to do them only when necessary. Markell was becoming a dilemma.

I finally finished cooking the dope and I stuffed it in a stash inside the car. I kept rubbing my eyes because the dope was starting to get to me. I was glad that Felicia had underground parking so I wouldn't have to worry about cops watching the spot. I walked back inside the house and decided it would be best I take a shower. I had a few clothes over at her spot. I was in the shower for about twenty to thirty minutes. Lonnie wasn't supposed to meet with me until another hour and a half. I could have watched a sitcom if I wanted to. Once I got out the shower the front door opened and closed. Glancing at the bathroom clock I realized that Felicia had made it in by then. I grabbed my robe to greet her.

"What's going on Pooh?" She greeted me first.

She was standing near the bathroom door when I opened it. We both stared at each other for a moment of lust. It was one of those times where you and another person know what each other is thinking. I didn't have a problem with tapping her young ass before I bounced.

"Let me jump in the shower real fast." She suggested.

I smiled without saying anything. Felicia was an exhibitionist like this stripper I used to mess with named Princess. I had pussy on the brain but another thought came to mind. If I involved her then I would have to be very careful.

Once she got out the shower she threw on body spray that instantly aroused me. Her body was still wet from the shower. Her aroma was from 'Bath & Body Works'. I grabbed her around her waist and stuck my tongue in her mouth. She put her arms around my waist as I slid my hands down to that plump ass. We kissed for a few minutes then I turned her around. I put both of her hands against the wall and lifted her right leg up from the back. I slid inside her as she bounced her booty against my pelvis. I grabbed her by her neck and choked her while she moaned.

"Oooh that's it Pooh, right there."

I learned through Janice that these young broads wanted you to be real rough with them. These young bitches were into choking, anal sex and all kind of freaky shit. I was willing to try a certain amount of things. I damn sure wasn't about to stick my dick up her ass though. That was still some gay shit to me. But I wore her ass out right in the hallway of her new apartment.

"You like the way I beat it up?" I joked.

"Hell yeah."

We lied on the bed since I had a little more time before I went to see Lonnie. She had some Kush but I didn't want to smoke before I made a drop off. So we decided to just talk.

"Did you hear about Nelly getting smoked in the Delmont Heights?" I asked.

"Nah, not Cornell?" She said in disbelief.

"Yeah those California Garden niggas is causing a problem. I got that detective that came asking about your sister asking me questions." I replied.

"About what?"

"He wanted to know what I knew about Nelly, your sister, Jake and some nigga out the California Gardens. I told him that three of the people he named I had love for; so I wanted the violence to stop also. He left me alone after that. I swear those stupid young niggas is making it hot for everybody." I lured her in.

"How can we get rid of those niggas that did that to our peoples?" She asked.

"I'm trying to figure out how to do it right now. But you might can help me if you want to." I replied.

"Hell yeah I want to!"

"Only if you want to. I don't want you caught up in this crazy shit Felicia. These crazy ass niggas don't have a problem with killing anybody. I'm not trying to have you risk yo life for this bullshit. I care too much about you to let that happen." I explained.

"Nah Pooh, if I can get those niggas for what they did to my sister then it's on and cracking." She shook her head.

"Well we will talk about it later." I glanced at the clock then kissed her on the lips.

"I got to take care of some business so I will probably see you tomorrow." I began getting dressed.

"Okay." She replied.

Lonnie met up with me at one of the spots we chose to meet up when it gets dark. He was like my number two but he didn't know where any of my spots were at. It wasn't that he couldn't be trusted I just was so precautious I never got around to it. I still had to worry about his cousin Chris that should probably get smoked if he's snitching. The difference with Nelly and Chris was that I didn't have any proof with Chris. It was just something I felt. Lonnie pulled up in good spirits but we needed to talk. I waited until he unloaded the product before I hollered at him.

"Look my nigga, we gon' have to lay low for a spell. That one detective that bumped us up at the hospital when Chris got shot pulled me over today." I explained.

"You bullshitting! That older dude that was in his forties or fifties right? Detective Barnes or some shit like that was his name. He's the one that got Fab-Five locked up." Lonnie replied.

"Yeah him. He pulled me over and had this long talk about people getting smoked. He talked about Nelly, Sissy, Jake and some nigga out the Gardens named Marquise."

"That was his name?" Lonnie glanced at me.

"Don't even worry about that shit but let's chill out for a while so that shit can die down."

"But that ain't totally up to us. What if those California Garden niggas get to tripping? We gon' have to protect what's ours." He subtly protested.

"I'm knowing. But I got a few things up my sleeve. I'll let you know what's going on once I put everything together."

We embraced then went our separate ways. I wanted to go to Janice's house but I was a little skeptical. She would be expecting to see me this early in the week. But after getting pulled over by Detective Barnes it had me really paranoid. I drove the Caprice to where the Range Rover was parked then drove the Range Rover home. I would have to switch things up to holla at Big Black for the recop. I almost forgot that he went up in his prices for each kilo. As my car drove towards Redlands I kept wanting to go to Felicia's house. But being in the Range Rover made me think they might have something that I can't find on it. It would be better to just go ahead to Janice's house. At least I know that they are following me. I figured I would get my dead homeboy Antoine's blue BMW when I make my run to holla at Big Black.

When I got inside to my surprise Janice wasn't in the bedroom. She was actually watching television in the living room. It somewhat startled me because that was not what she normally did. It appeared as though she was watching a movie while eating popcorn.

"What's that you are watching?" I attempted to break the ice.

"I threw in my old DVD 'Waiting to Exhale. Do you remember this movie?"

Aw shit; I thought. I wondered what kind of page she was on. If I told her I wasn't in the mood she would probably tell me that I was never in the mood. I decided to go ahead and face the music tonight so she could get shit off her chest.

"You know that Shanell told me that your friend Nelly got killed the other day? Why didn't you tell me that he got killed? Is this another one of those times when you want to bring that bitch Vanessa to the funeral instead of me?"

My face lit up in disbelief when she mentioned that. It seems like my sister Sharon had mentioned that she knew about the funeral but something made me change the subject. But it was obvious that I was surprised because it was written all over my face.

"Yeah, you didn't think I knew about that huh? I never said anything to you about it. But yeah I knew." She nodded her head.

She had her feet on the small end table while she leaned back comfortably. I leaned back on the couch right along side of her.

"She knew Antoine a lot longer than you did. I knew that it would break her heart if she didn't go. I knew you could have lived without going to the funeral because you didn't know him that well. You may have only talked on the phone with him a couple of times." I sighed.

"So you openly admit that you kept it from me to please Vanessa? You ain't shit Sherwin." She sneered.

"Now I ain't shit. She is the mother of my child just like you are. I show you respect and I show her respect. You don't even know her like that but she is call kinds of bitches. You need to calm your emotions and grow the fuck up. I don't have a problem with you going to Nelly's funeral. But every other day you have an attitude. Even on days when you are supposed to be happy you got a problem with something." I firmly replied.

"I got a problem with you not keeping your dick in your pants."

"You don't know who I'm fucking. You just assume that I'm fucking someone because you want to believe what you want to believe. As stingy as you can be about the pussy you shouldn't be worried about who I'm fucking anyway." I replied.

"I'm stingy because I know you fucking other bitches." She said incredulously.

"You just think that I'm fucking other bitches." I replied.

"It's some nights I don't see you for three or four days. My homegirl Shanell was fucking with a dude that had to move out of town and she said he came to see her every night. What happened to us Winnie?"

"What are you talking about? You don't know the shit I have to deal with day by day. Then here you come with yo petty shit. You know why I don't come home every night? Every time I leave this house I feel like the police are following me. I don't know how they found out about this house but they did. One of the detectives I've known for a few years pulled me over to talk about the killings on the west side."

She looked at me in disbelief and shock. Now I was on a roll and had to let her know to back the fuck up off of me.

"Yeah, they followed me from this house. I could get locked up for forever and a day and you worried about me coming home at night. You might have invited someone to this house that got the police hot on my ass." I continued.

"Damn Winnie I didn't know anything about that. That's why you haven't been coming home some nights. I haven't invited anyone to this house that you don't know about. Everything is in my name and in your sister's name so I don't know who could find out you live here." She explained with signs of sympathy.

"Are you sure?"

"I'm sure baby. Maybe it's time you got out the game and got into something else. If we put our heads together we might can come up with something that you can do to make a living and still have money coming in." She assured me.

"I got my mind on a few things anyway. Just understand that when I don't come home it ain't because I don't want to, I'm just skeptical."

"All you had to do was tell me that a long time ago and we wouldn't even be discussing this." She rubbed my arm.

"I didn't know how to tell you." I replied.

We made love that night and it was better than usual. My sex with Janice started to get dry. A nigga don't ever mind busting a nut but that was the only thing it had become. Before our dry spell Janice would get kinky and everything. It had gotten to the point where I didn't even like the act of sex with Janice. It was all about busting that nut. There was no sensuality and exploring of the body or anything. We did two to three positions quickly then I got my rocks off. But tonight was much more special. I guess her hearing about Shanell losing some cat she was seeing that 'had moved out of town' made her consider that she had a man. I appreciated the passion and pleasured her for most of the night.

We both got up that morning in a good mood. She left that morning to go to work but I chilled at the house. I knew I had to meet up with Big Black later on so I had to figure a way to dodge the police if I had a tail. I called my sister on the cell phone.

"What's up Winnie? When you gon' come by to see your nephew and me?"

"Real soon I promise. But I need you to let Marcus know that I need him to meet me at that spot like last time. But tell him to go blue this time." I explained.

Telling him to go blue this time was my way of letting him know to pick up Antoine's blue BMW parked at one of our businesses. He would drive the Range Rover back to where the BMW was parked then take his car back home once he was done with me. I talked to him about it in person a few weeks back. My sister got off the phone for a moment to let him know then came back to the phone.

"He said that's cool but he needed a number."

That was his way of asking me what time. It was already three in the afternoon so I told him ten. This was really a code that meant he would meet me there at four. I hung up with her and got everything ready. I wouldn't pick up the money from Vanessa's house until I got the car from Marcus.

When I got to the spot Marcus was already waiting on me in the car. This was a cat that was always about his business. We both got out the car then embraced.

"You are starting to do this a little more often. Is it starting to get too hot around here?"

"You don't have any idea. The police are pulling me over and everything nowadays." I replied.

"What they pull you over for?"

"Because a lot of people have been coming up missing on the west side. This shit gets real serious when the police start coming down on people. That's when you really know who can take what. But I take it in stride."

"Yeah, but if police is pulling you over for murders that's a hint that you might need to disappear. Get out of dodge if you know what I mean."

"I've been hearing that a lot."

10
WAR TIME

I'm like a rhino running through the roughest pack!
MC Breed

Frustrated and furious Markell threw the tennis ball at the wall. Casey sat nearby with his head down. They were going through a mourning stage. Markell really wanted revenge and had to think of a way to make it happen. He felt the pain of crying but tears wouldn't fall.

"I had love for that little nigga. That muthafucka Pooh is a dirty ass nigga Casey." Markell lamented.

"Yeah he smoked that nigga while he was with his bitch. You hear about some nigga under Pooh got smoked in the Delmont Heights? That nigga shooting niggas fresh out of high school. I know his sister Mercedes took that shit hard."

"Hell yeah she took that shit hard. I told her that I would take care of the funeral. My question is how in the fuck he got a line on Marquise? You think that bitch Bernice had something to do with it?" Markell asked.

"I don't think so she was pretty shook up about that shit. Besides, Pebbles been knowing that bitch her whole life." Casey replied.

"Well we need to touch some of Pooh's people. First thing we need to do is handle that shit over in the projects. We gon' take care of that nigga so he can do what we need him to do." Markell explained.

Casey didn't respond. He already knew what was next but Markell felt obliged to reiterate the plans. Markell began throwing the tennis ball against the wall again contemplating his next move.

He glanced up from his solo game of handball to see someone running towards him. He quickly reached for his gun but then had second thoughts as the person came closer.

"Ay that's Shelly, Pebbles' little sister." Casey remarked.

"Yeah, I thought someone was running up." Markell replied.

Little Shelly was about sixteen years old but was only about 4'11 in height. She was a darker version of Pebbles but her dimples were much deeper. Everybody thought she would grow up and surpass her big sister one day. The young guys all wanted her but the high rollers she was after was always too old. They looked at her as jail bait.

"What's up Shelly? Yo sister sent you over here to tell me something?" Markell asked.

"Nah Killa Kell, some nigga pulled over on me after school today asking if I was Shelly. I said 'Who wants to know?" and he handed me two hundred dollars." She pulled the two crisp hundred dollar bills out of her pocket.

"Then he was like, a nigga named Pooh wanted to have a meeting with you. He called you Killa Kell and everything. I didn't want him to think I knew you so I didn't say shit. But he kept going like he knew for sure that I knew you. He was saying that ya'll need to work something out and he gave you a number to call him at." Shelly handed him a piece of paper.

"Niggas is talking too muthafuckin much. How did the nigga look that handed you the number?" Markell asked.

"He was a light brown nigga with a taper fade. He looked like he had a little bit of paper too." Shelly replied.

"What was he driving?"

"A Sebring but it was a rental."

"Yeah that's some of Pooh's people alright. A nigga rolling up on a broad he better not be in his own whip so she could point him out. He's gon'e make sure he rolls in some shit she can't see him in again. Good looking out Shelly."

Shelly walked away smiling as if she was rewarded for her information. Casey stared at her as she walked off.

"Man that little bitch gon' be bad when she grows up." Casey said.

"You think this nigga is up to something?"

"His people didn't start blasting on the spot like before. This time he had someone get at you. I think he might be willing to talk." Casey replied.

"We still gon' take over that spot in the projects. We'll have the meeting with that nigga Pooh but still keep our plans. He can't blame us if that nigga Kramer gets smoked by his own little homies. But let's go inside, that nigga Boom-Boom supposed to be calling collect. I don't want my grandmoms to pick up the phone." Markell said.

When Markell and Casey walked in the door the phone began to ring. Markell rushed to the phone as his grandmother yelled downstairs.

"I got it grandma. Yes I will accept the call."

Markell waited for a minute to make sure the operator had cleared the call.

"Hello?" Boom-Boom said.

"What's happening OG comrade? How are you holding up in that bitch?" Markell asked with enthusiasm.

"I'll be out in a little bit. How's everything on the street. Ya'll been getting ya'll grind on lately?" Boom-Boom asked.

"Yeah but we just lost one of the young homies to one of Pooh's people. I think we gon' have to lock horns with that nigga."

"Be careful though. That nigga Pooh is a smooth muthafucka. He knows the game well that's why my boy James ain't around. Don't underestimate this nigga." Boom-Boom insisted.

"Nah not like that at all. But he reached out and he wants to have a sit down. He got one of his peoples to walk up on this female we know. Should I even go to this shit?"

"Yeah go ahead and go. He's probably trying to avoid a war. Don't let him know shit about what you got going on but try and get what you can out of him. He's smart than a muthafucka though so I doubt if you get anything but try anyway." Boom-Boom explained.

"Fa'sho! I've got yo books covered until you touch down. What's up with that thing we talked about?"

"I got you covered young nigga. I'll be shooting that information through this broad named Latrice. I was able to get in touch with her folks so I can shoot that to you." Boom-Boom replied.

"Well that's enough over the horn. I'll wait until we are face to face to go from there." Markell replied.

He hung up the phone then he and Casey stepped outside. Markell began throwing the ball at the wall again.

"You know that nigga Boom-Boom said we should go ahead and meet up with that nigga Pooh. He was saying we need to be careful though."

"Oh yeah? What did he say about that connect?" Casey looked up.

"He gon' connect us to this bitch named Latrice. Then we can buy bricks for a cheaper price. We probably can cook that shit up ourselves. Once we cut out the middle man we gon' really be bringing in the dough. And we're about to take over the projects too." Markell said with excitement.

"Yeah that shit will be bomb. You should have that nigga smoke Kramer while we having the meeting with Pooh. That way he can't move on anything because he sitting with us." Casey replied.

"Unless he brings the nigga with him to the meet. But I doubt it though because Kramer is a hot head. Pooh more than likely gon' bring some niggas that's gon' be calm about this shit. Boom-Boom said this nigga is real smart."

"Well call that number so we can make this shit happen. I want to see how this nigga Pooh looks anyway." Casey said.

115

"I heard he was a pretty boy nigga." Markell replied.

Markell pulled out his cell phone and began dialing the number. The phone rang twice before someone picked up.

"Yeah!"

"Somebody told me to call this number. Who is this?"

"The nigga you want to talk to."

"The top nigga?" Markell asked in surprise.

"Yeah!"

"So what's up you wanted to meet up?"

"How about Saturday at three."

"Where at?"

"Baker's across the street from San Bernardino Valley College."

"Alright."

"One hundred nigga."

Markell heard the phone go out then closed his cell phone. It felt good for a moment because he was on the level where a boss nigga wanted to talk to him. He knew fom that point that he had Pooh's full attention. When he pondered on it a little longer he didn't know if it was a good or bad thing. He was struggling with the idea of Pooh knowing how he looked as much as him seeing how Pooh looked.

"So what that nigga say?" Casey interrupted his thoughts.

"We gon' meet up a Baker's over on Mt. Vernon this Saturday."

On the other side of town Detective Barnes has taken a young homicide detective under his wings. He likes the fact that he was a young black man with some street smarts. Detective Ronald Bowen was recently granted the position of detective. It was an honor for him to have such a position at a young age. Detective Barnes very seldom seen his own kind move up in the ranks unless they were an undercover agent for drugs. He wanted to give him as much information as possible.

"Listen here Detective Bowen…"

"That sounds so good. Just to hear my name with detective in the front of it is heartwarming." Detective Bowen interrupted.

"Well get over it. Because in the homicide division you have to prove you can solve murders. You won't hold that title too long if you can't prove you deserve it. Now as I was saying, there might be a war beginning on the west side of San Bernardino. I think that some young guns are going after the head supplier of cocaine in San Bernardino. He goes by the name of Pooh in the street but his legal name is Sherwin Daniels born 09-16-82. Recently a few bodies have dropped from out of his crew. In retaliation a few bodies have fallen in the California Gardens. The two most recent killings are Cornell Davenport and Marquise Caldwell. Mr. Davenport was connected to Mr. Daniels and Mr. Caldwell was from out of the California Gardens." Detective Barnes explained.

"So the California Gardens is beefing with this Daniels guy?"

"I can't say if it is a gang war or not. I think it all began with a robbery/murder in the Dorjil's apartment complex. A young man by the name of Jacob Chandler was the victim. Now I know that Mr. Daniels has a few people hustling over there. I believe this young man was working for Mr. Daniels." Detective Barnes continued.

"So why don't we go after Mr. Daniels to prevent more murders?"

"He's guarded and if anything he's calling the shots for someone to get murdered. He's not the one doing the murders. What we are trying to do is get someone under him to give us information to what's going on." Detectives Barnes shrugged.

He waived his hand for the young detective to follow him. They walked out of the police station and into Detective Barnes' brown Crown Victoria. Several blocks went by before anyone said anything. Finally after a prolonged silence Detective Bowen sighed.

"Where are we going?"

117

"We are going down to the County Jail so that we can talk to one of Mr. Daniels' shooters. He's fighting a murder case for the last few years. He's been doing hard time because the county jail is hard time compared to the penitentiary. The date has been set back without the judge granting him bail. Maybe he is ready to start talking. He has a daughter and a woman waiting on him." Detective Barnes replied.

"Oh, so we plan on getting him to turn on Mr. Daniels in exchange for some type of leniency?"

"Exactly!"

They pulled up to the county jail parking lot. They nonchalantly walked in the office. After showing their badges at the front desk they were let upstairs. They were brought into an office where they awaited the man in charge. After several minutes a San Bernardino Sheriff in uniform walked up to greet them. He had three stripes on his uniform indicating he was a sergeant. He held out his hand to Detective Barnes while walking up. The stern faced white man with a tan strongly shook the detectives' hands then forced a smile.

"What can I help you with? I'm Sergeant Brenner."

"I'm Detective Barnes and this is Detective Bowen and we wanted to talk to an inmate by the name of Fabian Gilmore. We wanted to interrogate him about recent murders."

"That'll be fine. We will find a room for you to question him." Sergeant Brenner walked off.

He quickly walked out of the room and within thirty minutes returned with a Sheriff Deputy.

"He will show you where you will need to go."

Once they made it up the elevator they passed a few doors in the hallway. The third door swung open by the Sheriff Deputy and sitting at the table was Fabian Gilmore. They walked inside and immediately sat adjacent to the suspect with only a table between them.

"How are you Mr. Gilmore?"

Fab-Five just nodded his head without responding.

"You've been locked up for several years with your case pending. Maybe if you let us know some things we can probably do some things for you."

"I don't talk to police." Fab-Five firmly replied.

"You know you are looking at thirty years with an L. If you give us some information you might get to see your daughter and your girl sooner than you think."

Fab-Five smirked then turned his head. That puzzled Detective Barnes momentarily. He must know something we don't know he considered.

"We can do something for you if you do something for us." He insisted.

"I don't talk to police. Unless you got another murder charge to put on me can I go back to the recreation room? I was winning in dominoes and I was in my last house. I was doing good until ya'll called my name." Fabian playfully fussed.

"Shut up. I thought you don't talk to police?" Detective Bowen replied.

"I remember you because you were there when I got arrested but now you got a nigga around my age working with you." Fabian pointed at Detective Bowen.

"I guess you and Mr. Daniels are a couple of smart asses. But you think he gives a damn about you. Yeah so did your friend Cornell Davenport but now he is in the grave." Detective Barnes nodded to confirm his statement.

Fabian shook his head in disbelief. He tried to hide it but he was visibly shook up behind the news.

"I see you didn't know anything about that." Detective Barnes frowned.

They walked out the door and both detectives glanced at each other. No words were spoken until they reached the elevator.

"He was a little shook up behind that; couldn't you tell?" Bowen asked.

119

"Yeah, we will check on his case in about a week and see where he is standing. Once he realizes we're not lying about Mr. Davenport we might try again." Barnes smiled.

Detective Barnes decided to pull up in front of the police station. Silently he parked the car wondering how he could prevent an inevitable war. He always hated war time in the streets because it meant more work. With more work there was more stress and more stress brought about more mistakes. Now he had the burden of training a young detective with an ego. The thoughts raced through his head while he pulled into a parking stall.

"Damn that girl is pretty as hell. Let me out right here so that I can talk to this fine ass woman." Bowen said with excitement.

"Who are you talking about?" Barnes asked impatiently.

"You missed her because she's walked behind that SUV. She was a pretty light skinned girl with a banging body." Bowen quickly jumped out the car.

Barnes turned off the engine and sat in the car. He pondered on the times he would chase after women. He had grown tired of such antics. His marriage had taken a lot out of him. His thoughts kept dwelling on the drug war he knew was about to happen.

"What can be done to prevent this?" He said aloud.

Bowen came running back to the car swinging open the passenger side door.

"I got that number. She was even prettier when I got up close. She was fine as hell."

"What was her name?" Detective Barnes asked.

Pooh made it up to Baker's around two-thirty. He wanted to be prepared and set up when Markell arrived. He had a good idea what kind of person Killa Kell was. He just needed it to be confirmed. It was a difficult thing to consider. Pooh understood that Killa Kell was one of those cats in the game that got rid of his problems through violence. You could never show a sign of weakness to this kind of hustler. He was the type that preyed on the slightest weakness. He had to be firm but sharp. Lonnie stood up behind him while he had few people posted outside. He figured it wouldn't be any problems if it was broad daylight. But he had three of his boys outside packing just in case something jumped off.

Markell also showed up early. He came in about ten minutes before two walking up with who Pooh assumed was Casey. Markell sat in the same booth but on the other side of the table. They both nodded at each other without breaking eye contact.

"Stand up for a minute and lift your shirt up." Pooh led by example.

Markell followed his lead. He understood perfectly well what Pooh was doing and went along with the program.

"Alright take off ya shoes and lift up your pants."

After everything was checked and once Pooh felt comfortable he glanced back at Lonnie.

"Let us talk."

Markell glanced at Casey but he had already caught on to what was going down and had moved back already. Pooh noticed the sharpness and nodded his head in respect to Casey.

"The game is the game." Pooh began.

"What you want to do? You want to make some money or you want to gangbang. I've been hearing that you're a shot caller over in the CGs right about now. I want to work something out with you. I can break you off a brick for thirty-four on consignment already cooked up." Pooh explained.

"That's what I'm doing now. How about you offer me a whole bird for sixteen-five to seventeen even. I can cook the shit myself." Casey replied.

"I can go seventeen even but still cook it up for you. But you got to give me half of seventeen to show good faith." Pooh offered.

"I'll have to think about that." Markell replied.

121

There was a moment of uncomfortable silence. Markell tried not to show his anger. He must think I'm a damn fool if I let him cook it. He will stretch that shit and get another seventy-five hundred off the kilo I bought, Markell thought.

"People have been hit on both sides. If it is on some business shit we got to do what we got to do. But muthafuckas on both sides got straps; it's just a matter of who gon' win before the police win everything." Pooh explained.

"Yeah that's real talk. If I can make my money then you can make your money. I just lost a young comrade the other day. Some niggas smoked him at a hotel room. I had major love for that nigga and now he's gone." Markell passionately explained.

"Yeah but I lost a few comrades. A nigga got just cause to go after every nigga he thinks got something to do with my peoples getting smoked. But the better thing is to make this money and respect each other's hustle. A nigga can make this paper without bringing on 'One Time'." Pooh firmly replied.

"If I don't have to worry about any of my people then you don't have to worry about any of yo peoples." Killa Kell said.

"We good then nigga?"

"Yeah we good."

Pooh reached out for him to shake his hand. Markell shook his hand and he began to get up from the booth.

"Before you bounce, take this phone that only got one number on it. That way you can holla at me if you want to get one of those things. You holla at me with this number I will know it's you."

Markell nodded then stood up and walked out the door. Casey followed closely behind him. They noticed the three men standing by in the parking lot. Pooh gave them a nod as if to indicate they were cool to keep going. Both Markell and Casey noticed the exchange.

"You see that shit my nigga?" Markell whispered.

"Yeah those niggas were ready." Casey replied.

122

Markell didn't say anything else until they got inside the car. He started up the engine then smoothly drove off.

"That nigga Pooh is a pretty boy nigga." Markell said, they both started laughing.

"Yeah but I can't take that nigga lightly. Boom-Boom was saying he was the type of nigga you wouldn't expect to be as cold as he could be. I'll tell you this that nigga tried to play me by offering to sell me a brick for seventeen even but he was gon' cook it." Markell said with disgust.

"He would have stretched that shit and still would be getting paid an extra seven thousand plus." Casey replied.

"I'm saying." Markell replied.

Markell shook his head wondering how to play this. He knew that he couldn't avoid a decision for too long. He already had a connect that Boom-Boom was hooking up for seventeen even of cocaine that hadn't been cooked into crack yet. So he knew he couldn't buy any of Pooh's dope based on what he was offering."

"We gon' have to go to war with this nigga if I don't give him an answer soon. I plan on holding out as long as possible. But we gon' let that nigga he got over in the projects get smoked but let it be blamed on one of his own homeboys. I heard that nigga Kramer is a bully anyway. That will buy us time if he thinks some project niggas smoked they own homeboy." Markell explained.

"Then once we got that connect we don't even have to fuck with that nigga altogether." Casey understood.

"If he would have connected with us when we first reached out we would be under his thumb right now. He would be supplying us birds but we would have to answer to him. Now we got this new connect we can build up and ain't got to answer to anyone." Markell smiled.

"Yeah, that's cool. Is that all he was offering?"

"Yeah but that nigga wants us to forget about all the homeboys that got smoked. That nigga talking about he lost people too. I won't ever forget that shit. He was saying that the police make it hot when people get their caps peeled. What we gon' do is take over the projects and then build up our paper so if this nigga gets to tripping we can stand up to him." Markell nodded.

"For sure my nigga. We gon' go to war with this nigga for real." Casey replied.

11
KILLERS AND HUSTLERS

I keep them scattering like roaches when the light come on!
DMX

I ordered food from Baker's after Killa Kell and Casey left. I knew what kind of niggas they were after a few moments sitting across from him. I knew what was about to happen so I decided to ponder on it while eating. Lonnie sat across from me and ordered something as well.

"So what's up Pooh? Are we supplying those California Garden niggas now?" Lonnie asked.

I could hear the slight tone of disappointment in his ear. He was trying to hide it but I picked up on it. No need in giving him eye contact.

"We won't be supplying anything to them niggas. I offered them an amount and they said they would think on it. They were just trying to buy time because they have another connect. They want to build up their muscle then come after me."

"How do you know that? They might really want to think on it."

"They want the top spot. They only agreed to meet up with us because they don't want us giving them problems while they stack their cake. Once they get the money right then they can go at us full blast." I explained.

"Where are you getting all this from? You just think they're those types of niggas or what?" He seemed dumbfounded.

Slowly I chewed on my hamburger finishing the last remnants of the sandwich. Lonnie sat impatiently hoping that I would quickly answer his question.

"Yeah they are those types of niggas. See some niggas get rid of problems by organizing, some niggas get rid of problems by throwing money at it but some niggas get rid of problems by killing muthafuckas. That's how Killa Kell and Casey roll. They want people to bow down to them and whoever doesn't has to go. They wanted to see us so they could get a scope on us but they weren't about to agree to shit. Think about it, why kill a nigga from another man's clique so they could cop dope from him. From the jump they wanted to ride on us because we were making all the money. So now that they got a little change in their pocket they want enough time to get ready for whatever we gon' bring." I explained.

"So why didn't we just kill them niggas when we had the chance?" Lonnie frowned.

"Because when all this shit hits the fan with the police we gon' need someone to take the fall." I replied.

"I feel you my nigga. So when the police start getting hot they gon' go after them."

"You got hustlers and you got killers. Killers don't last too long in the game because they always make the police look like they're not doing a good job. Police always hunt them down first. That's why it's always good to have a nigga that thinks like a gangster as a boss. He won't get rid of a nigga unless he really has to. When someone disrupts some shit or causes some kind of problem that may have some repercussions then that's when he has to go." I taught Lonnie game.

He sat back in the booth seat and pondered on my words. He was deep in his thoughts before I tapped him for us to leave.

"I know we are not gon' let them hit us first before we hit them?" He asked while climbing out of the booth.

That's when my phone began to ring. The number was blocked so I was reluctant to pick it up. I thought about how many people knew this number and decided to answer after a second thought.

"Hello?"

126

"This is J-Rock from out of the projects. You know little Jason that serves for Kramer?"

"Yeah I know who you are. How did you get this number?"

"I grabbed it from out of Kramer's pocket. Some niggas just smoked him in broad daylight then ran off. I went to get something to eat for me and him and when I got back he was laid out dead." He explained while on the verge of crying.

"Are you fucking serious? Did you see who it was?"

"Nah but it had to be some niggas from over here. He was too deep in the projects for someone to just walk in here and its broad daylight. Plus it was close range." He replied nervously.

"Alright calm down."

I waited for a moment so that he could catch his breath. He was jittery and upset and it would be best that he kept his calm so he could think clearly.

"Look J-Rock, meet up with Lonnie in about thirty minutes at the liquor store on Baseline Blvd. Then from there we will tell you what you need to do. You feel me?"

"Alright I'll be there."

I hung up the phone and stopped in my tracks. Lonnie looked at me wondering what happened. It was somewhat perplexing because it could have been anybody. Kramer was quick to swing on a nigga for pissing him off. I had to figure out if it was personal or if it was business.

"Look here Lonnie; I need you to meet up with J-Rock at the liquor store on Baseline. Kramer just got smoked by someone over in the projects. You need to read that young nigga and see if he had anything to do with it." I said.

"I can't read niggas like you can Pooh." He replied.

"Just feel him out the best you can. Ask him a lot of questions and see how he responds. See who he thinks could have done the shit. Meet up with me later and we'll go over this shit then."

"I'll head over there right now."

We both walked out the door and headed towards the parking lot. Lonnie went towards his car while I walked up to Travon, Main Man and Willie. Willie was a young rider that worked under Travon in the Delmont Heights. Main Man was proving to be a reliable shooter for us. He usually worked under Lonnie's cousin Chris but he's been working out in other ways. Travon had a slight smirk on his face when I approached.

"We could have served them CG niggas if we wanted to." He gloated.

"I wasn't trying to have some shit crack in broad daylight. If we gon' handle a nigga we want to handle it right. But check this out here. Ya'll niggas get ready because we might be caught up in a full scale war. Kramer just got killed in the projects and it could be one of his own homeboys." I explained.

I gave them time to lament. Travon and Willie knew him but Main Man wasn't too familiar with him. Travon had that look of pain which meant he was ready to put in work. I wasn't ready just yet though.

"I'll holla at ya'll when we need to chop it up. It's too many funerals for the police not to start tripping. We got to be smart about this shit." I continued.

My eyes were beginning to hurt by now. I rubbed them after we all started walking back to our cars. I felt like I was losing control of everything. Kramer was a knucklehead but he was a down ass dude. It fucked with me a little bit that I wasn't going to see him alive anymore. Once inside the Range Rover my stereo instantly started playing old school Scarface. He always set the right mood for me. About ten minutes into the music I decided to call up my cousin. The phone rang several times before someone picked it up.

"Hello?"

"What's up Big Mel?"

"Who is this? Turn yo music down so that I can hear you." He yelled through the phone.

"This is Pooh." I said after turning down the music.

128

"What going on with you?"

"I need you to hit me on another number ASAP."

That was my way of letting him know that he needed to go to a payphone. He hung up the phone right after that. About twenty minutes later he hit me back from an unfamiliar number. By that time I had made it to a phone booth and had gotten a hold of some change. I had just crossed the bridge on Mt. Vernon that went over the 215 Freeway. He picked up the phone on the first ring.

"What's up nigga?"

"I need to get at you face to face. Some crazy shit been going down and I'm gon' need every soldier I can muster." I replied.

"You know I got yo back. Don't even worry about that. Where do you want to link up?"

"How about we link up at L's house around the corner from the park? You know where he stays at near downtown?"

"Nah, but I know what park you're talking about. Let's meet up at the park then I'll follow you from there."

"That's cool."

I pulled up to the park about five minutes before he did. By that time I called Lonnie and let him know that we were meeting at his house. He was already there when we pulled into his driveway. He stepped outside on the porch when he seen the lights from inside. We walked up his driveway and he met us there. After we all embraced that's when Lonnie began to talk.

"I think that nigga J-Rock is on the up and up. I don't think he had anything to do with Kramer getting smoked." He said.

"Kramer from over in the projects got killed?" Big Mel asked.

"Yeah that was what I wanted to holla at you about. What was J-Rock saying?" I directed my last question to Lonnie.

"He was saying that when he went to get something to eat someone started shooting. When he got back to the spot he seen Kramer laid out on the ground. He didn't have a cell phone to call

129

anyone so he grabbed the cell phone sticking out of Kramer's pocket. He dialed the number that said the letter P thinking he would get you and he was right. That little nigga was shook up about that shit." Lonnie explained.

"Did he say if Kramer was beefing with someone? Did he get into it with anyone over in the projects?" I asked.

"He said no. He told me that Kramer had been doing cool lately. He was making his money so he wasn't tripping with anyone."

His words rang in my ear. It had to be over territory but I still wasn't a hundred percent on that. I lowered my head trying to see how to handle this.

"I need you to gather one or two niggas to start peeping out what's going on over in the projects. If they moving weight over there right after Kramer got hit then that means someone got him for his territory. Those niggas Markell and Casey are the number one niggas to start looking at." I explained.

"What if it stays quiet?" Lonnie asked.

"Then we just need to put someone over that spot to take his place. We gon' have to bury our homeboy and try to find out who had a beef with him enough to where they wanted to murder him." I replied.

"Who the fuck is Markell and Casey?" Big Mel asked.

"Some little young guns coming out of the CGs that's trying to take my spot. You need to saddle up big cousin because we're about to go to war with these fools."

"You ain't said nothing but a word." Big Mel shook his head.

"Alright then…" My phone started ringing.

I looked down at the caller ID and realized it was Ace. After putting up my hand for them to hold on I answered on the second ring.

"What's going on old man?"

"No baby this is Aunt Thelma. Earnest told me to call you because he needs to talk to you as soon as possible."

"Is something wrong?"

"I'm at the hospital with him right now but you need to come and see him. He made me call you right away." She replied.

"Okay I'll be at the hospital in about an hour. Is that cool?"

"Okay baby I'll see you here."

Once I hung up the phone Big Mel was staring right at me.

"What's up with Ace?"

"I don't know but that was Aunt Thelma telling me I need to see him quick. Ya'll niggas gather the homies so we can start putting in work. If they want to go war..." Lonnie's girl Lisa stepped on the porch.

"Can I get any of you something to drink?" She asked.

We all shook our head then Lonnie looked back at her. He gave her a glare that would have made anyone shudder. I observed his demeanor as he waved for her to go inside.

"That bitch was just being nosy." Lonnie commented.

"We gon' meet up tomorrow at that hotel over in Riverside. The one by the Galleria. Once we know what we working with and who we're working with then we straight. I'm leaving it up to you two niggas to get the soldiers in place."

"Okay." They said simultaneously

Big Mel was parked behind me so he moved his truck from behind me. I pulled the Range Rover out the driveway and sped away. Big Mel and Lonnie continued to talk after I left.

Speeding on the 215 Freeway then connected to the 10 Freeway I headed toward the hospital. My thoughts were racing while wondering why Ace needed to see me so bad. I began to think that he was on his deathbed or something. With so many things on my plate it was difficult to focus. Preparing for another war was just too tiring. But the streets make you proactive or you won't survive.

When I showed up to the hospital Auntie Thelma was outside in the hallway. She looked really tired and drained. Her eyes were red, her mouth was sticky and her face looked as though

131

it was stained with tears. We embraced once we noticed one another.

"Sherwin baby it is so good to see you here. Earnest has been asking about you ever since I got off the phone." She said while still hugging me tightly.

"I'm going in there right now. Let me check on him and see how he's doing." I replied.

She loosened her embrace and allowed me to go inside his room. He appeared as though he was asleep as I attempted to creep towards his bed. As I got closer he opened his eyes and stared at me for a moment as though he didn't know who I was. He appeared to be peaceful and calm. It was the same Ace that I've always known. He always studied me and was very observant about what was going on around him.

"What's up with you Sherwin?" He coughed.

"I'm wondering the same thing about you. Auntie Thelma told me that you wanted to see me right away." I replied.

"Yeah, I wanted to tell you face to face that I'm about to die." He said, like he was walking a dog.

"What the fuck do you mean you are about to die? I mean, how do you know that you're about to die?"

"It's just my time that's all. But don't be doing all that crying and shit. I'm already getting enough of that from Thelma. Everybody has their time and mines is coming up." He sharply replied.

"Yeah but the doctors told you that there wasn't that much time for you to live or what? How do you know?"

"I just know. I can feel the cancer eating away at me. I lived a lot longer than I thought I would. All my brothers are dead and those were some mean ass niggas. But I outlived all of them. I'm seventy-one years old and I lived a full life." He explained.

"You say it like you're glad to go."

"I'm tired but I'm not glad to go. It's one of those things where you don't want to go but you don't really mind if you do. I've been married to a good woman for thirty something years.

Our daughter is grown, graduated from college and happily married in Maryland. I never had a son but my brother had a son that I love as though he was my own. Life has been hard but it has been good."

"Aw Ace you shouldn't even talk like that. You might actually pull through then we can sit down and have some Jack Daniels and laugh about the time you were in the hospital thinking you were about to die." I half heartedly laughed.

"I don't think so this time. But I'll tell you what; if you reach under that bag we can have that drink." He coughed while laughing.

I walked over to the chair and grabbed the bottle of whiskey. He had two plastic cups already sitting next to the bottle. I chuckled to myself after seeing the set up.

"What's so funny nigga?" He snapped.

"You and that whiskey."

"Well you know how that goes. So what's been going on in the streets of San Bernardino? Some of your people got touched huh?" He asked like it was any other day.

"Yeah, it looks like we're about to go to war. Another muthafuckin war. I'm getting tired of this shit. But I got some young up and comings out of the California Gardens dropping my people every chance they get. Remember when I told you the police detective pulled me over a few miles from the house? He was talking to me about murders happening on the west side."

"Then don't go to war. Back away from that shit and go about your business." He suggested.

"They're killing my peoples and they're supposed to get a pass? Fuck that, it don't work like that on this end. They at least got to know that if they cross my tees I'm gon' dot their eyes. That's the game." I shook my head.

"Yeah but after awhile somebody might get the upper hand. The west side is hot territory where a lot of young niggas coming up is trying to lay claim. In that kind of environment you can't be the top dog forever. At some point you got to swallow yo pride.

Yo father was stubborn like that and wouldn't let shit rest when he should. God knows I loved my brother and I hope to get to see him when I leave this place. But he didn't know when to quit."

"I see what you saying but I at least got to make sure my peoples are in a position to feed their families. That's only right." I frowned.

There was a moment of silence. It was surprising considering that Ace always had a comeback for what I said. I figured he was too drained to argue about something I had to do. At least I felt I had to do.

"Snitches get to coming to the surface when murders start piling up. Some niggas can't handle the pressure. It brings out the worse in niggas. And even if you win the police still might hand you yo ass." He coughed.

"You got to bring ass to get ass!" I commented.

"If yo mind is made up then I can't say anymore."

"Let's talk about other things. I don't want you to worry about my problems especially when time is so valuable. Does Big Black know what's going on with you?"

"I was chopping it up with him right before I came to the hospital. He told me that I didn't sound the same. After coughing severely for days Thelma took me to the hospital. I guess I wasn't paying attention." He chuckled.

I smiled but deep down I was hurting inside. He was the closest to a father figure I had. We talked about my mother and sister. We talked about Big Mel and his growing new family. We even talked about Vanessa.

"That's the woman you should be with. She's had yo back from day one. If anyone of these broads are worth keeping it would be her." He firmly suggested.

I knew he was right so all I could do was nod my head. When I finally left the hospital I had mixed emotions. I allowed a tear to fall down my face because I knew that he would be leaving me soon. But I also felt really good about the conversation we had. He was a straight up hustler since he was coming up with his

134

brothers. Ever since he's known me he's schooled me to the game. He was giving me street knowledge when I was still a toddler. I promised myself that I would visit him every day if I can. Taking at least an hour out of my day to chill with my uncle can be arranged. I hopped back on the freeway wondering whose house I would stay. It was the middle of the week so Janice expected me. Felicia hadn't seen me in a few days so she might expect me. Instead I chose to go over to Vanessa's house. That way I was still in the city of San Bernardino and I was with the one that meant the most.

As I was transferring back to the 215 Freeway my phone began to ring. I slipped it between bunches of paperwork so it was difficult to find. When I finally got a hold of the phone it had rang three times. Glancing at the caller ID was when I seen Shanell's name pop up. I was actually surprised to hear from her of all people. I took care of her family while Fab-Five was locked up but she usually didn't have to call me.

"Hello?"

"What's up my nigga?"

"Fab-Five?"

"Yeah, man that muthafuckin lawyer you got for me finally was able to grant me a release. They kept setting the court date back without granting me a release. Talking about I'm a danger to society and shit. But a muthafucka is home and I want to celebrate." Fab-Five said with enthusiasm.

"I'm cool with that. We can have a big ass party this weekend. Where is your girl right now?"

"She's driving right now while I'm in the passenger seat. My license expired and everything. But a nigga gon' get back on his feet for real. You and I need to talk about some things anyway."

"Well you don't have to worry about paper because you good on that. As a matter of fact we can sit down on that whenever you like." I replied.

"Nah that goes without saying my nigga. You took care of me and my family so I'm not tripping about that. I'm talking about some leaks in the faucet. Somebody is running their mouth." He replied.

"Oh, that's what you're talking about."

"Yeah, I'll give you the run down when we are face to face."

"How about we link up some time tomorrow? I'll give you the run down on everything that is popping since you've been locked down." I suggested.

"That's cool; right now I'm glad to see my two favorite females after doing that county jail time. So some time tomorrow will be good."

After hanging up the phone with Fab-Five all I could do was think. Ace was an old school hustler that was about to die. Then my next call is from a young killer that feels more alive than ever before. Maybe the game was changing. Maybe hustlers are being wiped out by the killers. Maybe somewhere down the line the game changed and I missed it. Fabian getting out of jail was bittersweet for me. I was glad he was home but I was losing an uncle in the process. An uncle that I admired my whole life I might add. My plan was to spend as much time with him as possible.

12
TRAGEDY

Death got to be easy because life is hard!
50 Cent

I drove down the street calmly taking my time to holler at Fab-Five. I had a lot on my mind and I knew he would be fired up. He was a free man that did two plus years of county jail time. County jail time is harder than when you are in the pen. The pen is built for you to do a bunch of years so they accommodate the place for that long period of time. The food is better and you are set up to be there for a minute. But Fabian was in County jail for two years fighting a case. It would have been easier if he would have done two years in the penitentiary. He would want to really enjoy himself and be in the best of moods. I wasn't in the best of moods. I was drained from all the stress but I had to put on a game face. I had to look like I had everything under control.

When I pulled up to Fabian and Shanell's apartment complex the Nelly situation came to mind. It was as if I could visualize it while I sat outside. My mind dwelled on that for a moment until Fab-Five started knocking on the passenger side window of the Range Rover. I didn't even see him walking up.

"Aw nigga you were slipping for real." Fabian teased.

"Yeah, I was thinking about some shit that's all. How have you been my nigga? Man it's good to see you touchdown." I said enthusiastically.

"It feels good to be home. I hadn't had any pussy in two years. I hadn't had any good food in two years. Shit...I haven't slept in a decent bed in two years." He smiled.

"So I take it you've already eaten?"

137

"Yeah Shanell cooked breakfast for me. But I'm down to get some beer and go somewhere to chop it up."

I decided to pick up some beer and go up to the park behind Valley College. It was in the cut and we could play catch up for a while. He seemed loose after getting that beer in his system. We laughed about when I first got out and how hungry I was. He teased me about taking so long to kill King James. I decided to have a conversation with King James before I killed him. It was actually refreshing to talk to Fabian. He was a comrade instead of someone in my clique I had to look after. We were getting reacquainted. After laughing for about a half an hour we got down to business.

"So what were you talking to me about over the phone? You were saying that someone is running off at the mouth." I asked.

"Oh yeah!" He swigged his beer.

"That one detective that arrested me came in with some hot shot young detective trying to get me to turn snitch. I laughed at those muthafuckas. I'd rather die than live on my knees as a bitch for the police. But they kept coming back as the case kept going. I knew the case was getting weaker every time they came. But the young detective slipped up talking about they knew Greg owed me money. Only a few of the homies knew about that fat muthafucka owing me money." He explained.

"Why in the fuck were you speaking up on murders to anyone in the first place?" I snapped.

"I thought I was around some stand up niggas." Fab-Five replied in shock.

"Some niggas break under pressure. It's always good not to speak up on that shit Fabian and you know that. You could have gotten life for that dumb shit." I firmly replied.

I never talked to Fab-Five like that. He was surprised but at the same time understood my anger. More importantly he knew that I cared. He lowered his head and slowly shook it.

"I fucked up homie for real. But it still doesn't dismiss the fact that we got somebody talking to the police."

"Yeah I think I know who it is but I can't speak on it until I know for sure." I replied.

"By the time you know for sure we might all be sitting on a hundred years. Let me know and I'll handle that shit." He glanced at me.

"Nah, because if I'm wrong you will still be looking at the nigga funny. I know you my nigga, let me find out for sure then we will move when we need to move. It's some complicated shit if it is who I think it is." I explained.

"Alright then Pooh, but don't say I didn't warn you."

I understood that perfectly well. We might all get caught up if I don't weed out the snitch. All I know it could be more than one snitch in my clique. I had too many landmines in my way.

"So some young niggas coming up got rid of the homeboy Nelly huh? I heard he was smoked in the Delmont Heights. Somebody is trying to take the homeboy Travon's top spot over there or what?" He asked, interrupting my thoughts.

"Nah but somebody over in the projects took care of Kramer. One of his homies from his own neighborhood got him. Travon is holding it down pretty tight over in the Delmont Heights." I tried to dance around the question.

Fab-Five wanted to know who killed or was suspected of killing Nelly. But it was too much of a touchy subject for me to indulge in.

"So it was the California Garden niggas that crept over there to get the homie Nelly huh?" He persisted.

"Let's bounce." I climbed off the park bench.

He followed close behind without saying a word. He must have realized I was avoiding the question. He already knew that we were going to war so I just let him assume. It might have broken his heart to know that Shanell was messing with his homeboy. It was time to get him reacquainted with the west side so we were first going to link up with Lonnie.

We pulled up on Lonnie at the park near his house. We were doing a lot of face to face talks because everyone was nervous. He was sitting in his Dodge Charger when I noticed Chris on the passenger side. Chris got out the car looking cool and calm but I was instantly nervous. How was I going to get rid of this nigga without making it obvious I didn't want him there? Lonnie and Chris quickly embraced Fab-Five once they were close enough. While Chris and Fab-Five were talking Lonnie pulled me to the side.

"I hope you don't mind me bringing Chris? When you called and told me Fabian was out he wanted to see him like I did." Lonnie explained.

"I ain't tripping but next time let me know ahead of time."

I was kind of tripping because I knew that I couldn't discuss business with Chris around. I believed that Lonnie was a stand up nigga but I couldn't trust his cousin. That put me in a fucked up dilemma.

"Do you let Chris drive yo whip?" I asked.

"Yeah, if he needs to." Lonnie replied.

"I won't have time to get all the liquor for Fabian's party tonight. So tell Chris while we're talking to handle that for me. I'll be killing two birds with one stone." I said.

At that moment Chris and Fab-Five finished reminiscing and walked over toward us. Lonnie glanced at me and turned to Chris.

"Look here little cousin, I need you to go to Stater Brothers and pick up a bunch of liquor for Fabian's party."

Chris glanced at me then glanced at Lonnie. He looked a little disappointed but appeared to understand. I considered the eye contact while we handed him money for the alcohol. Lonnie gave him the keys to his car and he was in the wind.

"So we got a few things to draw these niggas out of the California Gardens if we have to. There is dope moving over in the projects right now. So you might want us to take care of that right now. J-Rock told me today that a young nigga named Shawn

140

but they call him Corn is hustling over there. He's making serious paper too." Lonnie explained.

"Yeah we gon' need to take care of that right away. So I need you to have Main-Man and Willie handle that with J-Rock leading the way. He don't have to put in the work but make it easy for those two niggas." I replied.

"Three is always better than two. I can creep up in there and let some niggas have it also." Fab-Five offered.

"Nah nigga, I can't have you doing dirt so soon. You just touched down so you need to stay out of dodge for a minute. I got some young shooters that can handle this punk shit. Besides, we might have a full blown war and I'm gon' need you to be ready for that." I explained.

Fab-Five just nodded understanding what I was saying. I noticed a growth in Fab-Five that I appreciated. He had a maturity about him that I knew would be beneficial. I couldn't fully explain what I seen but there was something different. He was always street smart and had street knowledge but it seems like the County Jail made him wise as well.

"Once we get the projects back do you want J-Rock running that spot or you gon' put somebody else over there?" Lonnie asked.

"He's kind of young and that scares me. I thought about putting Main Man in the projects and putting Fab-Five over in the Dorjil's where he used to be. But that might be too dangerous for Main Man so I still got to think on how I'm gon' do this shit." I replied.

"Yeah Kramer was got over there and he was from over there. However you want to handle it though." Lonnie said.

"How about we put Main Man over the spot on Mt. Vernon and put Chris on the Dorjil apartments? Fabian can be the nigga schooling the youngsters on how to put in work." I commented.

"But I'll be sitting idle when it ain't a war going on. A nigga like me wants to earn his keep." Fab-Five replied.

141

"Yeah but you a nigga that done paid some dues so you don't have to be on the front line. That muthafucka Detective Barnes is probably itching to catch you up on some shit." I said.

I looked at the time and realized it was almost time for me to visit Ace in the hospital. I figured I could be a half hour later than the time and it wouldn't make a difference. I wanted to stop and make sure the spot was secure for Fab-Five's party tonight. He told me he wanted to have the same kind of party I threw for my cousin when he got out. I rented a spot and hired strippers for Big Mel after he had done ten years in the pen. I decided to rent out the same spot and do it the same way. I found this stripper named Paradise's old number and she agreed to bring her friends. She also understood that anything goes. That meant that we were about to have an orgy up in the spot. I figured I would have to call her when I left the park to make sure she and her girls were coming through.

"I'm about to bounce. Tell Chris to bring the drink up to the spot around eight. He can close up shop early and everything." I said.

"Well that club is cracking on Thursday nights. We might be able to get a scope on those niggas if they show up." Lonnie said.

"Nah they gon' be prepared for that. Remember what I told you about hustlers and killers. We might be able to find a better way to handle this shit without them knowing we're coming at them." I shook my head.

I climbed in the Range Rover after embracing Lonnie and Fab-Five did the same. We rolled a little ways before Fab-Five broke the silence.

"What did you tell Lonnie about killers and hustlers?" He asked.

"You got to handle them differently that's all. The young guns coming out of the CGs is killer type niggas. So they always are ready for war even when it ain't one." I explained.

"I guess I'm like that too." Fabian replied.

142

The silence continued after that so I called up Paradise on the way back to Fab-Five's house. She picked up on the second ring. She sounded sort of sluggish when she answered the phone.

"Hello?"

"What's up with you girl? You and your girls gon' be ready for this party tonight?" I asked enthusiastically.

"Yeah we will be ready. It's at least six girls coming with me but they expecting ya'll to spend big bucks."

"That ain't a problem. As long as ya'll make it worth our while. I really want ya'll to take care of my boy Fab-Five."

"Don't worry that nigga gon' be well taken care of." She giggled.

"Alright then, you remember how to get there right?"

"Yeah, I got the directions written down but I remembered where it was when we had it a few years back. I'm just trying to take me a nap before these bitches pile up at my house. Oh by the way, Princess is back working up at the club again. You want me to tell her to come also?"

I couldn't believe my ears when she said that. Princess whose real name was Nakia stole three kilos of cocaine from me. At the time she did the shit I wanted to break her neck. It wasn't a big deal now but I was still wondering how I would deal with it.

"Pooh are you there?" Paradise interrupted my thoughts.

"Yeah, I'm here. You don't need to have Princess come through. Don't even let her know that I'm still around. Just pretend like you ain't talked to me. She's doing her thing and I'm doing my thing." I replied.

"Okay! You probably wouldn't be feeling her right now anyway. She's lost a lot of weight and cut off all her hair. She looks like she was smoking dope or something. She just ain't the same." She gossiped.

"That's a tragedy. She used to look so good." I replied.

By the time I was off the phone with Paradise I was pulling up to Fab-Five's apartment complex. We firmly shook hands before he got out.

143

"I'll see you in about four or five hours my nigga." He said while climbing out the car.

"Fa'sho! Make sure Shanell let's yo ass out the house." I joked.

"Whatever nigga."

I backed up the Range Rover and pulled out of the parking lot. I jumped on the freeway so I could spend some time with Ace before the party. It took me about twenty-five minutes to make the drive to the hospital. Janice called me on the way. I knew she wanted to nag because I hadn't been home in awhile. I decided to pick up the phone and maybe get a reprieve because I was visiting my sick uncle.

"What's up Janice?"

"Are you coming home tonight?" Janice calmly asked.

"It looks like it will be a late one tonight. I'm going to visit Ace right now in the hospital. I'll come through tomorrow then maybe we can spend a little time together." I replied.

"Okay that's cool."

I was somewhat surprised when she said that. As I pulled off the freeway I wondered why I didn't get any talk back. You know what that usually means. She was considering other options. We were passing each other on the down slope of our relationship anyway.

"Alright then Janice I'll talk to you tomorrow." I replied.

Parking was easy at the hospital so I just found somewhere to park and went upstairs. Once again when I made it to the floor Ace was on; Auntie Thelma was in the hallway. She had her head down so I couldn't really see her facial expression. She must have heard my footsteps because she quickly looked up. The tears were still pouring from her face. No words came out of her mouth as I drew closer. It appeared as though it was difficult for her to speak. Finally after staring at me she said something.

"How did you know?" She asked.

"How did I know what?"

"That Earnest had passed away." She began to sob.

144

"I didn't know...is he in there now?"

Words couldn't come out of her mouth. Slightly she nodded trying to contain her tears. I barged through the door to see doctors standing over him.

"Excuse me sir but we need time alone with the patient." A doctor said.

I pushed him and another doctor to the side and went straight for Ace. Ace's eyes were closed and there was no air coming from his body. He had stopped breathing. He was dead.

"Earnest Daniels was pronounced dead at 4:52pm."

I cried out in anger. Both of my fists slammed into my head as I dropped to my knees. The only father I ever really knew was now dead. Tears began to fall uncontrollably. I continued to cry out until I felt warm hands on my shoulders. I turned my head towards my back to find Auntie Thelma behind me. She helped to lift me up and escort me out the hospital room.

"Baby we need to let the doctor handle what needs to be handled." She softly said.

We hugged and kissed each other goodbye before I staggered down the hall.

"I'll pay for all the funeral arrangements." I said.

"You don't have to worry about that. Your cousin Shanice had insurance on us for years. But I want you to stop by because Earnest wanted you to have something when he passed. You are the last surviving Daniels man besides your son and he wanted to make sure you had it."

I nodded but I was still shell shocked. For some reason it felt like the hallway toward the elevator was much longer than usual. Many things ran through my head. I decided to call Big Black to give him the news. Usually I would call with my number then we would arrange times on public phones. This time I allowed it to ring until it went to voice mail.

"My uncle is gone. He's in a better place now."

That was all I said. I hung up the phone and hopped on the freeway. I had a little time before Fab-Five's party got going. I needed a little time alone so I cruised down the street until I decided to stop by Felicia's apartment. When I walked inside her apartment she was in the room watching television. She jumped up from the bed when she heard me walk in. She could instantly tell something was wrong with me.

"What's wrong Pooh?"

"I just left the hospital and my uncle passed away today."

"I'm so sorry to hear that. Can I get you anything like something to drink or eat?" She sympathetically asked.

"No I'm fine. I can't really stay for too long because I got plans for later on tonight. How was that club the other night?"

"It's real cool. It's some thug niggas that goes to that spot all the time. Only reason it probably ain't any shooting is because the police be up there after the club let out." She replied.

"The police are up there every night after the club?"

"Every night." She nodded.

She came over and stood in front of me. She offered a hug and I accepted. She put my head in her bosom and gently rubbed it. I was numb up until that point.

"When I lost my sister I felt the same way you are feeling right now. But sometimes Pooh the people we love are taken away from us for a reason. At least he got to live to be of old age. Be thankful for that." She consoled me.

She leaned down to gently kiss me on the lips. I slid my hands down her waist to her ass. Our soft intimate kisses began to intensify. Standing up my hands was in her shirt so I lifted it up. She moaned as grabbed her and wrapped my hands around her neck. I had been holding back for some time now. I hadn't given her the high hard one for awhile. I stripped her totally naked tossing every particle of clothing on the floor. She smelled good as my lips began to explore her upper body. We kissed then I backed her to the couch. We climbed on top of the couch as I slid inside of her. She was extremely tight and wet. I pushed inside of her slow and smooth as she grabbed the back of my neck. Her left leg was leaning on the couch pillow while her right leg hung off

146

the couch. We kissed much more passionately than usual. This was sex with the common denominator being pain. I was hurting inside and she understood my pain so she wanted to make me feel better. I grabbed hold of her right leg and lifted it in the air and she moaned louder.

"Turn over on your stomach."

"Okay baby." She replied.

She lied on her stomach as I penetrated from the back. That round supple ass stuck up like a sore thumb. I continued to slide inside of her with hard and long strokes. She glanced back at me with her mouth wide open. We both began to sweat profusely. I could feel myself about to cum. Then suddenly I released inside of her. On second thought maybe it wasn't painful sex but more like angry sex. At least from my vantage point. I climbed off her as she rubbed my sweaty chest.

We sat and talked for a good hour. Then I laid out my clothes for me to get ready for later that night. She helped me pick the outfit I wore for the party. I still wasn't in the mood to party but I had to show my face. The girls would show up in a couple of hours expecting to get paid. I waited until eight before I jumped in the shower. I quickly threw on my clothes and headed straight for the spot.

When I made it there Lonnie and Chris were already setting up. It was Main Man, Pooly, Willie, Dre, Travon, Rasheed, Cory, Shake, J-Rock and Smokey falling in about twenty minutes after me. The music was playing and the girls came in a little after my boys showed up. Only two people were left that would make the party complete. Big Mel and Fab-Five hadn't shown up and I was beginning to worry. I didn't need any more bad news.

I decided to walk outside to check and see if either one of them pulled up. To my surprise they pulled up together laughing and joking. It actually brought a smile to my face. They got out of Big Mel's Dodge Truck half staggering with alcohol reeking all over them.

147

"Look at this nigga Pooh; he was probably worried about us. This is a stand up nigga fa'sho." Big Mel leaned on me.

"I love this nigga for real." Fab-Five slurred his words.

I smirked at those niggas. We walked inside as everyone began to greet Fab-Five and welcome him home. We partied hard with the stripper girls. I allowed Fabian to pick two of his favorites to take in the back room. We were having a good time into the late hours of the night. As it got later and I noticed Big Mel sobering up I pulled him to the side. Fab-Five had already pulled the two girls he wanted into one of the back rooms. Paradise was trying to get my attention but I was preoccupied so she would have to wait.

"I know we're having a good time and everything but I got some bad news to tell you big cousin."

"Aw shit what now? Everybody is here so it can't be anybody dead." He frowned.

"Ace died tonight at the hospital. The cancer got to him. I went up there to visit him and he was already gone." I replied.

"Damn...I had so much love for that old man. Is that why Auntie Thelma was telling you that he wanted to see you the other night?"

"Yeah that was when he told me he was about to die. I didn't tell you about it because I was hoping he would get through it. That shit is eating me up right now." I bitterly replied.

"It's a fucking tragedy that's what it is."

"I know."

"Damn Pooh, are you gon spend some time with me or what?" Paradise walked up on me.

13
THE WORD IS OUT

I call them April babies cuz they some fools!
Lil Wayne

William Stover walked into the hidden location for the drug enforcement surveillance team. He maintained his natural military posture that he abandoned while working undercover. He shook hands with several officers on the team until he reached the table of Detective Yates and Detective Hudson. They were both sitting behind the table shuffling through paperwork.

"What's going on fellas?"

"You've done well with revealing one of the residents of Sherwin Daniels. He doesn't reside there any longer. Is his mother revealing anything of substance to help us build on this case?" Detective Hudson asked.

"He pretty much keeps her out of the loop. If I casually get into a conversation about her son she changes the subject." Stover replied.

"Lean on her in other ways. She is involved in something that we can use to indict her. Maybe she will be willing to give up her son. You once said she was a very self centered woman." Detective Yates said.

"She smokes marijuana from time to time. I've found a certain amount of that in her possession. Maybe we can charge her with possession with the intent. With that hanging over her head she might be willing to give up her son." Stover suggested.

"That's too risky. She might be willing to take a marijuana charge for her son. See if we can get something that will make her

149

consider turning on him. At least enough that will get her to work for us." Detective Hudson replied.

"What's going on with the informant that Detective Barnes sent to you? It is somewhat frustrating to have this guy operate with immunity. There is a war about to take place and we might be able to save lives." Stover retorted.

"Wait a fucking minute Stover. Don't come to us about our lack of progress when you are in the same position. As a matter of fact there is already a war taking place on the streets of San Bernardino." Hudson replied angrily.

"Well do we at least know the people that Mr. Daniels is having this war with? Did Barnes' informant at least reveal that information?"

"Markell Brown and Casey Sanders are from the California Gardens and warring with Mr. Daniels. From my understanding they are killers that we need to get off the street. At least four homicides have been attributed to these two suspects including the murder of a woman in Rio Vista Park." Yates explained.

"Can we at least apprehend those suspects to perhaps stop the war?" Stover asked incredulously.

"They are smarter than that Stover. Every time we're coming inside the California Gardens in a marked or unmarked car they are warned by many people trying to win their favor. Besides, Sherwin Daniels is the primary target as far as I am concerned." Hudson replied.

"Okay…okay what is your next plan of action." Stover surrendered.

"How about we put something on his mother and get her to roll up to him? We plant a user amount of cocaine on her and threaten her with a charge. We don't actually charge her but bring her downtown and put her in the box. If she is as high strung as you say she is then we shouldn't have a problem if we suggest she is looking at serious jail time." Yates suggested.

150

Stover didn't immediately reply. He was stunned that they would even imagine such a thing. He shook his head in disbelief trying to choose his words carefully.

"I can't condone falsely charging Shirley for crimes that she hasn't committed."

"See, you have grown attached to the suspect. She is the target, Stover. Now you are too emotionally attached to the suspect's mother to make rational decisions." Hudson pointed out.

"That's bullshit Hudson! What Yates is suggesting is illegal. If we can't come up with a charge then that is one we lost in the shuffle. I'm not breaking the law to enforce it." Stover protested.

"Have you had sexual intercourse with the suspect's mother?" Yates asked.

"That's none of your fucking business. I was sent undercover to watch any illegal activity and that is what I have done." Stover retorted.

"I'll take that as a yes." Yates smirked.

"The point you are missing Stover is that we need to move fast before it is too late. Now that you have grown attached to Ms. Daniels it can compromise the entire investigation. We are not going to charge Ms. Daniels we are just going suggest a charge to roll her up to her son." Hudson explained.

"I can't be a part of it. It has nothing to do with if I had sexual intercourse with her or not. The fact of the matter remains that planting something illegal on a suspect is just as criminal as the criminals themselves. You are going to have to use another method. I gave you the address to his new home. I also gave you information on the deceased Cornell Davenport. I think our best bet is to press on our informant Chris Jackson and see if he can roll us up to someone."

Stover slammed his hand on the table and walked out the door. Both Hudson and Yates watched him walk out the door in disbelief. They then looked at each other.

"He's sleeping with her." Yates said.

They both started laughing. They went through the paper work trying to find some lead that can get them closer to the target.

"What if we could get someone else to turn in his clique? If we can find someone that is disgruntled about something then this case can have legs." Hudson pondered.

"Mr. Daniels takes care of his people as far as I know. If someone is disgruntled it would be difficult to find who it might be." Yates replied.

"There is a war taking place and whenever there is a war people always become disgruntled. What we need to know is who is going to hurt the most from this war among the people in his circle and begin invest..."

Hudson's phone began to ring. He picked up on the second ring. When he answered the phone it had become obvious that he was speaking to Stover on the other line. He nodded his head intently listening. Once he hung up the phone he jotted down a few notes. He turned to Yates.

"That was Stover saying that Mr. Daniels had an uncle who recently passed. We might want to put someone on the funeral. With enough pictures we might be able to find someone interesting enough to help build this case."

"Well at least Stover is giving us some information." Yates replied.

The San Bernardino cold had set in this particular night. The projects were buzzing with fresh product. Shawn had been making money hand over fist and was about to sell out of all his dope. He gazed at the stars happy to be related to Killa Kell because he was now making serious money. They were actually second cousins because Killa Kell's grandmother and Shawn's grandmother were sisters. He thought they were close enough for Killa Kell to give him product. He had his road dog Sammy posted up with him while he was on his grind. They were both strapped just in case someone tried to rob them. He wasn't particularly worried about someone coming up in the projects to

152

trip with him. The only nigga he was worried about was Kramer and he was dead as a doorknob. They thought about killing J-Rock and Smokey but it wasn't necessary. The only one that would have the heart to step to them was Kramer. The projects had become an open air market. He sighed smugly knowing that he would be out of product within the hour. He wrapped himself tighter in his coat hoping the crack heads would hurry up and cop. His dope spot was deep in the projects so he didn't have to worry about a drive by. His pleasant thoughts were interrupted when he heard someone playfully yelling.

"Toss the ball over this way my nigga. I'm about to go long."

He had to be one of the niggas from the projects because he was too deep in to just have wandered. But he couldn't put the voice to face and the dark made it difficult to confirm who it was. He didn't really worry about it because if the nigga was up to something he wouldn't have announced his presence so openly. He saw the man running towards him like he was about to catch a ball. Shawn looked up in the sky trying to see if he could locate the ball in the dark.

Before he had a chance to find the ball he heard gunshots go off numerous times. His mind told him to reach for his nine-millimeter but his body wasn't responding. He felt the sharp pain run through his torso in several places before he slammed into the grass. He moaned loudly trying to make sense of what happened. He scoured the ground with his eyes to find his road dog Sammy laid out dead with his mouth wide open. His eyes got big when he realized what was going on. He looked up to see two men standing over him with their weapons drawn. A tear fell down his left cheek realizing he was at their mercy.

"This is for Kramer nigga." One said.

The bullets riddled his body and face making sure there was no chance for an open casket funeral. The two killers ran off in the night while Shawn and Sammy lay dead.

Early the next morning Killa Kell's grandmother came knocking on his bedroom door. He had a long night and was only asleep for several hours. He moaned as she frantically banged on the door. Finally he climbed out of bed taking Pebbles' arm from off his chest. He cracked open the door still half asleep.

"What's wrong grandma?"

"Esther just told me that they found yo cousin Shawn dead over there where she lives. She said him and his best friend were both killed at the same time while up in those there projects." Her voice strained.

"Are you serious?" Killa Kell suddenly woke up.

"Boy do you think I wouldn't be serious about something like that? She said that poor baby was shot up pretty bad. It looks like it's going to be a closed casket and everything. Esther is over there grief stricken. I'm getting dressed right now because she might need some company."

She turned around and walked down the hallway. He closed the door behind her but walked in a daze. He made it to the bed and slumped hard on the mattress and box spring. His own family was coming up missing. His girlfriend Pebbles rolled over closer to him after feeling him sit on the bed. She wrapped her arms around his waist trying to pull him into the bed.

"Are you coming back to bed Markell?" She groggily asked.

He didn't respond. She turned over a second time in the opposite direction then she thought about it. She turned back around and drew her body closer to him. Why wasn't he getting back in bed?

"Is something wrong?"

Killa Kell didn't say anything for a moment. He was still in his thoughts trying to figure out what was next. He knew that Pooh would have to pay for this somehow. Now he was fucking with his family. His head began to hurt as he rubbed both his temples to contain his anger.

"Baby is something wrong?" Pebbles asked again.

154

"Huh…My grandma just told me that Shawn and Sammy just got smoked up in the projects last night. She's going over there to comfort my Aunt Esther." He replied.

"Oh no Markell; He was only nineteen years old. That is some fucked up shit. Who would do something like that?" She lamented.

"I don't want to talk about it."

Killa Kell had a strict policy about pillow talking. He told her just enough to know that he was bothered. He might not have told her if he wasn't for sure that someone else would get word to her. He knew the word was out that he was trying to take over the projects. He thought about all the different ways Pooh could have found out so fast. From what he understood Kramer had all types of niggas that had problems with him. Then he considered that Shawn didn't feel it was necessary to kill Kramer's workers as well. He insisted that Kramer was the problem. Killa Kell felt sick to his stomach knowing he should have listened to his own instinct. He rose from the bed gracefully sliding out of Pebbles' embrace. He glanced back at her and noticed the tears fall from her face. She can cry for the both of us he pondered. No doubt he was hurting inside but he never knew how to express it except through anger. But he couldn't make decisions anymore in anger. This nigga Pooh was calculating and he had to be that way too.

"This is a whole different level of the game." He said aloud.

"What did you say?" Pebbles asked trying to get some kind of reaction.

"Never mind." He replied while grabbing a shoe box from out the closet.

Inside the shoebox were two chrome nine-millimeter guns. Each pistol had sixteen in the clip and one in the chamber. He checked the chamber and the clips of each gun. They were brand new guns that he felt could now be used. Pebbles stared at him in amazement as he readied himself for war. He was going to have to rally the troops. He knew it was an uphill battle but Pooh had to fall.   He heard his grandmother walk out the front door so he stepped into the hallway. He called up Casey on the house phone.

"What's up comrade?" Casey answered.

"Shawn got smoked up in the projects. Sammy's dead too."

After a brief moment of silence Casey finally responded to the news. He banged his hand on the mattress while still lying in bed.

"That nigga Pooh got to get served." Casey gritted his teeth.

"I'm knowing."

"Are we gon' link up in a little bit?" Casey asked.

"Get some rest and in a few hours we gon' sit down."

"How is a nigga gon' rest after hearing that shit?"

"I got Pebbles here so we gon' have to link up in a few hours."

"Alright, one hundred."

That afternoon Casey and Killa Kell met up at Rio Vista Park. They both had a 40 ounce bottle of Old English Beer as they sat on the park bench. Killa Kell shook his head in sorrow before any one of them spoke.

"That nigga is fucking with my family Cay. We gon' have to step it up a little better than before." Killa Kell said.

"We need to get a hold of some people he's got love for and kidnap they ass. If we can get a hold of a broad or a kid or some shit like that." Casey replied.

"That's easier said than done. He's got his people out of dodge. It's got to be some shit that we can really pull off. We can smoke his homeboys all day but all that's gon' do is make him replace them with more. What's bothering me is how did he know so fast?" Killa Kell pondered.

"If I was in that nigga's shoes, the first thing I would find out was if product was still moving after my homeboy got smoked. Shawn and them made it look like it was a personal problem right? So once he realized the product started moving after Kramer got his cap peeled he knew it was over some territory type shit. That nigga Pooh ain't a dumb muthafucka." Casey explained.

"Yeah, but how did them niggas get at Pooh to tell him. Pooh got people he deals with face to face. I can't see him talking to one of Kramer's workers. Kramer was the buffer. He wouldn't talk to any low ball niggas to get that kind of information." Killa Kell considered.

"He must have for him to find out so fast. He must be doing more than just supplying the niggas in the projects. He might be cool with more than one person, maybe even some curb servers." Casey replied.

Killa Kell put the palm of his hand to his forehead. He lowered his head trying to make sense of the whole thing. He had planned to build some muscle in the projects before Pooh caught on. There wouldn't be any survival if he didn't get to Pooh first.

"Females!" Killa Kell exclaimed.

"Females? You think it was a broad that gave up some information like last time?" Casey asked.

"Nah my nigga. We need to use these females to get the information we need to nail that nigga Pooh to a cross. If we pimp these bitches out then these niggas is gon' get to talking." Killa Kell explained.

"Who are you thinking about using?"

"Pebbles, Bernice and Mercedes will get the shit we need to move on these niggas." Killa Kell wickedly smiled.

"You gon' use yo girl?" Casey asked in disbelief.

"Fuck all these hoes. That bitch will do whatever I tell her to do."

"Well let's make that shit happen then." Casey hopped off the picnic bench.

"Yeah we gon' spread them out and see what niggas is thinking with their dick that's a part of Pooh's circle."

"So when is yo cousin's funeral?"

157

"My grandma says its one week from today. It's a closed casket though. We gon' have to show that nigga Pooh about closed caskets." Killa Kell frowned.

"I'm knowing."

Chris jittered nervously in front of Detective Yates and Detective Hudson. He was always nervous around these two white cops. Now another war was in full swing and he knew they were going to ask him about it. But Pooh had been keeping him at arms distance. Lonnie was the buffer between him and Pooh; and Chris wouldn't dare give up his cousin. He wished like hell he would only be able to talk to Homicide Detective Barnes. At least he was Black, Chris pondered.

"We've been letting you sell drugs with immunity and you still haven't brought us anything substantial on Mr. Daniels. You are going to either shit or get off the toilet Mr. Jackson. And what I mean by that is either give up some information on Mr. Daniels or be indicted as part of a continuing criminal enterprise." Detective Hudson explained.

"You mean shit or get off the pot." Chris mumbled.

"Excuse me?" Detective Hudson asked.

"Never mind. What you might want to do is get on the people that are coming up in the California Gardens. The CGs got some young guns trying to take over the projects and everything. My homeboy Main Man told me that." Chris explained.

"Can we bring in this friend of yours 'Main Man' for questioning?" Yates asked.

"I don't think he would be too cool with that. As far as Pooh is concerned that nigga doesn't trust me. He's always making sure that I'm not involved with anything directly with him. If he needs something done by me he uses someone else to relay that shit to me." Chris continued.

"Well you need to give us the name of the buffers he uses to relay the messages to you. If we can get one of them to talk we can roll him up to Mr. Daniels." Hudson replied.

158

Chris didn't really respond. He slowly shook his head asking himself how he's gotten in this mess. I guess I was just hating on Pooh when he was probably doing the best he could. It wasn't his fault Chucky got smoked.

"Mr. Jackson are you paying attention to what we are saying?" Yates asked.

"I'll have to see about that. I don't know the people's government names." Chris lied.

"Could it be that you are related to one of them? A young man by the name of Lonnell Jackson happens to be your cousin. Tell us about Melvin Taylor or Fabian Gilmore. Fabian Gilmore was recently released after the courts couldn't find substantial evidence connecting him to a murder. Those are the buffers you need to let us know about." Hudson smiled.

Chris didn't say anything. He looked at both detectives and noticed the obvious smirks on their faces. He realized at this point that Detective Barnes must have given them this information. Chris lowered his head trying to figure a way out of this.

"I don't know them like that. My cousin is on the same level as me so Pooh keeps him at arms distance also." Chris lied.

"Look, Mr. Jackson we are growing very impatient with you. You have one week to bring us something or so help me we are going to bust you for narcotics possessions." Yates said in frustration.

"Narcotics Possession? You haven't caught me with any drugs." Chris replied.

"But you will go down just the same if we don't have what we need. So it is either you or your cousin. Better yet if you get us the main target then you will be free from any prosecution." Hudson explained.

"I told you everything I know." Chris blurted out.

"Nevertheless if you can't give us more than the word will be out that you are a major narcotics distributor. Your spot near Mt. Vernon will be through." Hudson smiled.

159

Chris dropped his head and lamented. He had made a deal with the devil and didn't know how to back out of it. He looked at both detectives and nodded his head. He slowly rose from the chair still with his head down. He was stuck between a rock and a hard place. Chris felt like crying as he walked out the office. He clicked off the alarm and climbed inside his Dodge Magnum. He started up the engine but took some time to pull off.

"What am I gon' do?" He said aloud.

A tear fell down his face. He backed out of the parking lot and drove off into the night. As he cruised down the street in his own thoughts it suddenly came to him. He knew only one way out. He was definitely frightened half to death just thinking about it. He picked up his cell phone and began dialing the number.

"What's up Chris?" Lonnie answered.

"I need to talk to you alone." Chris replied.

"Right now?"

"Yeah right now."

"Alright meet me at yo house in about fifteen minutes. I was watching the game but if this shit is important I'm on my way." Lonnie replied.

"It's real important."

Lonnie showed up to his apartment in about ten minutes. He knocked on the door then opened it when he realized it was unlocked. He seen Chris sitting on the couch with a facial expression like he wanted to cry. Chris turned down the game on his flat screen. He glanced at Lonnie for a brief moment but couldn't keep eye contact.

"What's wrong with you little cousin? You know I got yo back so tell me what's wrong." Lonnie said.

"I got something really bad I need to tell you?"

"Where's Nikki?" Lonnie looked around.

"She's at her moms' house." Chris sighed.

"What you got to tell me?"

"I've been talking to the police." Chris blurted out.

"What they pulled you over and they asked you some questions. They were probably sweating you because they didn't have shit on you. Ya'll keep that spot on Mt. Vernon trump tight…right?"

"I've been working as an informant for the police ever since Chucky got killed. Detective Barnes talked to me in the hospital before ya'll showed up and he talked me into giving up information because I was pissed at Pooh." Chris began to sob.

"What the fuck are you talking about? You mean to tell me you are a muthafuckin snitch?"

Chris began to sob even harder. Lonnie slammed his fist against the wall and began pacing back and forth.

"Nigga you gave up everybody?" Lonnie snapped.

"I fed them a bunch of bullshit for years but they want Pooh so bad that they told me if I don't get someone in a week they were gon' put my ass in jail for a dope charge." Chris continued sobbing.

"You are a weak ass nigga. I should smoke yo muthafuckin ass right now. A snitch is a snitch Chris." Lonnie went off.

"I know…I fucked up big time."

"The code says I'm supposed to peel yo cap. Blood or not nigga you supposed to come up missing. Fuck!!!" Lonnie shook his head in anger.

"Look, I got close to a hundred grand saved up from all these years. I was gon' just disappear and the police ain't got shit." Chris suggested.

"What the fuck did you tell them? Aw shit…that's why Pooh never would fuck with you. That nigga probably suspected all along. Since he couldn't prove it he might have gave you a pass. Nigga you could have gotten me killed too. Muthafuckas might think I'm a snitch too. I can't believe this shit." Lonnie panicked.

"That's why I'm gon' leave."

"What the fuck did you tell them?" Lonnie barked.

161

He asked the question several times as he walked towards the couch where Chris was sitting. He leaned down and looked Chris in his eyes. There was a level of disgust written on Lonnie's face. After repeating himself for the third time he just looked at Chris.

"I told them that Travon was working for Pooh in the Delmont Heights. I told them that Kramer was working for him in the projects and Nelly was working for him in the Dorjil's. That was shit they already knew though. I would tell them that Pooh never dealt with me directly but I never gave you up. I never snitched you out. I just found out today that they knew that you were my cousin. I think Detective Barnes put it together by our last names and they figured out we were related. I swear Lonnie that's all I said." Chris pleaded.

Lonnie took off his fitted baseball cap and rubbed his head. He had to think about what Chris just said.

"You sure that's all you told them. You don't have me or the homies walking into some shit; do you?" Lonnie asked calmly.

"Hell nah, I swear that's all they know." Chris replied.

Chris was somewhat startled by how calm Lonnie had become all of a sudden.

"Maybe you just weren't ever meant for this game. Well pack yo shit up so you can leave town. If word is out somehow that you've turned snitch I'm a dead man just as much as you. Pooh might know but ain't a hundred percent. START PACKING YO SHIT!" Lonnie yelled the last sentence.

Chris rushed in the bedroom and began packing his clothes. Lonnie paced around the living room dwelling on his new revelation.

"Call your girl Nikki and see if she wants to roll with you." Lonnie yelled from the living room.

After all he still had love for his cousin. Chris being kin was the only thing that spared him. His heart was broken but not to the point of killing someone in his family. He shook his head and gritted his teeth.

"If this nigga wasn't kin...if this nigga wasn't kin."

14
GETTING FEDERAL

They lock us up because government be wanting tax on the shit!
Juvenile

After the funeral of my uncle and father figure Ace, I climbed into the limousine. Janice rolled with me and my family. She kept glaring at me without saying anything. She was pissed off because I invited Vanessa to the funeral. It was crazy to me because Vanessa knew him a lot longer than her. In fact, Ace and Janice may have met twice. I'm not even sure if it was that many times. I know he came to a party my mother was throwing and she was there. It seems like they met somewhere else but I don't really remember. Vanessa on the other hand has sat down and had dinner with Ace and Aunt Thelma on numerous occasions. I honestly didn't give a damn what Janice was pissed off about. I was more worried if Vanessa was pissed off that she wasn't riding in the limo with my family. Besides, I was ready to go home and change into something more comfortable.

I was getting tired of Janice and her bullshit. It seemed like she was becoming more and more of a problem than a necessity. She bitched about everything or had some sort of attitude. It was like living with a tormentor at times. I was on the verge of dumping her ass but I always thought about my daughter. Shanee meant everything to me. But I knew that eventually I would have to make an exit strategy with Janice. I didn't even look her way the entire ride home from the funeral grounds. We all decided that the limo would take us back to my mother's house. I had the Range Rover parked there any way.

Even though I lost my uncle it was good to see Paula again. I hadn't seen her that much in the last few years. Her and my mother had been best friends for years. Paula still was looking good for her age. We talked for a little while so that we could catch up. She still lived in Victorville and was thinking about retiring from her job. The last funeral where we were together she'd done a really big favor for me. I'll never forget her for that. I also saw Big Black at Ace's funeral. He walked past the funeral grounds without stopping. I didn't blame him considering there were police hanging out nearby. I didn't know how to feel about that. I thought time was running out for me. I'm figuring because of all the murders on the west side of San Bernardino the feds might be getting involved. These things were running through my mind until we pulled up in front of my mother's apartment complex.

I quickly jumped out of the limo and Big Mel followed close behind. He was sitting next to me in the limo. My Aunt Thelma, my cousin Shanice and her husband Clarence were sitting across from me. My sister Sharon and Marcus sat next to Big Mel and me. While Janice and my mother sat next to Aunt Thelma on the other side. I received a call from Lonnie while I was still at the funeral. It seemed like it was urgent. I didn't respond to the call and just let it go to voice mail. Big Mel wanted to talk about the war with Killa Kell and his peoples before we went our separate ways. We walked a little distance while I was listening to my voice mail message from Lonnie. When I got off the phone I glanced up towards my family and Janice gave me another mean glare. All she was doing was pissing me off.

"So these niggas tried to set up shop in the projects by smoking Kramer? You just met with the niggas when they put that shit in motion huh?" Big Mel distracted me from Janice.

"Yeah my nigga! First they rob my people in the Dorjil's then they try to take my spot in the projects. To be honest with you I think they were able to cop because of what they did in the Dorjil's. They some grimy, kill a nigga over some shoes type

165

niggas. I wish it was a way to touch them. They are the reason the police is getting so hot." I explained.

"I seen those two white boys in the Jaguar parked on the funeral grounds near the entrance. Somebody is snitching." Big Mel replied.

"I'm knowing. At least they were smart enough not to be driving a Crown Victoria." I smirked.

"I know!" Big Mel laughed.

"You know those are the same pigs that arrested Boom-Boom when he tried to blast on me at the shopping center." I said.

"Are you serious? Then they've been on you for a while now. That's why they were at the funeral?"

"It's them from way back because one of them had that fucked up crew cut and they were still driving that same Jaguar. But being followed by those two is some recent shit. All these murders are what's doing it. I'm thinking about backing off this war shit. It brings too much muthafuckin heat. But I know if I back off, these ain't the kind of niggas that will respect that. They gon' keep coming for revenge even though they got at my people first. This shit is stressing me out from all sides. Now Lonnie is hitting me up about an emergency. If I don't get out of this shit quick I'm gon' either get stretched or get smoked. But I feel like I'm locked in." I vented.

Big Mel didn't say anything. I think he understood I was getting shit off my chest. He glanced up to see Janice walking up the stairs turning around sporadically to give me mean stares.

"What's up with Janice?" He asked.

"That's another thing. This bitch is getting on my last nerve. She's pissed off because I invited Vanessa." I replied.

"But Vanessa knew Ace way longer than her. Why would she trip about some shit like that at a funeral?" Big Mel looked stunned.

"Because she's petty than muthafucka. I'm about to give her those walking papers. I'm just worried she might do some

166

vindictive shit. But fuck her I got to bounce to see what's up with Lonnie."

"Alright family handle yo business but let me know when it's time to put in work." Big Mel said while we embraced.

I ran upstairs to holla at Marcus. I wanted to use his truck because it had tinted windows. I managed to pull him outside without saying anything to Janice. She rode with me but I knew that I could get someone else to take her home. I didn't let it bother me that she would be pissed off because she had to roll with someone else. I didn't give a fuck.

Marcus followed me down to the parking lot so that he could take his son's car seat out the back seat of his truck. We gave each other a firm handshake then went our separate ways. When I pulled from under the garage I noticed that the two white detectives had followed us back to my mother's house. I rolled past them without being noticed. I kept looking in my rearview but they weren't following behind. I cut on my cell phone and called Lonnie.

"What's up peoples?"

"You know that's some gang shit in Chicago. I got family out there that told me about when you say peoples or folks it represents someone's set. Anyway, I need to holla at you about something real fucked up." He said.

"Fa'sho! I'm on my way to that place not too far from yo spot." I replied.

That was my way of telling him to meet me at the park. He didn't really respond right away so I thought maybe he didn't know what I was talking about.

"Oh...fa'sho my nigga." He replied.

It took me about twenty minutes from my mother's house because I was fighting afternoon traffic. When I pulled up to the park Lonnie was already sitting on one of the park benches. I hopped out the car and we embraced. He seemed a little uneasy which made me be a little uneasy. He lowered his head without

167

speaking for several minutes. It was obvious he had something on his mind so I was patient. Finally he looked me right in my eye.

"Look my nigga Pooh; I got some fucked up news to drop on you. Its hurts me to even say the shit. So I'm gon' just say the shit."

I nodded for him to say what was on his mind. I thought maybe he thought that I wasn't paying him good enough. I was willing to hear him out on whatever negotiations he had. He was one of the last niggas I wanted to be disgruntled.

"My cousin Chris has been snitching." He blurted out.

I couldn't believe my ears when he said it. It was one of those kinds of things where you heard someone but you don't believe what you heard. I was stunned for a moment not even looking in his direction. My eyes were staring into the street. Finally I came to my senses.

"How do you know?" I managed to say.

"He admitted the shit. This is some fucked up shit Pooh but I swear my nigga I ain't ever cooperated with the police. This nigga done made my family look bad." Lonnie passionately explained.

"I believe you my nigga. I never had any doubts about your loyalty to the code. Where is Chris at right now?" I asked.

"I sent that nigga to Chicago because the police was putting pressure on him to give one of us up. He's my family but I should have smoked his ass huh?" He sincerely asked.

"It's hard to get rid of family because there is love there. Look Lonnie if I found out my family was snitching I don't know what I would do. Some niggas are weak and some niggas are strong and sometimes they're in the same family. Did Chris tell you what he gave up to the police?" I asked.

"He said he gave them a bunch of shit that they already knew. He was getting pressure to give up information that could get us all stretched. He gave them a bunch of petty shit but they threatened to lock him up if he didn't come back with something serious. But I'm like why in the fuck are you talking to 'one time' in the first place?"

"Did he say why he started snitching?"

Lonnie sighed before saying anything. He turned his head away from me from clear guilt. I could tell the nigga felt bad.

"He was pissed off about what happened with Chucky when they were shot up. He felt like you should have done more. But I told him that shit was taken care of. When he complained about it I brushed it off as him just venting. But you kind of knew all along that he was up to something. I must have been blinded because we are related." Lonnie shook his head.

"Yeah I felt something wasn't right with him. I can't explain what I was feeling but I knew not to deal with him directly." I replied.

"Look my nigga; I ain't a turncoat type of muthafucka. I never have and I never will." Lonnie said vehemently.

"You straight with me. It's good we got that shit taken care of though. Did Chris describe who was asking all these questions about us? Was it that Black detective that asked for our information at the hospital that day?"

"Nah he said he started talking to him but was sent to some white boys that worked in narcotics." Lonnie replied.

"Did he say if they were local or federal?"

"He didn't know."

That was good enough for me. I thought it was probably the same detectives that were at the funeral today. That was all I needed to hear. In my opinion Lonnie didn't have to tell me that his cousin was a snitch. He could have gotten his cousin out of the game and we wouldn't have heard from him again. But it bothered him so he had to drop that shit on me. That was the type of loyalty I had to reward. He didn't know how I would react to that kind of news. He was still my number two as far as I was concerned. I told him I wanted him to roll to Los Angeles with me. It was about an hour drive but I wanted to check something out.

169

When we got to L.A. I hopped off the Freeway and drove down the boulevard until I pulled into a parking lot. When he looked up to see the neon lights he chuckled.

"You're taking me to a strip club?"

"Yeah what's wrong with that?" I asked.

"I just figured it was on some business type shit."

"I just want to have some fun and check some shit out. We just got a monkey off our back so why not celebrate?" I smiled.

We walked in the strip club ready to have a good time. After paying the cover charge we walked in to see a familiar face on stage. Lonnie tapped me on the arm.

"Ain't that the bitch you used to fuck with back in the day?"

"Yeah her name is Princess." I replied.

Now I knew what Paradise was talking about when she said she lost weight. She had lost at least twenty five pounds. The weight loss affected her shape because she didn't have the ass she use to have. Her stomach was flat and she had the six pack abdomen but she looked malnutrition. She did a spin on the pole and when she finished she did a split and looked right at me. She was startled as I smiled at her. She stumbled to get up trying to keep her eye on me. I ordered something to drink then slid another twenty to the bartender.

"Is this her first dance or her second dance?"

"This is her first dance." The female bartender replied.

I sipped on my beer while she finished her song. When the song was over she hurried off the stage. She then came back to hurriedly grab her money from off the stage. This time she didn't come back out. The DJ began playing the second song but Princess never came out. I walked up to the security guard as quickly as possible.

"Can you get back in if you need to get something out of the car?"

170

He nodded indicating that he would remember my face. I quickly walked over to Lonnie while he was sipping on some hard liquor.

"Let me know if that girl that was just on stage comes back out."

"Alright."

I damn near jogged outside to catch her rushing to her car. She was so preoccupied with trying to get away she didn't notice me walking up on her. I calmly caught the door before she could close it.

"What's up Princess?" I smiled.

"Wh-what's Up Pooh?" Fear flashed across her face.

"Don't you owe me some money?"

"Aw come on Pooh I don't have yo money right now." She pleaded.

"So when will you have my money?"

"Uh…soon real soon. I got some things in the works right now to get that paper for you."

"What if I wanted my shit right now? This is a nice car. How about you sign over the pink slip to me right now?" I asked.

"I-I don't have the pink slip on me right now." She said.

"What is it of value that you have to let me know that you are going to give me my money? Or do we need to handle this in a different way." I grinned at her.

"Look I got about two thousand dollars worth of jewelry with me right now. You can have this shit and I'll have the rest for you in a week." She pleaded while pulling out her jewelry.

"How about in three days. You got a tendency to run from a nigga. I might not see you again." I pushed.

She shook her head in fear. I was just fucking with her honestly. I knew she wasn't able to pay me back all of that bread or replace the dope. I just wanted to see her reaction. But since she was offering all of this jewelry I thought I should take it.

"Girl I'm just fucking with you. You did me dirty though. If I would have caught up with you that night I would have probably killed yo ass. But I ain't even tripping?" I laughed.

She began to relax a little bit. I let go of her car door but she left it open when she realized I wasn't mad.

"So you must have linked up with some niggas that told you how to get off that product."

"Yeah they told me they were going to give me seven thousand off of each kilo. Those niggas only gave me two thousand off of each one." She admitted.

I laughed out loud when she told me that. I had to fuck with her after she told me that. It tickled me so much she began to laugh with me.

"What's so funny?"

"You could have made forty thousand off of each kilo." I continued laughing.

"Hell nah, you are fucking with me now."

"If you sold it whole sale you could have made sixteen to seventeen thousand. But once you cook it into crack you could have made forty thousand. I'm giving you game right now." I continued laughing.

"Come on Sherwin stop teasing me." She playfully frowned.

"That's what yo ass get for trying to steal from me. A ruthless nigga would have smoked yo ass, female or not." I chuckled.

It was too funny to believe. Even if the niggas would have stayed true to their word she would have been ganked for a lot of money. But they didn't even give her that. That's what her ass get for stealing some shit she didn't know the prices. We talked for a little while then she went back inside. I don't know what she explained to the owners as to why she didn't dance for the second dance. She wanted to keep in touch but she proved be untrustworthy so I declined. Lonnie and I stayed at the strip club

172

until it closed. I wasn't in a rush to make that drive back to San Bernardino. Besides, we were enjoying ourselves.

When I did drive back I decided to go to Janice's house. I didn't like being there that much but it was right off the 10 Freeway coming back from L.A. She was in a deep sleep when I walked in the door. I tried to be as quiet as possible while getting undressed. The following morning I heard much activity going on in the house. The television in the living room was up loud and it was only seven in the morning. I walked into the living room half asleep rubbing my eyes.

"Ay Janice could you turn the T.V. down I'm still trying to get some sleep?"

"Oh excuse me. I didn't think you lived here anymore since we hardly see you here. Especially after I had to get a ride home from Marcus and Sharon last night."

I ignored her and went back to bed. About thirty minutes after that Shanee came running into the bedroom.

"Daddy, Daddy could you take me to school?"

I couldn't tell my little girl no. I was pissed off because I knew that bitch Janice told her to come in there to ask me. I threw on a sweat suit then quickly brushed my teeth. When I walked into the living room Shanee came running into my arms. It was really good to see her. She grabbed my hand as we walked outside to Marcus' truck. Janice smiled at us as we walked outside.

"Ya'll have a good day."

She was being a smart ass. I had to get Shanee's car seat out of Janice's car and put it in the truck because Marcus had taken his. So after ten or fifteen minutes of dealing with that I was on the road. I dropped her off about fifteen minutes later. I thought about going back to Janice's house and have some choice words with her but I decided against it. I didn't feel like going through all of that. I decided to rent a room then visit Vanessa because I had some things to talk to her about. I wanted to rent the room because I didn't want to share my bed with anyone. But before I could get about two blocks away from my daughter's school an unmarked car pulled me over. When I glanced at the rearview it was that same familiar face. I couldn't make out the other face but it looked like he had a partner on the passenger side. He walked up this time without having his hand on his holster. Well at least he understood that much.

"So Mr. Daniels we meet again." He began.

"How is it Detective Barnes that you always tend to find out where I am? You don't have anything better to do but follow poor old me?" I said sarcastically.

"I don't bother you until the murders start increasing. What do you know about two young men being murdered in the housing projects?" He asked.

"Probably about as much as you know. I told you it is probably a bunch of knuckleheads that don't know how to be cool." I replied.

"For some reason I think you know more than that. You don't think that all these murders will not come back on you huh? With this kind of body count it is definitely going to go federal. All I'm asking you is to either stop the violence or give me information to how I can stop it. The streets talk and a man in your position definitely hears things that other people are not privy to." Detective Barnes insisted.

"Truthfully Detective Barnes I respect you as a good cop. You want to see people live and for that alone you get much respect. But you also have to respect that through life or death, freedom or jail I got to live by the principles I believe in. Even if I did know anything I couldn't talk to you." I replied.

"You don't think that your people won't turn on you the first time they get in a bind. Self preservation is the code in these streets. These young boys in the streets today will give up anybody so they won't have to do any jail time. Mr. Daniels there is too many murders on the west side for law enforcement to let it stand. Someone is going to take the fall for this. You better believe it will be you because your name is ringing out. When your people get into a tight squeeze they will not hesitate to put

174

you in the mix." Detective Barnes tried passionately to persuade me.

"They have to live with their decisions just like I have to live with mine." I firmly replied.

15
THE SET UP

Now they all lost for words like I beat them in Scrabble!
Ludacris

After copping from Big Black and cooking it up at Felicia's spot I decided to lay low. Only person I spoke to was Vanessa in a week. I let Lonnie know I would disappear for a week or two. Vanessa and I had to talk. I could never get used to Detective Barnes pulling me over. It was time to make moves for a way out the game. It's always a matter of having enough time to do so. You don't know what the police know. You don't know what nigga done turned snitch or informant. You don't know what nigga is creeping around the corner to peel yo cap. Death or jail could be right at your door and you don't have any way to escape. When I walked into Vanessa's house she smiled. I was happy to see her but didn't know why she was smiling like that.

"You know Janice called here asking where you have been." She chuckled.

"Are you serious?"

"That girl really doesn't like me. I tried to be cordial but she had a bad attitude the moment she got on the phone. I told her I would let you know she called. I thought it was my cousin calling from South Hampton because I just got off the phone with her."

"How is Patricia anyway? She hasn't been to Cali in a few years."

"Yeah she's been busy with a few things and she just had another baby." Vanessa replied.

"It seems like you told me about that. All the shit I got going on right now I can forget sometimes." I shook my head.

"So what's so important that you needed to talk to me so fast? I know you miss me Winnie but you were acting like it was life or death. Do you love me that much?" She teased with her hands on her hips.

"You know I do. But I'm hitting you up because I'm about ready to get out the game."

She didn't say anything right away. She looked me right in my eyes and studied me for a moment. It sort of reminded me how Ace would do when he was trying to figure something out. After really giving me the look for a while she turned away then walked into the kitchen.

"So it's finally burning you out?" She said from the kitchen.

I peaked around the open doorway of the kitchen while she opened the refrigerator. At this point I couldn't read what was going on. She didn't give me a happy or sad disposition. It felt like she was still reading me even though she wasn't looking in my direction. She pointed to the juice she was pouring asking me if I wanted any. I shook my head while leaning on the door entrance of the kitchen.

"Yeah it's about time I backed out of this here game. Too many landmines to last in this shit forever. I got to set something up totally different for myself. I'm almost off parole so it would be good to exit about the same time." I sighed.

She could sense the weariness in my tone. She sipped on her juice then gave a half hearted smile.

"If you are serious about this baby we can make it happen. When niggas become bosses they get addicted to that power and don't want to back up out of the game. That shit can be more addictive than crack." She said.

"I was always a reluctant boss. Wanting to be the boss of my own destiny put me in a position to become a boss. But once you get up there everyone wants to aim at you. I had that Black homicide detective pull me over again the other day. That was why I've been laying low. He pulls me over every time I'm leaving Janice's house. Somebody's snitching. I found out this young nigga was snitching but that's taken care of. Besides, he never knew where Janice lived. I don't know who could be talking. It's just too much drama for me." I broke it down.

"Well let's set it up so your people can be taken care of and you still can get out the game. If your people feel cheated then they gon' want to get at you."

"I'm knowing." I nodded.

"Let me jump in the shower and when I get out we'll map out what we plan to do."

"Okay. While you're in the shower I'm going to call Janice and see what's going on."

"You got some explaining to do." She smirked.

I waived my hand at her joke. After taking a deep breath I slowly dialed the numbers to Janice's house phone. I knew she wouldn't answer her cell if she was at home. I figured she would talk a whole bunch of shit and I really wasn't in the mood.

"Hello Ron?"

"No this is Winnie. Are you expecting a call from someone named Ron?" I asked with a tinge of jealousy.

"What if I am? You haven't been home for me to even think of you as my man. Maybe I've found another man to provide the things that you can't provide." Janice sassily replied.

"So you are saying that I don't provide for you and my baby?"

"I'm saying you don't provide the emotional stability I need. I like money but it can't keep me warm at night."

"I told you that the police have been hot over there by your house. Somebody is watching that house because I got pulled over twice leaving there. The cold thing about it is they don't even give a damn that I know they are following me." I explained.

"So that means you won't ever come home because you are worried about someone following you?" Janice asked in a condescending tone.

"You think?" I replied in the same tone.

"What about your family Winnie? Are we supposed to give up everything because you're worried about someone following you? We can't buy a new house." She snapped.

"Look Janice you can have that house. It means much more to you than it does to me."

"So it's like that? What about us Winnie are we through or what?" She sounded stunned.

"I don't know; what about Ron? Maybe it would be best we went our separate ways and just raised our daughter together." I suggested.

I could tell that she was hurt over the phone. The phone was silent for at least an entire minute. She was probably taking it all in. Then she sighed through the phone letting me know she hadn't hung up. I patiently waited for her to reply.

"What about the bills and the house note? What about Shanee and everything she needs?" She blurted out.

It sounded like strictly business but that was her armor. I guess she never thought that it would come down to this. Maybe because she was the one always breaking hearts she never expected it to happen to her. Janice is the type of woman men would crawl for. Her beauty was something that women envied. But you know the saying 'You show me a beautiful woman and I'll show you a man that is tired of her'. That was my sentiment at that very minute. There was no turning back at this point.

"I'll set you up so that you can take care of bills. And as long as I am able I will take care of my daughter. I might come by to pick up some things of value I might want but other than that I don't plan on coming back over there. You can bring Shanee over to my mother's house and I will pick her up and spend time with her from there."

"Fuck you Sherwin, you ain't shit! I hope yo drug selling ass get a hundred years; you low down muthafucka." She snapped.

"What are you talking about Janice I don't sell drugs? Not anymore." I calmly replied.

"Whatever nigga! All I know is that you are as crooked as a barrel of snakes. What goes around comes around and I hope you get everything you deserve." She continued to scream.

"What about our daughter? Why would you wish something terrible on the father of your child?" I calmly replied.

"Fuck you! You ain't good enough to be the father of my daughter. I'll find another nigga to be the father of my baby. I know you don't want to take me to court with yo criminal ass?" She teased me with her last sentence.

I didn't even reply. I was angry but I refused to let her know it. Now was the time to hang up the phone. Vanessa came walking in the living room in her bathrobe. She looked at me and could tell that I was upset. There was a frown on my face.

"What happened with you and Janice?"

"I told her it was over and she went off on me. She started talking shit about Shanee wasn't my daughter anymore and she hopes I get a hundred years in jail."

"She didn't mean all that; she was just pissed off so she was trying to piss you off." Vanessa said softly.

"I don't know Vanessa; she might have meant that shit. She started calling me a drug dealer over the phone and everything." I collapsed on the couch.

"Never mind..." The phone started ringing.

This time Vanessa looked at the Caller ID and noticed it was Janice calling. She pointed at the phone letting me know who it was. I shook my head as she waved for me to come closer to hear the phone call.

"Hello?"

"Hey Vanessa this is Janice. I was calling you to tell you that you can have Sherwin's trifling ass. I don't want that tired nigga anyway. I hope both of ya'll have a wonderful life together." Janice loudly stated.

"What are you talking about Janice? Winnie is the father of my child and that's how we keep it." Vanessa acted confused.

"Tssst yeah right! You know and I know that ya'll been probably fucking from day one. Don't worry about it though because I got me a new man. So I don't have to hear from Sherwin's tired ass ever again." Janice replied.

My cell phone began to ring so I walked away from the phone conversation Janice and Vanessa were having. I glanced at the Caller ID thinking Janice was trying to see if I was at Vanessa's house. When I looked at the number I noticed that it was someone I was expecting.

"Hello?"

"I'm going to hit you back in about ten minutes." I whispered.

I heard Vanessa wrapping up her conversation as I reached over to kiss her. She hung up the phone then glanced over at me as I was walking out the door.

"I thought we were going to set everything up?" She yelled after me.

"I promise you I will but this is something important." I said while walking out the door.

I rushed down the stairs and into the Range Rover in search of a pay phone. There was only one reason why I should have gotten a phone call on this phone from this person. Once I found a liquor store I made sure to grab a bunch of change so I could talk.

"Hello?"

"Don't say anyone's name but you remember what I told you about calling that number you called right?"

"Yeah everything is good."

"Okay out of the city. Is it one or two?" I asked.

"It's two! But what city?"

"Can you meet up with me before you go out?"

"Yeah I got a few hours."

181

"Meet at Valley College on the Auditorium steps. Order something from Baker's then find your way over there just in case you are being watched. In an hour." I explained.

I hung up the phone and called up someone very reliable. When he picked up the phone he was irritated. I could tell from the background that he was arguing with Shanell.

"I'm on my way."

"About how close are you?"

"I'm about a high two plus three away."

"Fa'sho!"

That was my way of telling Fab-Five that I was about twelve minutes plus three minutes away from him. Basically fifteen minutes from his house. About three and a half hours later I found myself in the parking lot of a Riverside movie theater. I had decided to rent a car just in case my vehicle could be recognized. I was looking for a tan Monte Carlo and eventually I found it. It looked like the couple were tossing and turning inside the car. If they weren't having sex it appeared as though they were. I smiled at the beauty of this thing. I didn't know what time the movie started so I had to wait until she gave the signal.

After I was waiting for about thirty minutes she decided to get out of the car. The woman had a body that made a man lust. She reminded me of that Commodores song 'Brick House'. I watched her walk up to the ticket booth and it appeared as though she was ordering tickets. I glanced at her then I glanced at the Monte Carlo. The guy driving was sitting down listening to music. I really couldn't tell what he was listening to but his mind was preoccupied.

I looked a few cars down in the parking lot and what I saw was what appeared to be a man that belonged to a biker club. He had on all the biker apparel those motorcycle clubs wore when they were on their motorcycles. He was by himself which wasn't usually the case. He took off his helmet and he had a black handkerchief covering his mouth and his nose. He was walking toward the ticket booth of the movie theater. He was walking in between cars somewhat at a fast walking pace. I glanced around to see what was going on around me. When the biker got close to the Monte Carlo it looked like he was pulling out something.

Suddenly I heard a pop go off twice. I slowly drove off as discreet as possible. I noticed that the biker walked off at about the same pace he walked up to the Monte Carlo. I didn't take the time to see all the details. I went around the block and I seen who I was looking for sitting on the curb on a big tree smoking a cigarette. I pulled up on her and she put out the cigarette and jumped in on the passenger side. I headed straight for the freeway.

"So how are you feeling?"

"I'm good." She replied.

"This kind of shit doesn't bother you a little bit?"

"Not really because that muthafucka had something to do with my sister getting killed. My sister never did anything to anybody. Shit you remember what Tupac said. 'Revenge is like the sweetest joy next to getting pussy'. But in my case it would be the sweetest joy next to getting money. You know dicks come a dime a dozen." Felicia laughed.

"Alright then. But you know you can't go back to that spot. Didn't he pick you up from there?"

"Yeah but I told him that I didn't know him like that so he doesn't know what apartment I stay in. Plus everything is set up for me to move to Texas."

"Yeah but I'm gon' use the spot every now and then for a few things." I replied.

"Yeah that's cool. Even if he told his people the apartment complex I lived in that doesn't mean he knows the apartment number or what section it's in."

There was nothing left to ask after that. I drove her to her car parked on this side road in Colton and she drove off. Then I drove to my final meeting for the night. It was in the parking lot of this shopping center right off the 215 Freeway. I pulled into the parking lot about twenty minutes after I dropped Felicia off.

Fabian was waiting for me leaning on his car. He was in a T-Shirt and jeans.

"Damn you changed out of those clothes quick than a muthafucka." I commented.

"Yeah I got rid of all that shit that might link a nigga. I had to do what I had to do." Fab-Five smiled.

"Real talk. I didn't really want you putting in any work since you had that little case pending. But I couldn't think of anyone that was more reliable to handle some shit like that. You feel me?"

"Yeah the little soldiers you got coming up in the game got heart to pull a trigger but they're not tactical niggas like me." He arrogantly replied.

I chuckled when he said that. I knew he was hungry to put in work because he had been locked up. I think because I held him down while he was locked up he had been wanting to show his appreciation.

"So who was the nigga we smoked tonight?" He asked.

"Aw this nigga from out of the CGs that robbed the Dorjil's and killed Lil Jake."

"Lil Jake got smoked? I haven't been over in the Dorjil's in a minute. I didn't even know the young nigga was serving over there. Shanell has been bitching about me not going over there so I've been avoiding that shit. That bitch has been giving me problems since I've been out. Complaining all the time and shit."

"I heard ya'll arguing over the phone when I called you. What does she have to complain about? You got money coming in right? Not to mention you gon' get a bonus for this work today." I said.

"I don't know why she's been bitching but I try not to lose my temper. She wasn't this way when we first started dating. She didn't even come at me the way she comes at me now. It's crazy." He slowly shook his head.

She probably felt guilty about the Nelly situation. I didn't want to tell him the dirt on his girl because I knew it might break his heart. The last thing you wanted to do was break the heart of a killer. Besides, I didn't want to be the messenger on that kind of shit. I allowed his thoughts to wander a little.

"Well I'm going to the house and get some sleep. It ain't too late, so I might get some pussy tonight." Fab-Five smiled.

"Hopefully." I replied.

We embraced one last time then we drove off. I decided to go back to Vanessa's house. She was probably asleep but I figured we could talk the next day. When I walked in the door she was actually on the couch watching television. It had to be close to eleven-thirty and I know she had to take Joshua to school in the morning.

"Don't you have to take Joshua to school or you want me to do it?" I asked while walking in the living room.

"He's spending the night at my mother's house. I figured you would come back over here so I told my mother to keep him another day. Did you take care of what you needed to take care of?"

"I did." I nodded my head.

"Come here then."

I came closer to her and leaned in and we began kissing. She stood up and lifted my shirt. She kissed on my stomach and my chest. It felt good to feel her explore my torso. She helped me take off my shirt then I slid off her night gown. All she had on under the night gown was a thong. Her beautiful chocolate frame glowed in the dimly lit living room. The moon peaked in the shades to add a glistening to her complexion. My hands began to explore her waist and her ass. We passionately kissed allowing our hands to touch different parts of our bodies. Locked in our embrace I managed to slide my pants off. I slid her thong from off her round supple bottom then gently laid her on the couch.

My tongue began to explore every part of her body. Every crevice and curve felt my hot wet tongue. After she couldn't take anymore she pulled me upward as our tongues collided in a heated

185

embrace.   I slid inside of her then went into deep hypnotic lovemaking.

This was something different.   It was as though we were sealing something that could not be sealed in words.   We brought about this new beginning in a way that could only be expressed on the highest level.   It verified that she was mine and I was hers.   It sealed our fate that we were one and would always be one.   We made love like we had never made love before.   It was a revitalizing or a rebirth of the enduring love we always shared.   I was at peace.   After making love on the couch we decided to climb into bed.   We got under the covers then she smiled at me.

"I have a pen and pad next to the bed.   So let's set this up." She smiled.

All I could do was smile back.

"Okay let's do it."

16
WORDS OF WISDOM

'One time' can't keep the law and order!
Ice Cube

J-Rock impatiently sat at the table inside the interrogation room. They were suggesting that he was an accomplice to murder one. He couldn't believe that he could get caught up in this mess. He wasn't the one that squeezed the trigger but the police were suggesting that he was just as guilty. The fact that it was two Black detectives didn't make his case better. In fact he knew it would be harder to run anything by them. They were making him sweat inside the small room. He had been sitting in the room for at least thirty minutes. They came to his mother's house to pick him up for questioning. His left leg continued to jitter as he wondered what to say once they walked in.

Detective Barnes peaked in at the young man from time to time trying to read his actions. He was definitely scared which might mean an opening for him to cooperate. He figured that good cop bad cop had played out and too many youngsters were becoming less intimated by the charade. He opted for a hard nose approach. He would suggest that J-Rock was responsible for the murders. He knew that the young man was only a curb-server selling dope on a minuscule level. He wouldn't expect to be sitting on a bunch of jail time. Detective Barnes decided to toss around some numbers at the young man and see how he reacts.

He walked inside the interrogation room with a smirk on his face. The middle aged detective with strands of gray hair looked down at the suspect. J-rock refused to even look in the man's direction.

"So Mr. Jason Phillips, we both know why you are here. You participated in a double homicide that could get you twenty-five to thirty years in prison."

"I-I ain't killed anyone." J-Rock's voice cracked.

"Yeah but we have an eyewitness that sees you at the murder scene during the time of the murders. You were the only person recognized with two other suspects in which you gave directions to within the housing projects. Our witness says that it was a calculated murder that you were full aware of and participated in. Now we know you are not the shooter so we might can work something out. But only if you work with us now. If we don't get what we need then you will be prosecuted to the full extent of the law. That means you will do the time for murders you didn't commit."

"Nah it wasn't like that. Pooh told me to show some people around so I didn't know anything about someone being killed." J-Rock nervously replied.

"When you say Pooh, are you referring to Mr. Sherwin Daniels?" Detective Barnes quickly asked.

"I don't know his real name." J-Rock sweated.

"He drives a white Range Rover SUV?"

"Yeah that's him." J-Rock nodded.

"Are you willing to testify that he told you to show the suspects the directions into the housing projects?" Barnes eagerly asked.

"Well I didn't hear from him directly. I heard it from 'L'. He was the one that told me to show some cats where the new spot was at."

"L? What is his government name?" Barnes persisted.

"I don't know. I just know him as L. He's light brown with a taper fade. He drives a Dodge Charger." J-Rock explained.

Detective Barnes walked out of the interrogation room to be greeted by Detective Bowen. He looked at the rookie detective and briefly smiled.

"I've got him talking. He says that a young man by the street name of 'L' told him to lead the suspects into the housing projects. I want to see if I connect anybody with that name to Mr. Daniels." Barnes explained.

"Do you think he would be willing to testify?" Bowen eagerly asked.

"I asked him if he would be willing to testify to Mr. Daniels and that is when he admitted that it was a man that goes by the street name 'L' that actually gave the order. Follow me to my desk." Barnes waved for him to follow.

They walked over to his desk which was adjacent to the rookie Bowen's desk. Barnes began to dig through many different drawers. He was searching for something but couldn't find it. Bowen leaned on his own desk watching Barnes tear up his work station.

"What are you looking for?"

"I'm looking for one of my old note pads. A young informant I visited at the hospital was working for Mr. Daniels. Mr. Daniels and several of his boys came to pay the young man a visit and I wrote down all their names. It's been several years since that pad has been in use. I wouldn't have thrown it away."

"Why don't you talk to your informant that works for Mr. Daniels and he might be able to point out who is this 'L' we are looking for."

"That's actually a good idea. You are catching on quick Bowen. It is good to follow all leads. Let me look in one more place then we can go…bingo here it is right here." Barnes pulled out a blue beat up notepad.

"What about the suspect in the interrogation room?" Bowen asked.

"We will keep him nervous for awhile by holding him in the room for awhile. We haven't read him his Miranda rights and we haven't officially charged him. We will grant him his phone call when we get back from chasing this lead. We will offer him something to eat to keep him on ice." Barnes explained.

They both walked past the interrogation room but Barnes opened the door to peek inside. The young suspect glanced up in anticipation wondering what was next.

"I'm following up on this 'L' character do you want something to eat? My treat of whatever you want." Barnes asked.

"I want a Burrito Supreme and some Nachos from Taco Bell." J-Rock sighed.

"What kind of drink?"

"A Sprite with little ice."

Barnes closed the door then walked out of the office with Bowen on his heels. Barnes flipped through his notepad while walking to his car. They hurriedly jumped into the Crown Victoria and drove off.

"The young man that might go by the name of 'L' might be Lonnell Jackson. In fact if this is the young man then he might be related to our informant Chris Jackson." Barnes explained.

"So we are headed to the house of your informant?" Bowen asked.

"No I gave his name to detectives that work in the narcotics division. They are some macho white guys Yates and Hudson. One of them actually has a crew cut as though he's in the marines. Their pretty hard nosed detectives that have been privileged to drive a Jaguar. It's a pretty car too I might add. They've been investigating Mr. Daniels for years but we can share information now that the murders have intensified." Barnes pointed.

In about fifteen minutes they pulled into a secluded area with a building hidden in the back view. Barnes wondered about showing up to this site without calling. He didn't know if Yates or Hudson were even here. He slowly climbed the stairs looking around to see if there was any life. When he knocked on the glass door it was Yates that came to answer the door.

"Long time no see brother. How is everything going Barnes?" They shook hands.

"Things are fine for the most part. This is my new partner Detective Bowen. Detective Bowen this is Narcotics Detective Yates."

They both shook hands then Yates escorted them towards the office area of the building. Yates looked over at the young detective and smiled.

"A young homicide detective huh? That's good to hear. So what brings the pleasure of two of San Bernardino's finest to our humble doors?" Yates asked.

"I was hoping to talk to Hudson and yourself about Mr. Daniels. I passed on an informant Chris Jackson to you guys and I wanted to know if I could talk to him about his cousin Lonnell Jackson." Barnes explained.

"Detective Hudson is in the head right now. When he comes out the restroom we can sit down and talk. As far as Mr. Jackson we asked him to get us information on Mr. Daniels and his people and he disappeared. We haven't seen or heard from him in a couple of weeks." Yates replied.

Noise from the restroom door closing alerted the three detectives. They looked in the direction of the restroom to see Detective Hudson walking out. Hudson was in his own thoughts when he looked up to see Yates, Barnes and an unfamiliar detective staring at him.

"Joe, how have you been? It's been a long time since you've come to visit us humble narcotics people." They shook hands firmly.

"I was stopping by to go over some information. I just heard from Yates that the informant I passed to you has gone AWOL. Do you think he's dead?" Barnes replied.

"No I believe that he has moved out of town. I personally drove by his place of residence and he had moved out. I checked several areas where he might be and he was nowhere to be found." Hudson sighed.

"You can't put out a search for him?"

191

"It would be easier if he was a convicted felon. Then he would have violated parole by leaving. But you must have him as an informant because he was dissatisfied about something. With no charge hanging over his head he was an informant with no leash." Hudson explained.

"Now that I recall he was a little upset with Mr. Daniels' organization and the way they handled particular things. I was able to get some information from him while he was in the hospital bed nursing a gunshot wound." Barnes remembered.

"Well we have a man working undercover that might bring in some charges to someone related to Mr. Daniels. What do you have?"

"We have a young man that may be willing to testify that Mr. Daniels gave the order to kill two victims found dead in the housing projects." Barnes replied.

"That would be a homerun score if you can get that. Most of Mr. Daniels' people can't speak on anything above the designated spots. I have a young man that doesn't feel he's being paid properly in the Delmont Heights. But he answers to a Travon Lewis and claims he hasn't met Mr. Daniels. I believe that Lonnell Jackson is the buffer between Mr. Daniels and the designated drug spots. But I envy what you have Joe." Hudson smiled.

"I believe this Lonnell Jackson is the suspect that goes by the name of 'L'. If we can charge him then we might have him testify against Mr. Daniels."

"Is this your informant that is willing to testify against Mr. Jackson?" Hudson asked.

"No my apologies this is my rookie partner Detective Ronald Bowen. He is assisting me on these murder investigations."

Hudson and Bowen shook hands momentarily but Hudson wouldn't make eye contact. Bowen felt the guilt from Hudson accusing him of being a suspect instead a cop.

"Well that's all we got right now. When we get more I'll be sure to give you an update." Hudson abruptly ended the dialogue.

"Okay thanks for the information. We will try to catch up with Mr. Lonnell Jackson then go from there." Barnes said while walking towards the door.

Bowen followed behind him without saying a word. He waited until they got inside the car. Barnes quickly drove off before the young detective could blurt anything out.

"So every Black man that he doesn't know is a suspect?" Bowen asked.

"I wouldn't worry about that. He knows who you are now." Barnes assured him.

"Yeah but that was clearly racial profiling. He didn't even ask who I was before he openly made his assumption." Bowen protested.

"You are making it bigger than it is. We have a job to do and sometimes people rub you the wrong way but that shouldn't distract you from your job." Barnes warned.

The car remained silent all the way back to the station. Both detectives were in their own thoughts until they made it back to their desks. Before Barnes made it to the desk he peeked in to check on his suspect.

"Damn I forgot the Taco Bell…where is my suspect?"

He opened the interrogation room to realize that he was gone. Barnes frantically looked around. No one was in sight to answer the whereabouts of his suspect. After several seconds another detective stood up from his cubicle.

"Your suspect received his phone call and within minutes his lawyer was here. It was so fast that he must have called him direct and the attorney was probably already in the building. A word to the wise Barnes in which you should know better; don't ever leave a suspect alone for too long."

Barnes stared at the white homicide detective with his mouth agape. He hadn't even read him his Miranda rights. He damn near had a confession and that fast he was out of his grasp. Detective Bowen seeing the defeat in his face calmly walked over toward him.

"Well I'll talk to you later because I got a date."

Killa Kell had enough. He knew Pooh had something to do with the death of his best friend. His heart was ready for war. He had to rally every shooter that had love for Casey in the California Gardens. If not he would have to do it himself. Casey and Killa Kell knew each other since they were toddlers. He couldn't believe it when Casey's mother Debra came to tell him the bad news. She said he was supposed to go on a date with a girl named Michelle. Killa Kell knew about the girl Michelle because they all met up at a club. He and Casey both believed the girl wasn't in the game. She carried herself like she was a square. He had a feeling she was more than what she pretended to be. Debra also told him that Casey was killed at a movie theatre parking lot in Riverside. He figured that Casey would decide to go to Riverside so he wouldn't get caught up anywhere in San Bernardino. He bounced the ball against his grandmother's house trying to clear his mind. Then he glanced down at his watch and realized that Boom-Boom might be calling. He walked into the house face sullen and cold. As he went into the refrigerator the phone began to ring. He grabbed a bottle of beer and went after the phone.

"Hello?"

"What's up young comrade?" Boom-Boom asked enthusiastically.

"I got some fucked up news." Killa Kell replied.

"Damn it must be bad. I'm in here and you are out there and I sound happier than you. Talk to me peoples."

"We lost the spot in the projects. My cousin and his homeboy Sammy got smoked the other day. Then I just found out today that my road Casey got shot in the head in a Riverside parking lot at the movies. I swear I want to serve this nigga Pooh." Killa Kell lamented.

"Aw that is really fucked up. That muthafucka Pooh got ways of getting at niggas. I saw how that nigga set up all my shooters with one move. You got to handle this nigga with smarts not anger." Boom-Boom sighed.

"Nah fuck that! I'm gon' start serving his people by myself if I have to. All of his spots I know about gon' catch heat. That's on everything I love. I even think he set Casey up with this bitch we thought was square that live somewhere in Colton. I'm killing all those niggas." Killa Kell cried out.

"That ain't the way to get at this nigga. That nigga Pooh will have a gang of people waiting to serve you once you get at his people. I say you lay low for a minute and stack yo money. Let the nigga get comfortable and think that he killed you off. Besides, you got some females in place anyway right?" Boom-Boom spoke sensibly.

"Yeah but I don't know when that's gon' happen. I'm supposed to wait until that shit pop off? What if it never does?"

"Don't place all yo bets on that shit popping off. Make that money and other things will come into play. Then you can make moves without doing shit yourself. Money makes people move for you. I seen my comrade James do that shit for years and he wasn't really a street nigga like that. He had a little bit of street but not like you, me or Pooh. He came into a connect and knew how to work it. But that nigga Pooh put an end to all that shit because that muthafucka was smart." Boom-Boom gave him game.

"Alright big homie I'm gon' listen to what you're saying. I want to make sure that when I get him, he knows I did it to him." Killa Kell replied.

"That's what I'm talking about young comrade."

Lonnie sat down with the lawyer and J-Rock at the law offices of Breyer & Klein. He sat next to J-Rock while they both sat adjacent to the desk of the attorney Seth Breyer.

"So what exactly did they ask you when they had you in the interrogation room?" Lonnie asked J-Rock.

"They said that they were told that I led someone in the projects to shoot those two cats Cornbread and Sammy. Then they got to asking me about you and Pooh." J-Rock nervously replied.

"And what did you say?" Lonnie persisted.

"Nothing except that I didn't send someone in there to kill but I showed some homeboys my neighborhood." J-Rock frowned.

"You weren't supposed to say shit. You're supposed to wait until a lawyer comes in and speaks for you. That's how they get a nigga to snitching by making him think he has to talk." Lonnie retorted.

"Mr. Phillips, did they read you your Miranda rights?" Breyer asked.

"My what?"

"Did they say you have the right to remain silent? Anything you say can and will be held against you in a court of law." Breyer explained.

"I've heard that before on T.V. but they never said that to me." J-Rock replied.

"Cool. They will probably come after you once you make it back to the house. If you did say something I'll know about it because they will have enough to arrest you. So let me know if you said something to them." Lonnie said.

"Nah I told them I know 'L' and that's it. Then they asked me if I knew Pooh and I said I ain't really spoken to the man before. That was it, I swear." J-Rock shook his head.

"Then all they did was detain you for questioning. They didn't have anything strong enough to arrest you so they were hoping you confess some shit so they could arrest you. Then after that they were going to offer you a plea deal for less time so that you could testify against Pooh or me. That's the game they play but don't fall into that shit. Snitches get stitches. I thought Kramer would have gave ya'll game on that." Lonnie explained.

"He did! I knew not to say anything to those police." J-Rock lied.

Both Lonnie and J-Rock stood up and shook hands with Mr. Breyer. Lonnie walked out the door feeling good about the results. They climbed into his Dodge Charger and sped off. While riding in the car he explained a few changes to J-Rock.

"Look here homie, if you do things right you and Smokey will hold down the projects and I'll put somebody over there with you to hold it down just in case a nigga tries to jack you. But you got to show me you are a soldier."

"Fa'sho! I'll grind that spot until it's dry."

"Alright cool."

Lonnie eventually dropped him off right outside the projects. To J-Rock's surprise the police weren't staked outside. He reluctantly walked towards his mother's house. He waved at Lonnie to drive off after he realized the coast was clear. Lonnie had plans to meet up with Fab-Five and Travon to get a bite to eat. They called Pooh but he couldn't make it because of a family emergency. He pulled up to the restaurant about ten minutes after dropping off J-Rock. He noticed Travon's truck but he couldn't find Fab-Five's Escalade. He walked into the restaurant to see them sitting at a table already. He walked over to their table without being escorted by the hostess.

"Check out you Baller niggas going out to eat at fancy restaurants and shit." Lonnie joked.

"What's happening comrade? We saved a seat for you." Travon replied.

"So did the young nigga talk or did he keep his mouth shut?" Fab-Five got to the point.

"He says he didn't give them anything. But we will see in a little bit. If he did give them something you best believe they gon' be knocking at my door. Or at least looking for a nigga." Lonnie replied.

"You think you should peel the young nigga's cap just in case he did say something?" Fab-Five asked.

"Nah because he doesn't have much to go on." Lonnie shook his head.

"I don't know nowadays. If a nigga ain't schooled right he might snitch without knowing. I was hearing about this kingpin law the feds got where you can get life or the chair if you get convicted on that shit. They can get a muthafucka on that charge just because someone started snitching." Travon replied.

"What did Pooh say you should do?" Fab-Five asked.

"I haven't got at him about it yet. I schooled the young nigga today and I think he knows what time it is. Ya'll niggas order already?" Lonnie asked.

"Nah we was waiting on you. Damn my phone is ringing...that's Shanell. She's been bitching a lot lately and I don't want to hear her mouth. Before I got locked up she was sweet all the time now she acts like she resents me or some shit. I think she was fucking with another nigga when I was locked down." Fab-Five complained.

Lonnie and Travon looked at each other without saying anything. Fab-Five caught the exchange and thought about it. They must know something he didn't know.

"What was that shit about?" Fab-Five asked.

"What?" Travon asked.

"Come on my niggas. Ya'll suppose to be my boys so if ya'll know something I don't know let me know. Why did ya'll look at each other like that?" Fab-Five asked.

The waitress walked up after he asked the question. She was a pretty Middle Eastern girl. Everyone ordered their food and waited for the waitress to take the menus. Fab-Five's leg was fidgeting waiting on the information they were keeping from him.

"Will one of you niggas spit it out?" Fab-Five said in frustration.

Lonnie sighed knowing that he would have to let him know. He didn't know the repercussions and didn't care to find out. But now the cat was out of the bag. He glanced at Travon then looked Fab-Five in the eye.

"That thing that happened with Nelly was because he was messing with yo girl." Lonnie said it plain.

"Are you fucking serious?" Fab-Five said in disbelief.

"Yeah we didn't want to break yo heart. I know you had love for both of them so one of them had to go. We read that nigga Nelly the riot act and he still was dealing with her. Pooh gave the order to lay that nigga down." Travon explained.

"Now it all makes sense. She probably figures that he got his cap peeled behind him fucking with her. So now I'm wise to what the fuck is going on. She is on some guilt shit and taking it out on me. I'm about to nip this shit in the bud." Fab-Five said calmly.

"Come on now Fabian that's yo baby mama. I ain't saying don't put her ass in check but you ain't got to take it there." Lonnie subtly protested.

"I ain't about to do what you think I'm about to do. I'm just gon' let her know in my own way that I got some dirt on her. Give her some words of wisdom to straighten her ass out." Fab-Five explained.

"It hurt all of us to handle that shit but Pooh probably hurt the most because he had to make the decision. I know it was hard because he's got love for you and he had love for Nelly; you know what I mean?" Lonnie said.

"Yeah I know what you mean. I got major love for that nigga Pooh. That nigga has always watched out for me. I'll walk through fire for that muthafucka. He's a gangster through and through. Ain't too many niggas you can say that about." Fab-Five firmly stated.

Lonnie and Travon nodded their head in agreement.

17
CHANGING OF THE GUARD

Go farther, go further, go harder, is that not why we came; if not then why bother?
Jay-Z

Now it was time to set everything up for someone else to take the reins. I had run my course and grown tired. I leaned on Vanessa's Mercedes contemplating my next move. The desert heat of the Inland Empire can be hot, sticky and thick at times. The beginning of summer was here and it was reflecting the turmoil in my life. I had enough by now. My money was long and I was able to put away a nice stash of money. After Casey was smoked the streets were quiet afterward. I wanted to breathe a sigh of relief but I knew what type of nigga Killa Kell was. The game always offered youngsters that would rise in the ranks and eventually be hungrier than you. I didn't want the game to get me before I got out. So now it was someone else's turn to be a boss.

The last time Big Black and I linked up I told him that I would be passing my operations on to someone else. It had taken me awhile to make a decision to which person it would be. I had my mind and my heart set on Lonnie when Fab-Five got locked up. But I had a problem with him because of the Chris situation. I knew Chris wasn't right and I also knew that he was a weakness for Lonnie. So I considered putting Nelly in charge until I found out he was messing with Fabian's girl. That was a clear violation of the code and bad business. When I warned him, he still continued to go behind my back so I had to finish him. It would have been messy from the jump and a bad judgment call overall. I had good enough reason to believe that under pressure he would make the same mistakes. When Fab-Five got out I considered him but thought otherwise. Fabian is a killer so he would handle things in that way. He wouldn't know when to pull back so he would need someone with more rationale to direct him when it was necessary to kill. Lastly I also considered Travon but that was quickly squashed because he wasn't a real leader. He was more like a mid level hustler that was comfortable with his station in life. He didn't have much in the ambition department. After considering everything and everyone I decided that my heir apparent would be Lonnie.

Lonnie rolled up about ten minutes after I drove up. We met at a liquor store out in Riverside that was on the side of a road. I had been watching the cars go by thinking about my life and what I would do after the game. I had a few hobbies that I could invest in. I glanced at Lonnie getting out of his Dodge Charger smiling like he didn't have a care in the world. I felt sort of bad because when he became a boss all of that would change. He would have to make decisions for himself and other people. I sighed as I pictured the last remnants of his innocence evaporate from the game. But he was pushing for it. One side of me wanted him to get out the game with me. That was the love I had for him. But the other side knew way too well that he would refuse such a proposal. Well if he's going to take the torch he had to be schooled.

"What's cracking Pooh?" We embraced.

"Just living that I.E. life. You feel me?" I replied.

"So what you got planned for today?"

"First thing I'm gon' do is show you how to cook this shit up. When you get this dope raw you got to know how to cook it."

Lonnie nodded. I could tell he was eager to get started. So I waved for him to get in the Mercedes. I hadn't cooked all the dope when I copped from Big Black. I knew that I had to show Lonnie how to cook cocaine into crack. I took him to Felicia's spot where I hid all the dope. Her lease was up in a couple of months. She already made her move to Texas. Sometimes I would

201

post up over there just to have some alone time. She left me the living room furniture but the rest of the house was cleaned out.

When we pulled into the apartment complex Lonnie looked surprised. He was staring at the scenery and the landscape while he followed me to her apartment.

"I wouldn't have ever thought this was where you had a spot. This is way in the cut somewhere. A muthafucka would have a hard time giving someone directions to this place." Lonnie laughed.

"You have to be thorough like that. You got to make sure that you got all ends covered and that you are one step ahead of everything; especially the law." I replied.

"Yeah I'm knowing."

"First thing you have to do is get you a broad that you know well enough to put her up in a house. You can have your square broad that takes care cleaning yo money. Then you got yo broad that's gon' have a spot you can cook up yo dope and sometimes get away from everything. This is the spot that you keep away from the world. It has to be a spot no one would expect you to be. Then you have yo bottom bitch or the one that is down for yo dirty drawers. She's the one that's gon' help you organize shit. She's the one that knows you the best and is yo friend also. But you still can't pillow talk with her." I schooled him while walking into the apartment.

He looked around and realized it was almost empty. So he went to the kitchen and leaned on the counter. I followed him then went under the sink to this spot I had under the drain. I pulled out four bricks of that raw Columbian cocaine. By the time it hit the states it probably was diluted about three or four times but it was about as raw as it could get while in the United States. I always gave him dope already cut up so he stared at the four bricks for a moment. While I was unwrapping one I continued to school him on being a boss in the game.

"The one that's down for yo dirty drawers is the one that's gon' come see you if you make a mistake and catch a case. Or better yet someone snitches on you. Snitching is becoming more like the norm nowadays. See Lonnie the difference between a gangster and thug is that a thug doesn't have any rules. Any nigga can be a common thug muthafucka but a gangster believes in organization. He believes in a code and lives and dies by that code." I explained.

"What about Tupac? That nigga was representing 'Thug Life' and he was one of the realest niggas in rap." Lonnie asked.

"That's that rap shit. Tupac was talking about street niggas in general but you would rather be a gangster than a thug. A gangster survives because of his rules." I replied while pulling the baking soda and procaine from out the refrigerator.

"It does seem like a lot of dumb niggas get caught that don't have they shit organized. Our clique always stay organized and we been one step ahead of the police." He commented.

"Hand me the glass pot from out of that cabinet." I pointed to the cabinet.

He handed me the pot and watched me pour water in the pan from the faucet. I grabbed the measuring cup from out of another cabinet. He watched attentively seeing each step I was doing. It was good that he was being as sharp as he was so I wasn't worried. Besides we had three more kilos to cook up and I was going to have him do the last three.

"As I was saying; yo bottom bitch or yo main girl got to have enough game to cover down on shit. She got to know where the stashes are and she has to know who to contact if some shit goes wrong. You still don't pillow talk with her no matter how much you love her. Women don't hide their feelings well in this game. You can maybe ask for some advice but ask her in a clever way. Some females will be down to do dirt with you but you still have to be careful. The less she knows the harder it is for the police to put pressure on her to talk. And if you complain to her about one of yo homeboys she might treat him different. Fuck what a nigga says watch how his woman acts around you. Usually women can't hide when they got a problem with you; which more likely than not means her man got a problem with you. She reflects whatever the fuck he's feeling." I explained.

"I see what the fuck you talking about."

I began adding the ingredients and watched the cocaine stiffen up into clay. I had already laid out some paper towels that had flower sprinkled all over. Then I poured out the water. I laid the dope out on the paper towels and gave it time to harden up.

"Once we let it harden up then we will cut it down and weigh it. With the shit I added we can get another seventy-five hundred off this one brick. That's how you stretch shit my nigga." I explained.

We took a break for a minute because it's easy to get a contact when you cooking up dope. I wanted him to see me do it then we could go from there to having him cook. We went into the living room and drank some beers that I had in the refrigerator. After posting up on the couch and sipping our beers Lonnie glanced up at me.

"So finish telling me about the three females I should have and how I should have them on my team." Lonnie asked.

"Oh yeah, yo main female has to be more than some pussy. She has to have some street game also. Your girl Lisa has a little bit of game but you might need to school her on some things. No matter what make sure she's happy even though sometimes it seems like a happy black woman is an oxymoron. She's the one that's gon' visit you when you get locked up. She's the one that's gon' put money on yo books. You got to know this before you make her yo main girl. And most of all you have to consider what she is capable of. Anybody can be capable of doing you dirty but knowing what lines a female will cross is what I mean by that."

"What about the other two females? What roll can they play?" Lonnie eagerly asked.

I put my feet on the coffee table and swigged my beer before answering. He was taking everything in and was paying attention.

"Yo number two girl has to be squeaky clean. She's the one you can wash yo money through. She has to be in some type of cash business. Females that do hair is real good. They always deal with cash and they can report what they want on their taxes. You can get you a stripper girl to be yo squeaky clean but most times they fuck with niggas in the game and if she knows too much about you she might get you robbed. The girl that is squeaky clean has to be able to report money to the government for taxes. She has to make everything look like she got all her shit legitimately. Her tax returns can justify why she's got this fly ass Hummer or Range Rover. You feel what the fuck I'm saying?" I continued.

"Yeah but why can't yo squeaky clean girl be the same as yo bottom bitch? I mean that's killing two birds with one stone if you got the same one down with you on both ends." He asked.

"Because if the police crack you for something anything in yo bottom bitch's name is gon' be part of the investigation. When the DEA comes their taking everything you own. But if you got a girl that can justify what she got and she's outside of the circle then they won't get everything. If she's an L7 female then that's really good. The police might think you're cheating with her but they will leave her alone if everything is in her name. You got to be able to trust her though."

"Man this is some deep shit you're kicking to me Pooh. I never expected the game to go that deep. I always looked at it as hustling without getting caught by 'one time'. Now I realize it's much more to this boss shit." He shook his head.

"Real talk! You have to play chess in this game. Even then it ain't that many niggas that can do the shit forever. Eventually the game gets you or the police. My time is about up so it is time for me to pass on the game. I'm getting too many signs and if I don't read them I'm gon' be caught up. A hard head makes a soft ass!" I replied.

He nodded as though he understood. I also could tell that getting out of the game was the farthest from his mind. I smiled because I knew he had the heart to make that money. There was also a tinge of hurt inside wondering what was in store for my young comrade.

"So what is the third female for?" He interrupted my thoughts.

"She is the one that you keep yo dope with. She doesn't have to know that you got dope in the house. A house cat will be fine but make sure she gives you time to cook up yo dope and stash it in the house."

"Is this the spot of yo third female right here?" He laughed.

"Fa'sho. She had never used her name for an apartment and I got her to get the apartment because she wanted a spot of her own. You pay the rent and help with the bills. Its way cheaper than renting a room every time you need to cook up some raw." I nodded.

We both stood up after that and went back into the kitchen. I began setting everything up so that he could cook the next batch. I handed him the glass pot and looked at him.

"Now it's yo turn to cook this shit up."

Lonnie had it down easy by the second kilo he cooked. If I seen him going astray I would easily point it out. It wasn't Chinese arithmetic or some complicated shit and Lonnie was a smart nigga.

We waited a few days before moving on to something else. I wanted him to understand the game all the way through. So I wanted him to decide which one of his boys he would have as his middle man. I pointed out to him that it would be wise to deal with one nigga in most cases. If you have to deal with another then only one more and it shouldn't be that often. After a few days it was time for him to decide.

"Okay I know that Fab-Five is the nigga I'm using for muscle. He's the nigga that's gon' put in work. So I'm thinking that Travon would be the nigga I have to hit the spots and collect the money. That's a down ass Delmont Heights nigga." He explained.

"Are you sure that nigga can handle that position? I mean, it's yo decision but make sure he's reliable." I replied.

"Yeah I think he's a stand up nigga."

"Alright if you are sure." I shrugged.

I was a little indifferent about it but I didn't think Travon was reliable enough to go outside of the Delmont Heights. It was Lonnie's call so I let him make the call.

"You decide what female you gon' put up in an apartment?"

"Yeah the dead homie Chucky's sister Cherise. She's nineteen now and she is fine as hell. She's always had a crush on me and we've been talking lately. But I don't know if Lisa should be my bottom though. She's insecure about too much shit." Lonnie explained.

I was hoping that he had everything in place within the next couple of months because once I was gone I was gone. I told him it would be good to get another car to roll around in. He would need a car in someone else's name. More than likely the police had his name because Detective Barnes had taken it down at the hospital several years ago. We decided to get something to eat when my cell phone began to ring. I looked down at my Caller ID and realized it was Janice. We weren't together so I didn't think she would trip. I decided to go ahead and answer because it might be something concerning my daughter.

"Hello?"

"How are you doing Winnie?" She jovially asked.

"I'm doing good. What about you?" I replied.

"I'm doing pretty good nowadays. I was wondering if we can sit down and talk some time soon. It would be good to see you. I talked to your mother when I dropped Shanee off last weekend."

"Yeah I went by there to see her for a little while." I stated.

I wanted to be sharp and to the point. It wasn't about being cold and heartless but she needed to know that I didn't need any nonsense.

"I know Shanee told me you took her to the park. You've always been a good daddy to her. But I was hoping that we could have a conversation face to face. We can even get something to eat." She suggested.

"I don't know Janice. We didn't leave on the best of terms and I don't need any more problems. You feel me?"

"I don't want any problems either. I just think we need to talk. I didn't like the way we left it either. We can at least be friends." She calmly pleaded.

"When are you talking about linking up?"

"How about in an hour?"

"Okay that's cool. We'll get something to eat somewhere in Riverside. I don't want to be anywhere near the house in Redlands." I pointed out.

We hung up and I told Lonnie that I would have to link up with him some other day. He wasn't tripping because he was planning to holla at Cherise anyway.

We decided on a restaurant in downtown Riverside. I was hungry by this time. I was ready to eat when Lonnie and I was about to get something but I had agreed to drive to Riverside to meet up with Janice. She pulled up in her BMW looking as good as she wanted to. She had on some tight 'True Religion jeans' with a pink half shirt showing off her belly button. She had a diamond inside her belly button accentuating her flat stomach. Her pretty light brown face glowed with clear lip gloss lightly glazed across her lips. She looked finer than a muthafucka. I shook my head in disbelief. It somewhat bothered me that she looked so good. We walked towards each other both with smiles on our faces. That moment reminded me when she was sitting at the table with my mother. That was the first day I saw her. She even had the pretty hairstyle. It was a ponytail that went to the side with neatly cropped curls at the end. Ponytails always did her justice because it brought out how pretty her face truly was. This was a trap.

"What's going on Winnie?" She smiled.

"What's going on with you? You are looking really good." I commented.

"Aw that's so sweet. Thank you baby, I must admit you are looking good yourself." She replied.

Her eyes scanned me up and down. I had on a blue button down from Rocawear. I had on Rocawear jeans and some blue and white Air Force Ones. We hugged one another. We met up right in front of the restaurant then walked inside. I followed behind her as the hostess quickly escorted us to the table. We order drinks before either one of us said anything.

"I was hoping we could spend a little time together. I think that as of lately we haven't been communicating that well. I know it is partly my fault and I was hoping that we could be better towards each other." Janice began.

"That sounds good. I think we can be better towards each other also. At least for the sake of our daughter we can be civil. You know what I mean?" I replied.

"Exactly! But you know Shanell and Fabian been having a lot of problems lately. She's been real bitter because she's lost a friend and she just hasn't been able to handle things at home with Fabian and..." She lowered her eyes.

I gave her time to think on her words. I wondered if she knew that I knew about Shanell and Nelly messing around. It appeared as though she was about to cry. I could tell she fought hard to hold back her tears. The waitress approached while she was trying to find the right words. We ordered our food and by that time she had regained her composure.

"I just think what we had been a little stronger than what they had. Don't get me wrong Shanell loves Fabian but I don't know if she is in love with Fabian. But we had a strong bond in the beginning that we lost somewhere." She explained.

"What happened to Shanell's friend?" I changed the subject.

I knew where this was going and I didn't really want to entertain it. She was trying to work something out with me but I was through. She looked good and everything but I knew the drama that came with her. Janice glanced at me in disbelief. She wanted me to respond to her words about our beginning. She caught her breath and went along with the question.

"He got shot and killed." She bluntly replied.

"Oh that's fucked up." I shook my head.

"Yeah I thought so too. Ever since then she has never been the same. I just think she may be taking it out on poor Fabian that's all."

"Why would she do that? Was he some nigga she was messing around with?" I slyly asked.

"Nah nothing like that. He was more like her brother or a friend." Janice lied.

I decided to play with fire. I didn't want to get on the subject of us getting back together so I wanted to see how far I could take it.

"When did he get killed?" I pried.

"A few months back." She quickly replied.

"Damn that's about the same time my homeboy Cornell who we call Nelly got smoked." I commented.

She glared at me with accusing eyes. Our plates arrived and I glanced at the entrees the waitress was sitting before us. We began eating our food which kept the table quiet for a few minutes. I was comfortable with the silence but she obviously wasn't.

"Do you think that you and I can work through our problems Winnie?" She calmly asked.

"We don't have any problems Janice. If we are friends than we should keep it that way. We both have to raise our daughter and like you said we can communicate better." I replied.

"But I'm talking about our relationship. You don't think we belong together baby?" She whispered.

It sounded more like whining to me. Probably because my mind was made up. I was trying to find the best way to tell her I didn't want to keep trying. I believe that I resented her a little. She knew that I was in the game and she added stress to the game.

If she didn't like the way things were she could have left. But she was into that money the game was bringing. She was addicted to the lifestyle that the game provided. While taking everything she wanted from the game she complained when she didn't like certain things. She made my life that more complicated. She should have fucked with a square 9 to 5 type of nigga. But then she would have complained about him not having any money.

"I'll always have love for you Janice. But I think we should just be cool with each other and not do the relationship thing. I'll respect your space and everything. You can keep the house and you can keep the hair salon as well. I want my daughter to grow up in a good neighborhood. As for us I don't think we see eye to eye." I explained.

She didn't say anything after that. We finished our meal but it was relatively quiet for the rest of the meal.

"What if I can't afford the house note Sherwin?" She sharply asked.

I handed her five thousand dollars right then and there. Her eyes welled up with water after that. I knew she would eventually ask for money so I went to one of my stashes before we met up. We both went our separate ways.

The next day I met up with Lonnie again. This was the day that he would meet Big Black. We met him near Pomona this time. When we got to the hotel room he glanced at Lonnie.

"You ain't a fag or anything are you?" Big Black firmly asked.

Lonnie was slightly offended by his facial expression. He adamantly shook his head.

"Hell nah!"

I chuckled to myself as I began to get undressed. He had the sweat suits laid out like always then he took us to another hotel. Once we made it to the other room he pulled a bag from under the bed.

"You told him it was sixteen-five for each one of those thangs right?" He asked me.

I nodded. Lonnie handed him the money in a duffle bag. He already put them in large bills like I always did. Big Black opened the bag and glanced at the money then nodded. Before Lonnie could check the product he went to the bathroom. Big Black decided to talk to me.

"So you were serious about the changing of the guard huh? Are you sure this young nigga is ready to run shit like you did. I mean are you schooling him right?" He asked.

"Yeah I'm schooling him. I think he's ready for the top spot." I replied.

"You think? You better know for sure or you gon' have this young nigga stretched out somewhere." Big Black frowned.

I didn't respond because Lonnie had came out the bathroom by then. He checked the dope and liked what he tasted. Big Black gave him the nod then walked out the door.

"Ain't you gon' count the bread?" Lonnie asked.

"I shouldn't have to. If you short changed me then you don't have to worry about doing business with me again." Big Black sternly replied.

Lonnie nodded and Big Black walked out the door.

18
DON'T FIGHT THE FEELING

You gone fall trying to ball while my team wins the pennant!
Lauren Hill

Killa Kell smiled as he saw Marvin and Mercedes walking towards him. Marvin was Mercedes' oldest brother. He had been locked up for about six years and had been recently paroled. Killa Kell remembered looking up to the soldier when his big homie Boom-Boom was out. Boom-Boom had convinced King James to let Marvin hustle product out of the CGs. He had proven to be a sound hustler until one of his curb servers got caught up and started snitching. The snitch gave him up then moved somewhere else to avoid being killed. Now Marvin who was nicknamed Game Face was out of jail. He was named that by Boom-Boom because no matter what problems he was having he kept the same facial expression. He was a dark brown man with sharp handsome features and a stocky build standing at 5'10 in height. He walked up to Killa Kell who he heard was moving weight and they embraced.

"I thought they took the weights from out the pen. It looks like you been hitting iron the whole time you was locked down." Killa Kell commented.

"I was doing a lot of push-ups and pull ups. I was doing dips and everything to make time go faster." He replied.

"What's up Mercedes, you can't speak?" Killa Kell asked enthusiastically.

"How are you doing Killa Kell? I just wanted to show my brother where you were at but I'm going back to the house. It's hot as hell out here." She replied.

She walked away while Killa Kell and Game Face walked toward one of the spots. Once Mercedes was out of ears reach Game Face glanced at Killa Kell.

"I heard you the nigga with all of the product. At least up in the CGs." Game Face asked.

"Yeah I'm moving a little something over here. I was trying to spread out but that muthafucka Pooh got shit locked down everywhere else on the west side." Killa Kell replied.

"That's the nigga that got my baby brother set up right? He's a nigga from out of the Dorjil's. I've been hearing about this nigga. He used to serve for King James back in the day. He had caught a case a couple of years before I did."

"Yeah that's that nigga. Fuck him and everything he stands for though. That shit fucked me up real bad when he got to Marquise. I think he had something to do with Casey getting smoked in Riverside too." Killa Kell sighed.

"I remember you and that nigga was always running together. My sister says you've been trying to war with that Dorjil nigga. Is that how my brother and Casey got murdered?"

"Yeah big homie that's exactly how that shit happened. We was trying to spread out and it wasn't happening. That nigga Pooh even had my cousin Corn from out the projects killed. That nigga got reach but Boom-Boom was saying I should be quiet until I see an opening." Killa Kell explained.

"That's smart. Wars make the police come around a lot more. One time gets to pressing on niggas and the next thing you know they snitching." Game Face frowned.

"Well my nigga, you know that you are put on with no problem. We all can be making this money."

"I'm gon' see what's up. There is a time and place for everything. I've been hearing that you've been down to put in work on a nigga. So I know you got heart. No matter what we gon' make some shit happen."

"Yeah my nigga don't fight the feeling and come get on a nigga's team." Killa Kell nodded.

Game Face nodded in return. He didn't really have too much to say. He decided to return to his house. He hated that he missed his little brother's funeral. He knew Killa Kell as a little boy and always thought he would make a good soldier but not necessarily a good boss. He pondered on the new state of the California Gardens while walking home.

William Stover, undercover DEA agent and boyfriend of Shirley Daniels contemplated his next move. His girlfriend was the mother of drug kingpin Sherwin Daniels a.k.a. Pooh. He made the phone call while in the public restroom at a local fast food restaurant. He set it up with Shirley for her to buy a large amount of marijuana for use. The problem was that it was enough marijuana to convince a district attorney that she was buying it for distribution. Detectives Yates and Hudson couldn't get anything to stick on Pooh so they decided to pin something on his mother. She might be willing to talk and give him up for the fear of jail. Stover felt bad about succumbing to the pressure of the two detectives. He believed that Shirley was high strung and arrogant but by no means was she a criminal. Her son might have been one and she might in some ways encourage him to be one but she hadn't committed a crime herself.

"Well she is just as guilty for accepting whatever illegal funds that he makes from his drug organization." Stover reasoned.

He walked into the dining area of the KFC and smiled at his girlfriend. She smiled back then waited until he was right next to her.

"You want the three piece with a biscuit and mashed potatoes right?" Shirley asked.

William nodded and turned around to look out the window. That was kind of strange to Shirley.

"What's wrong with you?" She asked.

"Nothing's wrong." He replied.

"You seem like you're distant or something. Are you that hungry? It's my fault we took so long to get something to eat but I will make it up to you later." She slyly flirted.

William half heartedly smiled then sat down at the closest table. Moments later they picked up their food and walked out to the car. Once they were inside the car police lights suddenly flashed. Marked and unmarked cars surrounded their car from all angles. Detective Yates and Detective Hudson jumped out of their jaguar and went to both sides of Shirley's Mercedes. Yates went to the passenger side while Hudson went to the driver's side. They simultaneously opened the doors and asked both William and Shirley to step out. They quickly handcuffed both of them and began searching for contraband. They were quickly able to find the bag of marijuana.

"You have the right to remain silent, anything you say can and will be held against you in a court of law." Yates began her Miranda rights.

Afterward Yates escorted Shirley to the back seat of the Jaguar while Hudson put William in a marked squad car.

After the spectacle and all the spectators cleared out it took about twenty minutes to drive down to the police station. Shirley looked around trying to see if she can find William anywhere. Finally she was put inside a small room where she was made to sit down alone for a few minutes. Yates chose to keep her handcuffed so that she could feel the reality of jail. He was hoping to peek back inside the room and find her in tears. Little did he know that Shirley was too proud to cry in front of strangers. She yawned and waited for someone to come in and talk to her. She wasn't as nervous as she should have been.

"I should have been scared." She said aloud.

The gray four walls surrounded her as she stared at the graffiti. People had carved their names in the walls with different instruments. There was also gang graffiti on the wall. She glanced down at the plain metal table and frowned at the décor.

"This is set up to make someone feel uncomfortable. This is probably what Winnie had to go through when he went to jail. Winnie…this is probably got something to do with him. They may have him locked up in another room somewhere." She spoke to herself.

Suddenly the door opened wide and Detective Hudson was standing at the door. He had a smirk on his face and his hands were behind his back. He sat down at a chair that was adjacent to her. He still had the smirk on his face as he revealed the bag of marijuana. He dropped it on the table as if it was a murder weapon.

"Who were you going to sell this to Ms. Daniels. We know that you were planning to distribute this illegal substance for sale. Give us the name of where you got it from and we might can work something out." Hudson firmly suggested.

"I don't know the people's name where I got the weed from. I wasn't planning on selling it I was planning on smoking it myself. It is only for personal use." Shirley frowned.

"With the amount you have you can be charged with 'possession with intent' Ms. Daniels. If you give us too much shit we can also charge you with conspiracy. You will be looking at three to five years in the state penitentiary." Hudson replied.

"Conspiracy? Are you serious? You actually want to charge me for all of that over weed?"

"We sure can Ms. Daniels unless you want to help us out. We need the information to your supplier or your headed to the County Jail to await trial." Hudson snapped.

"That's some bullshit. I want to speak to a lawyer or something." She screamed.

"He can't help you right now but I will call him if you like. Give me the number and I will contact him immediately. But if you cooperate we don't have to press any charges." Hudson pried.

"I told you that I don't know the person I got the weed from. He was friend of a friend that's all I know."

"Okay then since you want to be a hard ass then we will file the paperwork. I don't think it will look good on your resume as a middle aged woman with a recent felony. And that is after you've served your jail time." Hudson got up from the table.

He glanced at her to think about it then slammed the door behind him. When the door closed she began sniffling trying to hold back her tears. This is what they do when you go to jail, she pondered. Her eyes watered despite the attempts to keep her composure. She began wondering what they were doing to William. She began to panic but the handcuffs were still tightly on her wrists. She jumped up from her chair and began slamming on the door with her body.

"Let me out of here." She yelled.

The detectives heard her yelling but opted to allow her to release her rage. She finally calmed down after tiring from the ordeal. She staggered towards the chair and sat down to catch her breath. It took another twenty minutes before another detective walked in. She glanced up realizing it wasn't the same asshole as before. He seemed a little more sensible, she pondered.

"How are you Ms. Daniels? I'm Detective Yates of the San Bernardino Sheriff's Narcotics Division. Would you like a cigarette?" He politely asked.

"Thank you…what did you say your name was, Yates?"

"Yes ma'am! I'm Detective Yates. We have reason to believe that you were buying drugs with the intent to distribute. We don't want this to follow you for the rest of your life. We can easily take care of it for you but you need to help us out. If you help us out I guarantee that we can make all these charges go away. The most you might have is a fine." Yates nicely persuaded.

"What will I have to do?" She asked.

"Give us your supplier and you will be free to go I guarantee." Yates replied.

"Like I told the asshole detective a while ago I don't know who sold me the weed. I got the weed through a friend that knew a friend." She sassily replied.

"Well who was the friend that referred you to the supplier? Is it your boyfriend that was in the car with you?" Yates softly asked.

"I don't know where you are getting your information." She replied.

"Look Ms. Daniels it's okay he told us that you were the friend that connected him to the other friend. He claims that you had every intent to sell marijuana and he's willing to testify." Yates assured her.

"That's bullshit. I don't believe William would even say such a thing."

Yates gracefully got up from the table and walked towards the door. He didn't walk out but slowly opened the door. Standing on the other side of the door was William. Shirley looked up at him in disbelief. She quickly noticed that he was no longer handcuffed.

"What did you tell them William?" She screamed.

"Calm down Shirley and you can get out of this. They just want a little information about Sherwin. You give them what they want on him and you can go free." He said calmly.

"What does my son have to do with this? He didn't sell me the weed. What the hell is going on and why aren't you in handcuffs?" She nervously asked.

William walked into the room and sat down across from her. For a few seconds he didn't say anything. He wouldn't give her eye contact.

"I'm a Drug Enforcement Agent Shirley. I've been working undercover investigating your son since we met." He admitted.

"What happened to your plumbing business and all that shit? That was all made up to catch my son?" She asked incredulously.

"A lot of people have turned up dead on the west side of San Bernardino and we believe your son is responsible for most of these murders. Now when everything goes down you will definitely be indicted for conspiracy and part of a continuing criminal organization. It would be best that you cooperated with these detectives so that you can at least protect the rest of your family. You are a grandmother of three and have to think of them right now. All we're asking is that you give us information on your son." William explained.

"So you are not even a plumber? How did you fix my drain. Who are you really? Is your name even William Stover?" She snapped.

"Look Shirley I am actually William Stover. I was also in the military like I explained but I didn't mention that I was also an undercover police officer." William replied.

"So you buying that weed for me was all a set up? Us dating was all a set up? I can't believe this shit." Shirley began sobbing.

"Shirley you have a chance to see your grandchildren grow up if you cooperate. You or your family shouldn't have to suffer because of what Sherwin is doing. But if you don't cooperate I can't promise you anything. Your entire family can see the penitentiary and your grandchildren can wind up in the foster care system. Your son knows what he is involved in so he should expect the consequences. Think about your family Shirley. Be loyal to your family first." William continued.

His words were soft and gentle but she felt the threatening undertones. The tears on her face continued to pour. Shirley didn't know if she was more upset from William's betrayal or being faced with the choices. Either she did jail time or gave up her only son. Her mind was racing but her time was short.

"Don't fight the feeling of doing what's right and what's best for you and your family. If Sherwin goes to jail you can recover but if you all go to jail your family is ruined." William stood up.

He walked towards the door. She gave him a glare of hatred. He lowered his head but slowly began to close the door.

"We will give you time to think about." He said before completely shutting the door.

Stover, Hudson and Yates went into the hallway to discuss the situation. It was obvious that Stover was saddened that he had to reveal that he was a DEA agent. He felt the pain of betrayal through her eyes and it shook him to the core.

"Do you think she will give us what we need?" Hudson interrupted his thoughts.

"I think if we would have waited long enough we might have some charges on Sherwin Daniels instead of his mother." Stover snapped.

"Calm down William it is part of the job. You knew at some point you were going to have to reveal to her who you are. She's hurt and disappointed but her son is a criminal that needs to be off the streets." Yates replied.

"Ya'll just don't get it; do you? We are banking on the fact that she might consider that Mr. Daniels has already got a charge against him. If she asks for a lawyer and she finds out that he doesn't have any charges she might take the marijuana charge and we end up with nothing. I think we should have waited." Stover explained.

"I disagree! Mr. Daniels is very careful about his dealings and the only way we can get him is if we can get an informant in his inner circle. Someone has to be willing to talk about his business. That has always been the way to catch a drug dealer on his level." Hudson firmly replied.

"Well we can only wait to find out what she does." Yates added.

Bernice and Pebbles made their way through the Carousel Mall and out into the street. They carried numerous shopping bags while rushing to the car. Pebbles knew that her boyfriend Killa Kell would be looking for them real soon because he let her borrow the car. They still wanted to make a stop into the Galleria mall out in Riverside before they returned the car. They threw the bags in the backseat and quickly drove off.

"Girl Markell has been talking about buying me a car for months. If he wasn't on his hustle I probably wouldn't have gotten to roll this muthafucka in the first place." Pebbles remarked.

"It seems like he's been doing better business since Marvin's came home. Girl that chocolate nigga is fine. Too bad I used to mess with his brother because I sure wouldn't mind fucking him a few times." Bernice smirked.

"You better not let Markell hear you saying that shit. But that nigga is fine though. That nigga knows how to make money too." Pebbles smiled.

They made it out to the Galleria in about twenty minutes. They wanted to get outfits for the club. They met some niggas that was feeling them the other night at the club. Pebbles knew that her boyfriend Killa Kell might be interested in robbing them. They pulled into the Galleria parking lot and found the closest parking stall.

"If the Carousel Mall wasn't so weak we wouldn't have to drive way over here. I hope we find something before Markell gets to calling." Pebbles commented.

"We should because we haven't been gone that long. Let's hit a few spots and see what we can find. I wouldn't worry about that shit until he calls." Bernice assured her.

They walked through the mall and looked in different shops until they came across a few outfits they liked. After trying on several outfits they both chose three a piece. Now they were ready to go. As they were walking out of one of the stores Bernice held out her arm for Pebbles to stop.

"Hold up, isn't that the girl Vanessa that comes to the same beauty salon as we do? That nigga she's with is shining." Bernice whispered.

"So what about that bitch? You want to go over there and say hi to her?" Pebbles shrugged her shoulders.

"When Marquise was killed the people that did that shit followed us to the hotel. That was the only way they could have known where to find him. He had picked me up from the hair salon then we went straight to the hotel. I always thought one of those jealous bitches at the hair salon had something to do with setting up Marquise." Bernice continued to whisper.

"So you think this bitch got something to do with Marquise getting killed? Just because she's with a nigga that is shining doesn't mean he's that nigga Pooh." Pebbles whispered back.

"First of all bitch you talk too much. You was in that hair salon bragging and shit letting everyone know what yo man does. You didn't say he was in the game but you said everything that would make bitches realize he was in the game. And you even mentioned his name once or twice. If she's connected to Pooh she could easily give him the news. And didn't Markell and Casey say he was pretty boy type nigga. That nigga is cute but I don't know about pretty. But as grimy as Markell and Casey are I can see them saying he's a pretty boy." Bernice explained.

"First of all I wasn't bragging that much. You still haven't convinced me that that is Pooh." Pebbles replied.

"I just got a feeling. Vanessa was on the phone when Marquise came to pick me up. I remember that shit like it was yesterday."

"If you got a feeling then you should listen to it. Let's walk up to the bitch and speak then she will probably introduce us." Pebbles shrugged her shoulders.

"Bitch are you crazy. If that is him she's going to know we are on to her. I think we need to tell yo man Killa Kell to follow that bitch home and see what he finds. You connect him to someone that got ties to Pooh he's going to love yo ass forever." Bernice replied.

"It looks like he's about to buy her some expensive bling-bling. They are smiling and everything. Yeah that bitch is pretty and she is forever getting her hair done. He's got to be rolling in

223

some dough. Even if he's not Pooh he still might have enough money for him to get robbed." Pebbles remarked.

They decided to walk in the other direction of the jewelry store even though their car was in the opposite direction. They were on the second level so they walked to the other end to get on the elevator. When they reached the door of the elevator Pebbles' phone began to ring. She sighed knowing exactly who it was. She shifted her bags around so that she could answer the phone.

"Hello baby what's up?" Pebbles said in her sweet voice.

"Where are you at?"

"I'm on my way home right now."

"I didn't ask you that. I asked you where you are right now." Killa Kell replied.

"I'm at the Riverside Galleria." Pebbles admitted.

"What the fuck are you doing at the Galleria way out in Riverside? You told me you were going to the mall for a few things. I'm thinking you are talking about the Carousel Mall." He snapped.

"Don't be mad. We went up to the Carousel but we couldn't find any outfits we really liked. All we was able to get was some shoes and a few accessories. But we are leaving right now."

"Alright hurry yo ass up. I got shit to do." Killa Kell replied.

"But I got some good news for you."

"What's that? You bought me some new clothes?" Killa Kell said sarcastically.

"No but I might know the bitch that is fucking with that nigga Pooh." Pebbles replied.

"Tanya don't play with me like that." He firmly stated.

"Seriously baby it might really be her. Bernice was the one that pointed it out."

"We gon' have to see about that."

19
SYNONYMS

Still tote gats strapped with infrared beams!
Notorious B.I.G.

Vanessa and I decided it was time to get married. I had proposed to her right before stepping out the game. My money was real good and we had plans to relocate. I was considering somewhere in Orange County around a bunch of white folks. That way we wouldn't be too far away from our families but at the same time we wouldn't be too close to the streets. I called my mom to tell her the good news but she wasn't picking up her phone. I figured she was probably spending time with William at his house. It seems like every time I went to her house he was over there. Maybe he and my mother were getting tired of that. I called Sharon and told her the good news. She was happy for me but subtly suggested that moms wouldn't be. I was hoping moms would be happy but I didn't really care one way or another. I already knew she was the love of my life but Ace had to confirm it for me. I felt kind of bad about that. The plan was to make up for all the lost time the game wouldn't allow me to have for her. That was the only reason I believe she said yes was because I was getting out the game. That was what she meant when she said we weren't ready yet.

Lonnie had started copping his dope from Big Black on his own by now. I let him cook up his shit at the spot Felicia had until Cherise was able to get approved for an apartment she applied for. I appreciated how he was keeping it close. I told him to keep it that way. We talked while he cooked up his product. He got the hang of it pretty fast.

225

"I'm thinking about making Cherise my main girl with the money. I want Lisa to be the chick that keeps the yayo for me. I've already told her that we were moving and she's going to get an apartment in her name. I'll keep the dope at that spot when she moves. Once my lease is up at the other spot then I'll find a squeaky clean broad that I'll link up with at a college or some shit." Lonnie explained.

"So ya'll went to the club the other night? You know you gon' need to slow down from that shit after awhile. It's too many traps at the club." I changed the subject.

"Yeah I'm knowing. But it was some bad ass bitches at that muthafucka. I got the digits of this bad ass bitch with ass named Shelly. She was playing hard to get with a nigga but she knew I was shining. Travon was trying to holla at her friend Mercedes. That bitch looked good too but I seen her somewhere before I just can't put my finger on it." Lonnie said.

"Ya'll just trying to run up in these broads right? You gon' get enough of fucking with bitches at the club. That's like these bitches that fuck with niggas on the internet. You don't know who they know." I replied.

"Yeah I just want to hit. I ain't trying to wife any of those bitches. I think Cherise is the one that I really want to chill with. I mean, a nigga gon' be a player but Cherise gon' be my main girl." Lonnie laughed.

He was very jovial nowadays. The war was over and he was running shit pretty smooth. Fab-Five was his top muscle with some young shooters just in case some shit jumped off. He was a quick learner but I sometimes wondered about his cousin Chris. Sooner or later someone was going to disagree with a decision he made in his own clique. The code has went out the window for most niggas. I climbed off the couch and walked towards the door.

"Lock the bottom lock when you're done. I'm about to bounce." I told Lonnie.

"Alright my nigga." He yelled behind me.

226

I went to Vanessa's house to talk about the wedding. We just wanted to have a Las Vegas wedding with family and that was about it. I didn't even tell Lonnie about my recent engagement. When I got to Vanessa's house she wasn't even home yet. I sat down and had a beer. Then it dawned on me that she was going to an after school event with my son. I went to the last one so we agreed she would go to the next one. I was supposed to be getting all the arrangements for our drive to Las Vegas. We wanted to rent a limo once we were down there so I had to set the reservations. Plus I had to get reservations for my family to have somewhere to stay. It was a bunch of tedious things that I had to do. I jumped up off the couch after finishing my beer. It was time for me to finish everything.

Killa Kell waited patiently for Pooh to walk out of his girlfriend's house. He wasn't sure if she was his girl until he spotted Pooh. For the last couple of days he had been posted outside the apartment complex hoping he caught a glimpse of the high roller Pebbles and Bernice was talking about. He gasped for breath when he realized who it was. He would have given up after the third day. He had Game Face taking care of business at the dope spot. Game Face actually ran it better than him. Killa Kell was more about the hunt than anything. Sitting next to him was a young shooter he had recruited from the California Gardens. The young shooter went by the name of Dale. He was about an inch shorter than Killa Kell. He had his hair in cornrows and Killa Kell considered him a pretty boy but he was down to put in work.

They followed behind Pooh in his Range Rover as he turned out of the apartment complex parking lot. He appeared as though he was distracted. Killa Kell knew that Pooh was sharp and probably watching his own back. But he was on the phone looking totally preoccupied. He never imagined he would catch Pooh slipping like this. He had waited a long time to serve this nigga. They watched him switch lanes and cruise down the boulevard. He drove all the way into Rialto and even into Fontana. Killa Kell was growing impatient but forced himself to calm down.

"Once this nigga gets out the car wherever he's at we gon' put on these masks and start dumping on this nigga." Killa Kell ordered.

"So that's really that nigga Pooh?" Dale asked in surprise.

"Yeah nigga that's him. He's been out of dodge for a long time probably going to other cities to do his business. It's fate that we get this nigga. Bernice pointed that nigga out based upon that bitch he's fucking with. When we finished with him we gon' kidnap that bitch Vanessa and her son. I think she had something to do with Marquise getting smoked." Killa Kell explained.

"Yeah let's serve this nigga."

They sped up a little bit but kept a distance long enough for him not to see them following. Pooh was going through different streets that was busy until he hit a dark road right near the 10 Freeway. That was good for Killa Kell because it would be less of a chance of there being witnesses. He bought a bucket that he planned on ditching after they ambushed Pooh.

Pooh suddenly hit a back road and turned a right hard and fast. Killa Kell got nervous for a moment thinking he might lose him. When he turned the corner the Range Rover was nowhere in sight. He cruised down a road with empty fields in both directions.

"Where the fuck this nigga go?" Killa Kell muttered.

Finally he noticed the white Range Rover parked in the driveway of a house. It had gotten dark so he couldn't tell if Pooh was still in the car or if he was already in the house.

"Fuck it my nigga; we gon' wait until he comes out then we're blasting on his ass. Whoever is with him catches it too." Killa Kell explained.

They walked a little ways down the street. They wanted to be close enough to the car but not too close. Just in case there were witnesses that saw their faces before they put on their masks.

"Come on nigga lets roll."

Dale followed close behind as they pulled out the nine-millimeters they both brandished. They got up close on the Range Rover to realize that he wasn't in the car.

"Go on the other side of his car so we can pick this nigga off on both sides." Killa Kell whispered.

Killa Kell squatted down to make sure he wasn't seen while Dale leaned on the garage door of the house. They waited for about fifteen minutes before they heard anything. When they glanced down they both realized that it was a cat. Killa Kell sighed hard then put his gun behind his back.

Suddenly gun fire began to be released and Killa Kell couldn't find out where it was coming from. He heard Dale yell in pain then he peaked his head up to see what was going on. Before he could blink he took two shots to the right side of his shoulder. His gun flew from out of his hand and he winced in pain.

"Don't kill this nigga yet." Someone yelled.

He looked up to see Pooh with a handkerchief covering his face. He walked up with a guy that was much larger than him.

"Pull off the mask and see if that's the nigga." The large man said.

Pooh slid Killa Kell's mask from off his face. Pooh stared at him for awhile and nodded his head. Killa Kell looked at him with contempt even though he was looking down the barrel of a gun.

"Is his boy dead?" Pooh asked.

"Yeah this muthafucka is laid out." The large figure replied.

"So you came after me huh? I didn't think it would come down to this my nigga." Pooh said.

"Fuck you nigga you got my boys Marquise and Casey set up. You ain't any different than I am."

"Oh just because we in the game you think we're the same. You kill when you get the feeling but I kill when there is no other way." Pooh replied.

"That's bullshit nigga you kill when you get the feeling just like I do. Fuck it nigga do whatever you gon' do. I don't know why the fuck you're talking but I'm ready to meet my maker anyway." Killa Kell yelled.

"Come on Pooh don't have a long conversation with this nigga like you did that nigga James." The large figure protested.

"So you killed King James huh. But we different?" Killa Kell said sarcastically.

"Yeah he was a snitch though. I'm smoking yo ass because I know you won't ever stop coming. I seen yo dumb ass following me way back in San Bernardino. You was too eager to get me because you hate your enemies and that clouds your judgment. I beat my enemies and that's what makes us different." Pooh replied.

Pooh squeezed the trigger as bullets riddled Killa Kell's upper body and face. Pooh and the large figure hopped in the Range Rover and sped off into the night.

I was drained when I dropped Big Mel off at the house. I was being followed by that nigga Killa Kell and one of his little homies. I saw someone following me all the way from San Bernardino. I could tell they were waiting for me to stop somewhere so I called Big Mel. He was the closest person to me since he lived in Fontana. He reminded me about the vacant house that we would sometimes pass when we would visit Ace. It was near a back road off the 10 Freeway. I thought I was out the game but it is always someone that's telling you something different. It took a lot out of me to have to serve that nigga. I called Vanessa on her cell phone and told her not to go back to the house. I was going to have her rent a room until I figured out where I would put her and my son.

"Are you alright?" Big Mel interrupted my thoughts.

"Yeah I'm a little shook up behind that shit. I wonder how in the fuck that nigga found out where Vanessa lived. I thought I was finished with the game but the game ain't finished with me." I replied.

"That should be the end of that business though. You said he was the main nigga coming at you. Now you can put this shit behind you. Vanessa knows not to go back to the house so don't even trip. So…did you tell Auntie Shirley you were getting married to Vanessa?" He asked out the blue.

"I called her a few times but she hasn't been picking up the phone. I was gon' run by there to check on her after I finished my business but this shit came up."

"Yeah I wondered about that. She was so determined for you to marry Janice I wonder how she's going to react." He continued.

"I'm not about to worry on that shit. I got a few things on my mind other than who my mother thinks I should marry."

"How is Janice nowadays? Do you plan on letting her know?" Big Mel continued to pry.

I paused for a moment because I was still shook up from what just happened. Big Mel acted like it was a normal day. I've had to kill niggas before but when your mind state is set on doing different shit it's bothersome to kill a nigga.

"Nigga you act like some niggas ain't just tried to peel my cap. I'm wondering about getting rid of this Range Rover not what Janice and moms think about me marrying Vanessa." I retorted.

"Aw Pooh you need to calm the fuck down. That's how niggas do when they see you shining. That nigga don't care that you out the game he's worried about taking out the top dog so he can be the top dog. But you acting like we didn't handle the shit. It's over!" Big Mel assured me.

"Is it ever over?" I sighed.

We talked a little more then I drove to the hotel where Vanessa and Joshua were. Big Mel promised he would get rid of the guns while it was my job to get rid of the Range Rover. As long as my family was safe I wasn't tripping. Don't get me wrong; I want to live but I had chosen the life and knew that there were

231

consequences. I was hoping that I could slide out before the game got me. That's why a lot of niggas I know can't get out of the game. They think that the game won't ever let them out. Either they can't get a decent job or someone is out to get them for the past. Then there is the thing with females that's always a problem. Women will look at you different when you don't have money. I wasn't really tripping about that aspect of the game because I made sure I stacked my money right. Besides, Vanessa was down for my dirty drawers. I always wondered if Janice would be just as down if I was broke or working a blue collar nine to five. It was so many traps to staying in the game but I remained steadfast.

When I knocked on the hotel door Vanessa hesitated. She was worried at this point. Everything in the room went still for a moment.

"Baby it's me." I said through the door.

She peeped through the peep hole then finally opened the door. She hugged me tightly damn near in tears. Then she looked me up and down to see if I was wounded. Once she realized I was in one piece she sighed then walked over to the bed and collapsed. Joshua was already asleep so she decided to start grilling me.

"What happened with you Winnie? All you said was that I shouldn't go home. Then you hung up the phone. What the hell is going on?"

"Killa Kell must have found out where you lived or spotted me in traffic somewhere. I saw him following me in San Bernardino so I took him for a ride. I didn't know if he had people watching the house to do harm to you." I replied.

"So where is he now? How do you know you got rid of him?" Vanessa asked.

"I got rid of him. You don't have to worry about him anymore." I replied.

She nodded understanding totally what I meant. We went to sleep in the king sized bed holding each other. I had a lot on my mind but I managed to get a little sleep.

The next day I decided to go somewhere to get rid of the car. It was paid for so I knew there wouldn't be a problem getting something else. I had my sister meet me at a dealership and I traded it in for an Armada. I rolled off the lot with low monthly payments. In fact I gave all the money to Sharon so that she could pay it monthly. She had a bank account set up just for car note payments. We chatted before we went our separate ways.

"So have you talked to mama yet?" Sharon asked.

"Nah every time I call she isn't picking up. I didn't get a chance to holla at her yesterday because something came up. But I was planning on going by there today. First I want to pick up a few clothes from Janice's house. I need some clothes." I replied.

"You don't have any clothes at Vanessa's house?"

"Yeah but I don't know when I'm going by there. I'm thinking about moving her out of there for certain reasons. It might be too dangerous right now and I just want to get everything of value from Janice's house." I replied.

"This is a good time to go because it's Friday and she'll be at the shop all day. But if you're out the game why will it be so dangerous to go to Vanessa's house." Sharon asked.

"Let's just say some people might not want me out the game. But Vanessa has to get some clothes for her and Joshua sometime today. She bought a few outfits but it is other things she may need until we relocate. She and I might go there real late tonight but be extra cautious. You think you can stop by the hotel and watch Joshua while we handle that?" I explained.

"Yeah that's cool just let me know what time to be at your hotel room." She nodded.

"I'm looking at around one in the morning. Is that too late?"

"Nah that's cool. Saturday is our busiest day but I will let Janice know that I will be a little late." She shrugged.

"Cool!"

"I love you Winnie and I'll talk to you later." She said after hugging me.

"I love you too."

I drove over to Janice's house shortly after that. When I went inside I noticed a bunch of things that I wanted to take with me. I grabbed as many clothes I could grab. I practically cleaned out the closet of all the clothes that were mine. I had forgotten that there was a small safe inside the house. It had maybe fifteen thousand dollars inside plus the deed to the house. I also had miscellaneous paper work. After making several trips to my car I decided to come back for everything else another day. I figured this would hold me until I can make one last trip to Janice's house. After that then I could cut all ties except for my daughter. That reminded me to call my mother again to see what was up. I hadn't heard from her or anything. She usually kept Shanee on Friday and Saturday. I wondered if she was available for this weekend.

"Hello?"

"What's up mama where have you been?" I asked.

"In my skin boy I'm a grown woman." She snapped.

"Not like that I was just worried about you that's all. Are you picking up Shanee from school today?" I asked.

"Don't I always pick her up on Fridays? What's with all the questions Winnie?" She snapped.

"Mama what's wrong. It sounds like something is bothering you. I'm on my way over there to tell you some good news." I calmly asked.

"I'll be here!" She replied.

There was nothing but dial tone in my ear after that. I couldn't believe how hostile she was. She wasn't drunk or did I bring up anyone that might have pissed her off. My mother was predictable in most ways. It was hard to figure out what was bothering her now. I chalked it up to her probably having her first big fight with William. She was probably at his house and an argument ensued.

Still I reluctantly drove to her house. When I got there I knocked on the door. Even though I always had a key when she started dating William I never would use it. She opened the door and turned around without saying anything to me. That was uncomfortable. Not knowing what was fueling this cold shoulder I decided to press the issue. Maybe something can be unraveled about my moms' weird behavior.

"I have some good news for you mama."

"Ain't that what you said over the phone?" She said sarcastically.

"Mama if I done something to piss you off; would you just tell me. It seems like you're trying to be mean to me. I came over here in a good mood and everything." I bitterly replied.

"You know what Winnie you are right. Maybe I am acting a little nasty. I'm just irritated about some things. Tell me your good news and maybe it will cheer me up. I need some time alone after this and I'm picking up Shanee in a few hours." She waved her hand as if to surrender.

"Vanessa and I are getting married. About a week from now we are going down to Las Vegas and we are jumping the broom." I smiled.

"Well if that's what you want to do. Are you sure you're not messing up that girl's life Winnie? You know Janice called here the other day crying about your relationship?" She calmly replied.

There was no excitement or backlash. I didn't know what to think of how she handled the news.

"That's because I want to be with Vanessa and I just want to take care of my baby with Janice. That's probably why she was crying. I didn't mean to hurt her but you can't help who you love." I replied.

"Yeah you remind me of your uncles and your daddy. Picking and choosing different women at your whim. I never was big on you being with her but maybe I shouldn't be too big on her being with *you*." She said.

She walked over to the couch then sat down. She grabbed a cigarette from out of the cigarette box on the end table. She lit it up and just looked at me.

235

"What is that supposed to mean? After all these years you thought I was too good for her now you think she's too good for me?" I snapped.

She didn't say anything. She just puffed on her cigarette and lowered her eyes. There was an uncomfortable silence for a few moments. Then I just turned around and walked out the door. The shit kind of hurt me. But I wasn't going to let it get to me. I hopped into my Armada and sped away.

I couldn't have made it past the second stop light when the infamous Jaguar started flashing lights on me. It was the two white cops that was there when this nigga named Boom-Boom tried to blast on me at a shopping center years ago.

"Fuck!" I yelled in frustration.

The detective with the crew cut came walking up to the driver's side. He looked into the backseat of my car before he walked up to my window. I knew the police was on me but not to the point that they were watching my moms' house.

"How is everything Mr. Daniels?" Crew cut asked.

"I'm doing fine." I bluntly replied.

"Well we wanted to talk to you. Can we have permission to search your car?"

"Do you have a warrant? This is some racial profiling or something like that; ain't it?" I snapped.

"You know we can detain you until we receive a warrant?" He replied.

"Well that's what you're going to have to do. I haven't done anything for you to be pulling me over. I'm tired of being treated like a criminal." I protested.

"You're synonymous with the most ruthless criminals that I've had the displeasure of meeting. You just happen to be a smart nigger that's all." Crew cut hissed at me.

I just shook my head. He wanted to be provoked but I wasn't about to be that stupid. I stared at him wondering what he was capable of. He looked around then back at his Jaguar where his partner was still on the passenger side. I followed his eyes wondering what he might be up to.

"I see you have a new car. You need to enjoy it why you can."

I still didn't respond. He seemed frustrated from my apparent disregard for his words. I was too worried to reply.

"Get the fuck out of here Mr. Daniels." He gestured with his head.

I drove off without having to be told twice. I looked in my rearview to see if they were following me. It didn't seem like it but you never knew. I pulled up in a parking lot to see if they put a low jack on my car. Once I realized they didn't I breathed out in relief. I left my mother's house upset but now I was just happy to be free.

20
THE FINAL STRAW

The new Ice Cube; muthafuckas hate to like you!
Eminem

Vanessa and I had enough. When I made it back to the hotel I let her know the sordid details to my bad day. The crazy thing was I didn't know if they had followed me from my mother's house or they had been following me from Janice's house. I had to assume that they had all my phones tapped and everything. I wasn't trying to get caught up like that. That's the kind of case where you end up doing life in jail. We both agreed that it was time for us to get out of town. Too many muthafuckas would have a problem with me being out the game.

I made plans for Vanessa and my son to move out to Victorville until I decided what we would do. My mother's friend Paula had offered to let us stay there until we relocated. We would have to take Joshua out of school. My life was feeling like a rollercoaster and my son didn't need to experience it. I decided to try and spend time with my daughter so I asked my mother to meet me somewhere.

"Why can't you come over here and visit Shanee?"

I didn't understand the hostility. Even though I offered to fill her tank up she nagged about it. Finally I just admitted to her my dilemma.

"Two white detectives pulled me over on the way home from yo house. It was two white boys I had a run in with before; many years ago. Now they pulled me over calling me all kinds of niggers and everything. I don't want them following me because I don't know if they followed me from yo house or Janice's house. I'm out the game and I don't want any problems." I explained.

"What do you mean you're out the game?" She asked surprisingly.

"Yeah I've backed away from the game. I'm trying to take things to a whole different level."

"Are you serious Winnie?" A hint of excitement went through the phone.

"Yeah mama I'm dead serious." I replied.

"Well I'm on my way. Maybe that girl Vanessa is exactly what you needed." She hung up the phone.

She met me at a shopping center around the corner from the hotel. When my daughter seen me she jumped into my arms. It felt good to see my mother and my daughter. Moms was in a much better mood than yesterday. Shanee and my mother rolled to the hotel with me in the Armada. Paranoia had me looking in every direction and through every rearview mirror.

When we went inside the room Shanee ran right at Joshua after seeing him. She definitely loved her big brother. Joshua came over to hug his grandmother while we talked in the hallway. My mom gestured that both Vanessa and I follow her in the hallway. I didn't understand why but it was something she didn't want to say in front of the children.

"First of all Vanessa I want to apologize for the way I have treated you for so many years. You are a good woman to my son and I will never forget that." She began.

"Don't worry about that Ms. Shirley." Vanessa replied.

"No because I need to clear the air with you, child. I was in a relationship with a man I thought loved me but I recently found out different. He was..."

"You and William are having problems?" I interrupted her.

"Let me finish. I recently found out that William is an undercover narcotics officer for the DEA."

Both Vanessa and I took two steps back simultaneously. We couldn't believe what we were hearing. By this time my

239

mother was in tears. She began sobbing uncontrollably for the first time since my father was killed. It was the only other time she had cried in front of me. I was heartbroken seeing her like that. We had to wait a few moments for her to regain her composure. I opened the door to check on Shanee and Joshua and they were playing video games on the bed. Eventually she calmed down after wiping her eyes with Kleenex.

"They wanted me to become an informant because they caught me with five ounces of weed. William told me he knew someone that sold weed for large amounts for a good price so I checked it out. I never considered how he could get that connect when he doesn't smoke weed." She began sobbing again.

"Mama don't beat yourself up over that. There are plenty of people that don't smoke weed that know people that sell it. You didn't know that he was setting you up." I replied.

"I was beginning to love that man. Anyway, he told me to consider my grandchildren because you were going down. He said that everyone connected to you including our entire family would fall. He even threatened that my grandbabies would end up in foster care. So none of this would happen, he asked me to give you up. I hated the position I put myself in." She cried.

"It's okay mama because I don't hustle anymore. We'll hire you a lawyer that can get that weed charge cut down to a first offense misdemeanor. You won't be looking at any jail charge over weed." I assured her.

"Well I had to let you know why I was acting like I was yesterday. It was hurting my heart baby."

"I'll get the lawyer on the phone and we'll clear this up. As for Vanessa, Joshua and me we plan to move out of state soon after we are married." I explained.

"Aren't you still on parole?" My mother asked.

"Yeah but I got to get out of here. I have about nine more months before I'm off parole. I think if I informed her that I was moving out of town she will let me go. She hasn't had any problems with me. I very seldom have to report to her for a piss test. I'll see what's up with that but until then we're moving up to Victorville with Paula."

"Are you serious? When you go up there let me know so I can ride with you. My girl hasn't been down to San Bernardino in awhile. Ever since I was talking to William we mostly talked on the phone. We've been shopping maybe once or twice in the last seven or eight months." Mama smiled.

The whole ordeal my mother was going through further convinced me that I needed to get out of town. She told me that the two white detective's names were Hudson and Yates. She said the white boy pig with the crew cut was Hudson. I could never forget him because he was the one that called me a nigger. My mother was appalled when I told her that. I took some time after our talk to take my son and daughter out to the park. By Wednesday Vanessa and I had plans to be in Las Vegas for our wedding.

The next day I received a phone call from Janice. She had a nasty attitude once I got on the phone.

"What's Up Janice?"

"Next time you need to let me know when you're coming over to *my* house. You can't just walk in here and expect to roam freely; especially when I'm not here. You gave up that right when you moved out."

"First of all that is not one hundred percent your house. If I'm not mistaking someone else's name is on that lease besides you." I reminded her.

"I know who the fuck's name is on this house. Look *Sherwin*, if you can't respect my boundaries then we're going to have a problem. Oh by the way, I heard that you're getting married."

"Who told you that; my sister?" I asked.

"Yeah and I think she was trying to be spiteful. I offered to buy her out for her half of the salon and she got pissed. Well congratulations I hope you're both happy." She said sarcastically.

241

I chuckled to myself. That was the real reason she was calling. It didn't bother me that Sharon was being a little messy but I figured Janice probably provoked it. I know both women involved and Sharon has to be antagonized to be like that.

"I was telling her that she doesn't do any hair, nails or massages so she should quit. Sell me the other half of the shop because her manager skills is okay at best. We wouldn't skip a beat if she was here or not. She was late yesterday and we still was operating like nothing had changed." Janice sassily explained.

"But from what I've been hearing the hair stylists at the shop like Sharon more than they like you. Except for Shanell you don't have a lot of friends in that shop. Maybe if Sharon left a lot of hair stylists might jump ship also. And me and you both know that you and Shanell are on and off friends anyway. Ya'll call each other up when one of you are having man problems." I replied.

"Fuck you *Sherwin*! Don't just pop up at my house anymore nigga."

She hung up the phone in my face. I had bigger issues to tackle. Vanessa was gathering all the money I had from my hustles in the game. I always made sure that I had more than one stash just in case someone found one there were at least four others they had to discover. For the most part though Sunday was a rest day. We planned on leaving for Victorville on Monday. My mother took Shanee back to her house so that Janice could pick her up but Shanee didn't want to go. She wanted to keep playing with her brother and being with us at the hotel. Mama took her anyway because we didn't want Janice to find a reason to gripe.

Early Monday afternoon I received a phone call from Lonnie. I was days away from getting rid of the phone altogether. He hit me up and I quickly told him to follow the routine. I wasn't in the game but too many things were happening for me not to be worried. I went down to a phone booth and called his cell phone. Then he called me from another pay phone and we began to talk.

"You know Fab-Five caught another case? He caught a murder charge for J-Rock." Lonnie began.

242

"What makes them think that he did that shit? Do they have any evidence that supports the shit?" I asked.

"I don't know but he says it was enough to charge him. He thinks somebody is snitching. Or they are just fucking with him because they didn't get him on another charge." Lonnie replied.

"Somebody go check on his family? You know we got to see what's up with his peoples." I explained.

"I made sure he had a lawyer but he told me he wasn't fucking with Shanell anymore. But he does have a daughter by her."

"Don't worry about it. I'll go by there to check on her and put some money on his books. You got to remember to take care of yo peoples. You feel me?"

"I'm knowing! Ay did you hear that nigga Killa Kell got served somewhere out in Fontana? He's dead than a muthafucka." Lonnie commented.

"Nah I didn't know shit about that. Holla at me later so we can chop it up."

I got off the phone with Lonnie and went back to the hotel with Vanessa and Joshua. I walked in the door and she gave me a look like something was wrong. Never underestimate the power of woman's intuition.

"What's going on where you have to go use the pay phone?" She asked.

"Lonnie hit me up telling me that Fab-Five caught another murder case. I want to stop by his girl's spot and check on his family. I'll make that run then we can drive out to Victorville."

"I know you are hard headed so I'm not going to tell you not to go. Just be careful." She replied.

I hurriedly dipped out the door wondering what she was worried about. I would have usually listened but I couldn't leave Fab-Five hanging like that. It took me about twenty minutes to get to her house because of the traffic. I pulled up and seen her car parked out front. I double parked the car and ran upstairs and knocked on the door. The door swung open after the first knock.

243

"What are you doing here Sherwin?" Shanell glanced around outside the door.

"I heard what happened to Fabian and I wanted to offer a little help. How is everything?" I asked.

"You know what, I don't need shit from you. As far as I'm concerned you're responsible for Cornell's death. He ends up dead because he was running errands for you. Yeah I was in love with Cornell. I love Fabian because that is the father of my daughter. But I wasn't in love with him. And in my opinion you are one of the people responsible for me losing the love of my life." She snapped.

"Nelly...I mean Cornell was in the game and that is how the game is. He knew the consequences once he got in the game. As far as you being in love with him I didn't know anything about that." I lied.

"Nigga Please. You probably knew all along. You were more loyal to Fabian because he was willing to do your dirty work. You probably knew all along. Cornell told me you might know that we were seeing each other. Then the first night he gets this 'promotion' he ends up dead. Just leave me and my family the fuck alone." She lashed out.

"I'm sorry you feel that way. But both Cornell and Fabian was my peoples and I had love for both of them."

"I can't believe you can look me in the eye and bold face lie. That's the final straw. I'm not fucking with you, Fabian or Janice for that matter. All of ya'll are a bunch of twisted muthafuckas." She slammed the door.

I walked down the stairs somewhat stunned. I came over to help and had to listen to that shit. I quickly drove over to the hotel room and tried to shake off what just happened.

"Did you take care of everything you needed to take care of?" Vanessa asked me when I walked in the door.

"Yeah we are good. Next time I'll listen to you when you don't want me to go anywhere." I replied.

"Why what happened?"

"Let's just say that what I was trying to do wasn't appreciated."

"Yeah we gon' leave all of that behind so don't even worry about it." Vanessa smiled.

We hopped in the Armada and drove up to Victorville. It was a peaceful ride. It gave me time to clear my head. It sort of reminded me of the day I came home from Corcoran State prison. Besides my mother nagging I was able to take some time out and think. My mother came along for the ride to see Paula but this time she was quiet the entire ride. This was another major change in my life and I was getting the time to think it out. Shanell going off on me like that was a clear sign that the game was a part of my life that was now over.

When we pulled up to Paula's house she was already outside watering her grass. She had a three bedroom house with no family. I think she was just as excited about us visiting as we were excited about having a place to lay low. She took us in with welcome arms.

That Wednesday Vanessa and I drove down to Las Vegas to get married. We went down to a chapel and had a quiet ceremony for just the two of us. We had complete strangers to be our witnesses. My mother wanted to go but she had to stay back to watch over Joshua.

Later that night we made love in one of the suites at Caesar's Palace. We just sat in bed and ordered room service and talked.

"We should move to Virginia and live with my family out there." Vanessa suggested out the blue.

"When did you come up with this idea?"

"I've been thinking about it for some time now and I was thinking of a way to ask you. We will be away from the game totally." She explained.

"I doubt it if my parole officer will let me out of the state. I wondered about her letting me move to Orange County but Virginia is a whole different thing." I replied.

"Well it won't hurt to ask. You haven't had any violations since you've been out. You only got about nine months on your parole so she will probably grant you that much." Vanessa assured me.

"You know what, let's do the shit. I've been in Cali my whole life and I want to see other parts of the world. We'll drive the Armada out there and have the Mercedes shipped to us."

"Are you serious Winnie?" She got excited.

"I'm serious as a heart attack."

She jumped up to hug me. We laughed and talked until we both dozed off. The next morning we went to the casinos and rolled the Las Vegas strip. I went to the crap table and lost a little bit of money. After taking a few souvenirs we decided it was time to drive back to Victorville. On our ride back we laughed at our wedding pictures and for the first time I was at peace. It was different for me. I was ready to make that move to Virginia and start all over.

"Do you got everything you gon' need before we leave?" Vanessa asked.

"I have that safe at Janice's house with a little bit of money in it. But I'm not worried about the money as much as I'm worried about personal items in there. I got my high school diploma, my social security card and a few other pieces of paper work that I need to grab. After I get those things then we can leave the next day." I replied.

"Do you think Ms. Janice is going to let you come up in her house and get those things? She might give you a problem or two." Vanessa pointed out.

"How about I wait until Friday morning and we leave right after that? She'll be at the hair salon at that time. Then we will hop on the Freeway after that we're gone forever." I smiled.

"That sounds good to me." She smiled back.

21
BURNED

Watch for 'one time' as I speak because they do dirt like fools in the street!
PaPa Sak

Detectives Yates and Hudson stood in front of their informant grilling him for more information. Hudson paced in front of the young man trying to get the man they were really after.

"We want Mr. Daniels what information do you know about Sherwin Daniels?"

"I don't know who Sherwin Daniels is?" The informant cried.

"You may only know him as Pooh." Yates calmly replied.

"Oh you're talking about Pooh. He's not in the game anymore. He stopped hustling. I can only tell you about the murder done by Fabian. He shot that nigga J-Rock in the head for talking too much. That's why you got to make sure I'm taken care of." The informant explained.

"We will really take care of you if you hand us Mr. Daniels on a platter. All we ask is that you testify that he ordered the murder of Jason Phillips." Hudson replied.

"I told you man I'm not testifying. As far as Pooh goes I wouldn't testify against him anyway. He always was a stand up nigga to me. Plus he's not even in the game anymore. Ya'll clutching for straws now. That nigga Fabian is foul though. That nigga will smoke his own homie over fifty dollars. I got love for him but he's a different breed of nigga." The informant explained.

"Look Mr. Johnson you were caught selling dope to an undercover cop. You're looking at eight to ten years because you

247

have a prior and you're on probation. You've never been to prison but you are on your way. You are also implicated in the murder of Cornell Davenport in the Delmont Heights. So you need to listen to what we are telling you and obey." Hudson impatiently explained.

"Okay...Okay, Travon is the main nigga out of the Delmont Heights. J-Rock was the top nigga in the projects until he was killed. Some nigga named Main Man is the nigga hustling over off of Mt. Vernon. The top nigga in the Dorjil's is some fool we call 'Sheed'. That's all I know." The informant explained.

"Who do these top guys cop their dope from? Give us the name of the person that supplies all of these spots." Yates said.

"That nigga 'L' is the one that supplies all the spots." The informant sighed.

"When you say 'L' you mean Lonnell Jackson?"

"Yeah I think that is his name because we sometimes call him Lonnie. But he hates being called that shit over the phone. I've met him a couple times when he was working under Pooh. But I was hearing that he might make Travon his middle man." The informant explained.

"Okay most of this is new to us. So we have the entire crew except for Mr. Daniels. We can't help you too much Mr. Johnson if you can't testify. You will have to testify against someone in court." Hudson replied.

"Well just send me to jail. I'm not going to be known on paper as a snitch. I might as well sign my own death certificate. Ya'll white boys know the game. But I'm better if I'm working on the street for you. We can both pretend that you didn't find the dope and I can get you information on everybody. If Travon gets promoted more than likely that means so will I. I'll be running the Delmont Heights and I'll be in the inner circle. Ya'll muthafuckas need to think about this." The informant passionately explained.

"We're willing to work something out but we want Mr. Daniels. He's into something we can pin to him." Hudson replied.

"Ya'll act like ya'll hard of hearing. I told you he ain't in the game anymore. I haven't heard anything about Pooh for a little over a month now; probably longer than that. He's the one that got away." The informant smirked.

Suddenly a tall middle aged Black man walked into the building. Following behind him was a younger Black man and they both wore business suits. It was obvious to the informant that they were police. He refused to give either one any eye contact. The middle aged taller Black cop stared at him momentarily then glanced at Yates and Hudson.

"How can we help you Detective Barnes and Detective Bowen?" Hudson asked.

"Can I talk to you privately?" Barnes asked.

Hudson and Barnes walked toward the back into one of the various offices. Barnes made sure to close the door.

"You know the young man Markell Brown was found dead over in Fontana. He was killed right in front of a vacant house. He was the kid out of the California Gardens that was giving Mr. Daniels so many problems." Barnes explained.

"How did he end up in Fontana? Where did you get this information from anyhow?" Hudson asked.

"I have a friend that is a homicide detective in Fontana and he informed me of the recent murder when he realized the victim was from San Bernardino. But that is not the only thing that is interesting. A witness said they seen two men drive off in a white Range Rover." Barnes replied.

"Are you serious? Was the witness able to get a license plate number?"

"There is no license plate number but it is at least enough to implicate Mr. Daniels in the murder." Barnes suggested.

"I'm recently hearing that he is out of the game by my informant. When I last talked to Mr. Daniels he was driving a black Armada." Hudson informed him.

"He's out the game huh? Well you win some and you lose some." Barnes surrendered.

"As long as he is in town he can get indicted on various charges. He's still on parole which means he can't leave so he's still our number one target. What do you know about Lonnell Jackson who goes by 'L' or Lonnie?" Hudson asked.

"He's Mr. Daniels' number two. Fabian Gilmore who recently took a murder charge was his muscle. But if Mr. Daniels is out the game then that probably makes Mr. Jackson the top dog." Barnes replied.

"So what the informant is saying is true." Hudson really said to himself instead of Barnes.

"That's your informant outside. He looks familiar as though I've seen him in the Delmont Heights area." Barnes asked.

Hudson didn't really respond. He was trying to piece together a way to bring everyone in under the kingpin law including Mr. Daniels. He kept rubbing his chin while Barnes observed him for several moments.

"I'll talk to you later Hudson. I have some other things to do." Barnes interrupted his thoughts.

"Okay Barnes I'll talk to you later. Thanks for the information."

Hudson followed Barnes out into the hallway. Bowen, Yates and the informant were in the main room sitting quietly. Barnes waved for Bowen to follow and both Black detectives walked out the door.

Yates looked at Hudson and noticed the perplexed look on his face. He glanced at the informant then chose to handcuff him.

"Give us a minute." Yates said to the informant.

They walked to the back down the hallway without going into the offices. Yates was curious to know what Barnes said to get Hudson's wheels turning.

"What did Barnes have to say?" Yates impatiently whispered.

"He said that Markell Brown from out of the California Gardens is dead. They don't have any suspects but a white Range Rover was spotted leaving the murder scene." Hudson explained.

250

Yates' mouth dropped. He knew exactly who that was implicating but he allowed Hudson to continue.

"They don't have the license plate number but Mr. Daniels is the only drug dealer I know that had a problem with Mr. Brown."

"So before he left the business he finished one last part of business. I feel like we got burned. He does all this dirt and gets away with murder...literally." Yates retorted.

"Not necessarily. If we put this dope on Mr. Daniels that we found on Mr. Johnson then we can begin the wheels to turning. He will have violated parole and with Mr. Johnson as an informant we can tie everyone in." Hudson suggested.

"But how will we catch up with Mr. Daniels. He's probably in the area but I doubt if he returns to his mother's house or Ms. Martin's house." Yates replied.

"Since his mother hired a lawyer and pled down her charge he might feel free to go by there. What we can do is post two unmarked cars at both places of residence and when he shows up to either we will plant the drugs and place him under arrest. Then we can tie him with everyone else on conspiracy charges." Hudson explained.

"Okay I'll move on that right now. What are we going to do about the informant?" Yates asked while walking to the phone.

"We will let him go but he will report to us as a confidential informant."

The very next day early Friday morning Hudson and Yates got a call that Mr. Daniels had returned to Janice Martin's home of residence. They quickly grabbed the evidence and weapons and hurried out the door. They didn't have much time because of the morning traffic. Even if they put on their sirens it would take them about twenty-five to thirty minutes to arrive.

Pooh set his clock for early that Friday morning. He was very familiar with Janice's schedule on the weekend. She always left the house around eight in the morning to take Shanee to school. Then she would go to the shop and stay there until late. His mother always picked Shanee up from school so Janice had a social life at her job. He had plans to only be inside the house for about twenty minutes tops. Then he would carry on with his life and never have to see the state of California again.

Vanessa got up with him. They didn't bother taking baths. They brushed their teeth, threw on some clothes then headed towards her house. They didn't say too much on the ride over there. Pooh asked Vanessa to drive for some reason. He had a premonition that something might go wrong so he felt more comfortable with her behind the wheel. After the silence of only the radio playing Pooh glanced over at Vanessa.

"If I didn't have this important paperwork I wouldn't even show up to this place. My stomach is upset worrying about going over here." Pooh admitted.

"Baby everything is going to be alright. All you have to do is grab what you need and leave the rest there. You still got that game in you so you worry still." Vanessa assured him.

"You know me better than that." Pooh replied.

"Yeah you are usually right but you have to get your birth certificate, social security card, high school diploma and everything else. It's one of those things you have to do. Let's just pray for once that you're wrong and it is more of being nervous." Vanessa smiled.

It took fifteen minutes to pull up on Janice's block. He told Vanessa to park a little ways down the street. He didn't want anyone to see the car out front and alert Janice. He could have called Janice for his things but he knew she would give him the run around for the sake of being difficult. He didn't need anything stalling his trip out of town. He went up to the door and tried the key and it worked. He walked inside of the house and ran straight toward the safe. He quickly did the combination to the safe and unlocked the safe door. He then grabbed a pillow case from off the bed and unloaded everything in the safe into the pillow case. He quickly walked outside to see Vanessa eagerly waiting for him.

He dropped the bag in the back seat of the Armada then glanced up at her in the driver's seat.

"I'm almost done but I got all the real important stuff. I'll grab everything else I want and then we are out of here. It will take me two to three minutes." He smiled.

She smiled back at him while he rushed off to finish getting his things. He walked back into the house and grabbed the other pillow case reaching for a few miscellaneous things. He was done in less than two minutes and was walking out the door.

"I can't wait to see you either baby. I'll be here waiting for you." A familiar voice said.

Then the front door swung open. Both Pooh and Janice looked at each other in shock for a moment. She looked down at the pillow case he was holding and reached at his arm.

"What the fuck are you taking from my house Sherwin?" She yelled.

"Let me go. All this shit belongs to me." Pooh snatched away from her.

She began grabbing him and pulling on him trying to reach for the pillow case. He pushed her to the side and began trying to walk out the door.

"I'll be damned if you walk out my door and I don't know what the fuck you are taking." She began swinging on him.

Her fists came slamming down on his face and chest. She was relentlessly trying to bring him down with her punches. He tried to hold her off with his arm but she was hysterical.

"Give me that fucking bag Sherwin." She continued screaming.

She wiggled past his arm and threw a couple more punches at his face. He had to cover himself trying to protect his body. Finally, in order to escape, he rose up and popped her in the mouth with an open hand. She fell to the ground stunned. He tried to rush out the door but she grabbed a hold of his leg.

"What the fuck are you doing Janice this is my shit? You don't ever have to see me again. Just let me get the fuck out of here." He yelled.

"Nah muthafucka; because I told you not to come to my house without asking. This is my house and you are no longer permitted to come and go as you please."

"Bitch you tripping, I'm out." He reached for the door knob.

She was growing weak from her hysteria. Her grip on his leg began to loosen as he opened the door. When the door swung open a black man was standing at the door. Both Pooh and the man stared at each other momentarily. Janice looked up and noticed her guest.

"Ron this muthafucka done broke into my house!" She screamed.

"Broke into your house? I have a key because my family owns part of this house. I just came to get the rest of my stuff and you won't let me go." Pooh said incredulously.

"This muthafucka slapped me in my mouth." Janice yelled again.

"I was just trying to get you the fuck off of me. I don't have to explain myself I'm out this bitch."

"You do have to explain yourself to a judge. You're being charged with domestic violence." Ron calmly said.

"Who the fuck are you to be talking about I'm being charged with something?"

"He's a detective you dirty muthafucka." Janice retorted.

"I am homicide detective Ronald Bowen with the San Bernardino Sheriffs' Department. You have the right to remain silent, anything you say can and will be held against you in a court of law."

Pooh listened to him read the Miranda rights and just lowered his head in defeat. He was quickly handcuffed while Ron gestured for Janice to call the police. In about five minutes a black and white police car pulled up to the driveway. Pooh glanced back at Janice who had a smirk on her face.

"I didn't think that you would be messing with the police. You ain't about shit Janice." Pooh bitterly said.

She waved her hand with the same smirk on her face as if she was dismissing him. Two uniformed cops escorted him down to the police car while Ron was inside checking on Janice.

When Pooh got in the car the two uniformed officers went back to talk to Ron about the charges. After explaining the charges to the officers he picked up the bag and asked Janice if she wanted what was in the pillow case. She looked inside and shook her head.

"Put this with his property when you take him to the station." Ron replied.

"What is his name?" One officer asked.

Ron glanced over at Janice and she took a moment to gain her composure.

"His name is Sherwin Daniels."

Ron's mouth dropped in disbelief. He glanced at Janice feeling as though he wasn't hearing her correctly.

"Did you say Sherwin Daniels? The Sherwin Daniels?" He asked in disbelief.

"I just know his name is Sherwin Daniels. I don't know about 'the Sherwin Daniels'."

"I've heard his name plenty of times in major drug and murder cases but I never took a look at his file. My partner has pulled him over numerous times near here and I never put two and two together. I always stayed in the car when he questioned him. Look officers, book him for the two charges of domestic violence plus assault and battery. When I'm done making sure she is okay then I'll come down to the station and follow up on these charges." Ron explained.

The two officers turned around and walked out the door. Pooh started feeling the heat of the sun beam into the car while handcuffed in the backseat. Vanessa being worried rolled past the police car to see him in the backseat. Pooh seen the tears fall down her face but he motioned with his head for her to keep driving. She reluctantly drove off as she seen the two uniformed cops walking out of the house.

They hopped into the vehicle and drove Pooh off to jail. Moments later after they left the block a Jaguar pulled up. Hudson and Yates jumped out the car and ran toward the unmarked car. One of the officers looked at them walking up.

"I didn't notice him until he was being hauled off to jail. Whatever he was doing he was caught by some detective who just handed them to two uniformed officers." The officer explained.

"Fuck!" Hudson replied.

They walked up to Janice's house and knocked on the open front door. To their surprise Detective Ron Bowen answered the door. They both looked at each other.

"What are you doing here Detective Bowen?" Hudson asked.

"I'm dating the young woman that lives here. What are you doing here?" Bowen replied.

"We were trying to catch Mr. Daniels but it appears that we are a moment too late." Yates frowned.

"I suppose so. He didn't have any contraband but he is being charged with one count of domestic violence and also assault and battery." Bowen replied.

"You got to be fucking kidding me. The biggest dope dealer on the west side of San Bernardino gets a domestic violence charge?" Hudson said in disbelief.

"He wasn't caught for anything else. I'm sorry guys. If you don't mind I'd like to get back to my friend." Bowen frowned.

"Well what if we added a possession charge to his other two counts?" Hudson suggested.

"He wasn't caught with that. If I'm going to arrest him for that I need to catch him doing that." Bowen said. He showed clear undertones that he was offended.

"Okay detective but realize you are letting a known drug dealer and murderer off with a slap on the wrist." Yates commented.

"I wouldn't if I caught him doing the crime. Good day gentlemen I'll be down to fill out the paperwork on Mr. Daniels shortly."

After Pooh went through the long process of being booked they finally sent him off to the County Jail. He was sent to the dorm where it held forty-eight beds. One of his dorm mates was Fabian Gilmore. They embraced and talked about the charges against them.

A few days later Pooh's probation officer came to visit him. She was a middle aged white woman. She was always polite and respectful because Pooh was always handling his business with her. They had developed a rapport after all these years. So she didn't mind telling him the status on his case.

"You can plead down to misdemeanor assault and misdemeanor domestic violence and you will only be violated. You can fight the case but you probably will still have to serve your time in the County until the trial is over."

"So if I take the plea you will violate me? And if I fight it I still will have to serve County Jail time while I'm fighting the case? I might as well just do the time."

"That's what I would suggest. You can finish your time in prison and you will be off parole. Once you were charged for the crime you were violated even if you are guilty or not. But you can serve the rest of your parole and will be a free man and don't have to report to anyone. Though I did get reports from several detectives suggesting you are the most ruthless drug lord in San Bernardino." She explained.

"That's just people that have a problem with me. I'm not in the game anymore." Pooh assured her.

"Well you haven't been charged with anything like that so that is just conjecture. But I thought you needed to know that."

"Thank You."

Pooh stood up from his meeting and looked straight ahead. He had about eight months according to his Parole officer before release. He took it in stride and didn't look back. He was still married to a woman that loved him. He walked back to his dorm feeling like a man. He had jail time but he wasn't compromising himself for anyone. He left jail a man and went back in as a man. Janice burned him but wounds can heal.

22
THE FINISH LINE

If poverty is the mother of crime, stupidity is its father!
Jean de La Bruyere

8 months later

This day I came home from prison once again. I was released from Corcoran State Prison. This time around my wife Vanessa came to pick me up. I hopped into our Armada and we drove off. I kissed my beautiful wife who stood by me the entire time I was incarcerated. In the back seat was my growing son. I reached toward the back seat and shook his hand. Everyone was all smiles. Vanessa explained to me that she sent her Mercedes to her cousin in Virginia. She had a trailer attached to our SUV stored with everything we were taking with us. Now that I was out we weren't stopping until we reached the state line. Leaving all the drama behind was the objective. It really felt good to be out and free. Though I was happy I still remained silent for most of the ride. My thoughts were running after me.

I heard a lot of things while I was locked up. The one that hurt the most was that Lonnie had got set up by this broad named Tanya who everyone knew as Pebbles. Rumor has it that she was once Killa Kell's girlfriend before he was killed. That sort of broke my heart. He was my young protégé. I also heard while I was locked up that Willie Johnson from the Delmont Heights was snitching. Word gets around fast on the I.E. car when you're locked down. I was respected in the pen because niggas heard I was running shit on the outs. But I still knew to keep my mouth shut and just do my time. Luckily enough for me I didn't have any problems. Fab-Five on the other hand caught a life sentence behind Willie snitching. Whatever police he was snitching for was sloppy about keeping him confidential. He ended up dead about three months after I went in.

I was leaving town but it still bothered me that some of the homies I would never see alive again. It changed my whole perspective on life. I knew that was part of the game and I was one of the best at the game. But it still was hurtful to know that those that lived by the code couldn't live to enjoy the fruits of their labor. As for me the game was done and I had stacked enough money to live good for the rest of my life. I definitely don't encourage this lifestyle in order to make money but I understand why it's done. Honestly, I am one of the few that is able to escape the game and live to talk about it. Especially if you consider the level I made it to. I wondered about Big Black and how many years he's been in the game but is able to still function. There are a few out there but not that many. Most of us don't know when to get out the game until it's too late.

One of the last things I remembered hearing was that this nigga out the California Gardens was running shit now. He was supplying a number of spots on the west side like I once was. His name was Marvin but he went by the name of Game Face. I actually knew of him because he used to hustle for King James back in the day. He was locked up for about six to eight years and I remember hearing he was a sound hustler. Now he was a boss nigga. Thinking about that I chuckled because in my heart I felt like he could have the game. He could have the top spot because everyone is taking shots at you when you're at the top. Well he can have all the stress that comes with the game and with being a boss.

"We're across the state lines. Now we can stop somewhere to get a room for the night. Let's first stop to get something to eat." Vanessa suggested.

"I'm with that." I replied.

Joshua just nodded but not looking up because he was in the backseat playing with his Game boy. Yeah I'm with this. Big Black once told me that if I ever want to get out the game I should at least have a million dollars saved up to go legit. He explained that sometimes the game forces you out and you don't get to meet that goal. Well I was okay in reaching that goal and much more. My money was long and my game was strong and I had my ride or die chick next to me while my son was in the back seat. Only thing I was regretting was leaving my mother, my sister and her family and my daughter Shanee. My mother only got probation for that weed charge. Once her probation was up she was planning to come out to Virginia and live with us. My sister and her family would stay in California and watch over my daughter Shanee. As for Janice and her new boyfriend they had plans on getting married. According to Sharon, Janice is having the same problem with him that she had with me; not coming home at night. My excuse was the game while his excuse was his job. I didn't care one way or another. I was going to fight to have Shanee visit me in Virginia for the summer. Other than that I was through with everything else. That part of my life was dead.

Big Black opened the hotel door to see the handsome young man walk through the door. He had a stern no nonsense facial expression that Big Black appreciated. The stern young man stopped and looked at him for a moment studying him while Big Black was studied him.

"Big Black?" He asked.

"Yeah that's me. You ain't a fag are you?" Big Black asked.

"Hell Nah." He firmly replied.

"Cool then, change out of your clothes right in front of me then change into this sweat suit." Big Black ordered.

"Are you serious?"

"Does it look like I'm serious?" Big Black firmly replied.

They both began getting undressed. They quickly changed into the sweat suits laid out on the bed. Big Black told the young soldier to ride with him to another hotel after receiving the money.

"Sixteen-Five for each one right?" Big Black asked.

"Yeah it's all there, you want to count it?"

"Nah, because if you cheated me I'll never do business with you again."

They hopped in one of the SUVs Big Black had on stand-by and drove to another hotel. He took him upstairs and opened the door to another room. The young soldier walked in and grabbed a duffle bag. He tasted what he was getting then quickly taped it back up.

"Call me when you're ready to re-cop at this number. Don't leave a message but put in 909 so that I will know that it's the cat from San Bernardino. Last but not least what will I call you and don't give me any government name because I'm not giving you one." Big Black bluntly explained.

"They call me Game Face."

"I like that young comrade, I like that." Big Black nodded.

THE END!!!

PaPa Sak eventually sat down to write his first novel, after many years of running from his calling. He experimented with many different genres, and then decided to write about the things that he was most passionate about. He found that his passions lied in stories that reflected his experiences in love, street life, and struggle. He began to write the stories of those that have been subjected to violence, poverty, despair, abuse, and unhealthy love. He wanted his stories to be a beacon light for society to recognize the social ills that plague us. His first published novel was published in 2005, 'The Wages of Sin', a gangster story. Ever since his first published book he has hit the ground running. Though his genres may change, he will always stay true to the voice of his community. He will stay true to the passion, pain, dialect, culture, love, richness, vantage point, and glory of the Black experience through his literature.

PaPa Sak is a voice for the streets and the Black community for those that are usually misrepresented and misunderstood. His goal is to bring humanity to these characters and to bring understanding to other unpopular perspectives. His characters come from people he has known or interacted with at one time or another. One of his main focuses is to shed spiritual insight on stories that should be told in the Black experience and abroad. He is also a profound orator and inspirational speaker ranging in spoken word poetry, gang & street lifestyle, male and female relationships, manhood training, spirituality, Hip Hop and history. He is definitely a literary force in the new Millennium. You can also find him on my space at URL: http://www.myspace.com/papasakkingpen, Facebook as Novelist PaPa Sak, Twitter as Sak Dog71 and www.ensbooks.com

Order now
@ **www.ensbooks.com**

Coming soon

Order now
@ **www.ensbooks.com**